Poul Anderson

Conquests

A PANTHER BOOK

GRANADA
London Toronto Sydney New York

Published by Granada Publishing Limited in 1981

ISBN 0 586-05041 8

A Granada Paperback UK Original
First published in the USA under the title of
Seven Conquests
Copyright © Poul Anderson 1955, 1956, 1957, 1958, 1963, 1964, 1969

These stories have appeared previously, in a somewhat different form, and are copyright as follows:
'Kings Who Die,' Worlds of If, *May 1963. Reprinted in* The 8th Annual of the Year's Best SF, *published by Simon & Schuster,* © *1963 by Judith Merril.*
'Wildcat,' The Magazine of Fantasy and Science Fiction, *November 1958.*
'Cold Victory,' The Magazine of Fantasy and Science Fiction, *May 1957.*
'Inside Straight,' The Magazine of Fantasy and Science Fiction, *August 1955.*
'Details,' Worlds of If, *October 1956.*
'License,' The Magazine of Fantasy and Science Fiction, *April 1957.*
'Strange Bedfellows' (*under the title* 'To Build A World'), Galaxy Magazine, *June 1964.*

Granada Publishing Limited
Frogmore, St Albans, Herts AL2 2NF
and
36 Golden Square, London W1R 4AH
866 United Nations Plaza, New York, NY 10017, USA
117 York Street, Sydney, NSW 2000, Australia
100 Skyway Avenue, Rexdale, Ontario, M9W 3A6, Canada
61 Beach Road, Auckland, New Zealand

Set, printed and bound in Great Britain by
Cox & Wyman Ltd, Reading
Set in Intertype Times

Granada ®
Granada Publishing ®

TO GEORGE W. PRICE

Contents

Foreword

The first duty of science fiction, as of any art form, is to entertain. But entertainment can involve much besides telling a story. It can be an examination of the real world and the human situation therein. Now reality is more than the little bit we have directly experienced. It includes everything we do not yet know, or never will know – all the infinite possibilities in a space-time that reaches through billions of years and lightyears. By suggesting what might conceivably happen, science fiction tries to throw some light on what has already come to pass and what exists at this moment.

Here lies the justification for a book that might otherwise seem very narrow, a one-author one-theme one-genre collection. In effect, we shall be looking at the same thing several times, through the same pair of eyes but from different angles. Thus we may begin to understand how complex and mysterious the thing must be.

Our subject is human conflict leading to institutionalized violence. The key word is 'institutionalized'. Societies have generally found ways to keep murder, battery, rape, and riot within some bounds. When they fail to do so, throughout history it has been a symptom of their breakdown; they are soon replaced by new systems or whole new cultures virile enough to guarantee the ordinary peaceful person a measure of security in his daily life. But no government thus far has established a similar protection against war: for this is a proceeding of society itself.

The prayers, prophecies, denunciations, pleas, studies, conferences, and political restructurings of several thousand years have not done away with war. Our generation is unlikely to get further with its noisy peace parades and its mealy-mouthed observances of United Nations Day. The violence of the state remains legitimatized, and often glorified, because it serves the ends of the state. And these ends are not always evil; ask anyone whom Allied forces liberated from Nazi concentration camps. Such considerations demonstrate the fallacy of pacifism.

Nevertheless, whether the cause be good, bad, or indifferent, the human flesh caught in the middle is just as dead and maimed, the wealth is just as wasted. In an age of nuclear explosives and nerve gases, it is alike irresponsible to assume that war will come to a permanent end when a number of people speak up for peace and to assume that wars can go on as usual without the gravest consequences.

In trying to deal with the problem, we are almost fatally handicapped by the fact that we don't understand the phenomenon. He who claims to have final answers to the questions of why men fight and how to stop them from fighting, is merely showing his own ignorance. Perhaps no one will ever find any solutions; perhaps none exist. But our duty is to keep trying.

Someday men may succeed in abolishing war – though they may discover that the price is high. Or they may at least work out methods of limiting its destructiveness, to the spirit as well as to the body. If so, for them, as well as for us today, the saving virtues will remain the old-fashioned ones of courage, calm, and compassion, together with the more modern one of open-mindedness!

It is to this last quality, open-mindedness, the willingness to give a fair hearing to any suggestion whatsoever, that science fiction most appeals. I hope you will enjoy these stories simply as stories. But still more do I hope they will make you think, and come up with better ideas than those you find here.

POUL ANDERSON

Kings Who Die

It is obvious that technological change forces change in the manner of conducting human activities, including war. What is not so obvious is the degree to which it affects the very nature of those activities.

Luckily, Diaz was facing the other way when the missile exploded. It was too far off to blind him permanently, but the retinal burns would have taken a week or more to heal. He saw the glare reflected in his view lenses. As a ground soldier he would have hit the rock and tried to claw himself a hole. But there was no ground here, no up or down, concealment or shelter, on a fragment of spaceship orbiting through the darkness beyond Mars. Diaz went loose in his armour. Countdown: brow, jaw, neck, shoulders, back, chest, belly . . . No blast came, to slam him against the end of his lifeline and break any bones whose muscles were not relaxed. So it had not been a shaped charge shell, firing a cone of atomic-powered concussion through space. Or if it was, he had not been caught in the danger zone. As for radiation, he needn't worry much about that. Whatever particles and gamma photons he got at this distance should not be too big a dose for the anti-X in his body to handle the effects.

He drew a breath which was a good deal shakier than the Academy satorist would have approved of. ('If your nerves twitch, cadet-san, then you know yourself alive and they need not twitch. Correct?' To hell with that, except as a technique.) Slowly, he hauled himself in until his boots made magnetic contact and he stood, so to speak, upon his raft. Then he turned about for a look.

'*Nombre de Dios*,' he murmured, a hollow noise in the helmet. Forgotten habit came back, with a moment's recollection of his mother's face. He crossed himself.

Against blackness and a million wintry stars, a gas cloud

expanded. It glowed in many soft hues, the centre still bright, edges fading into vacuum. Shaped explosions did not behave like that, thought the calculator part of Diaz; this had been a standard fireball type. But the cloud was non-spherical. Hence a ship had been hit, a big ship, but whose?

Most of him stood in wonder. A few years ago he'd spent a furlough at Antarctic Lodge. He and some girl had taken a snowcat out to watch the aurora, thinking it would make a romantic background. But when they saw the sky, they forgot about each other for a long time. There was only the aurora.

The same awesome silence was here, as that incandescence which had been a ship and her crew swelled and vanished into space.

The calculator in his head proceeded with its business. Of those American vessels near the *Argonne* when first contact was made with the enemy, only the *Washington* was sufficiently massive to go out in a blast of yonder size and shape. If that was the case Captain Martin Diaz of the United States Astromilitary Corps was a dead man. The other ships of the line were too distant, travelling on vectors too unlike his own, for their scoutboats to come anywhere close. On the other hand, it might well have been a Unasian battlewagon. Diaz had small information on the dispositions of the enemy fleet. He'd had his brain full just directing the torp launchers under his immediate command. If that had indeed been a hostile dreadnaught that got clobbered, surely none but the *Washington* could have delivered the blow, and its boats would be near—

There!

For half a second Diaz was too stiffened by the sight to react. The boat ran black across waning clouds, accelerating on a streak of its own fire. The wings and sharp shape that were needed in atmosphere made him think of a marlin he had once hooked off Florida, blue lightning under the sun ... Then a flare was in his hand, he squeezed the igniter and radiance blossomed.

Just an attention-getting device, he thought, and laughed unevenly as he and Bernie Sternthal had done, acting out the standard irreverences of high school students towards the psych course. But Bernie had left his bones on Ganymede, three years ago, and in this hour Diaz's throat was constricted and his nostrils full of his own stench. He skyhooked the flare and hunkered in its harsh illumination by his radio transmitter. Clumsy in their gauntlets, his fingers adjusted controls, set the revolving beams on SOS. If he had been noticed, and if it was physically possible to make the velocity changes required, a boat would come for him. The Corps looked after its own.

Presently the flare guttered out. The pyre cloud faded to nothing. The raft deck was between Diaz and the shrunken sun. But the stars that crowded on every side gave ample soft light. He allowed his gullet, which felt like sandpaper, a suck from his one water flask. Otherwise he had several air bottles, an oxygen reclaim unit, and a ridiculously large box of Q rations. His raft was a section of inner plating, torn off when the *Argonne* encountered the ball storm. She was only a pursuit cruiser, unarmoured against such weapons. At thirty miles per second, relative, the little steel spheres tossed in her path by some Unasian gun had not left much but junk and corpses. Diaz had found no other survivors. He'd lashed what he could salvage on to this raft, including a shaped torp charge that rocketed him clear of the ruins. This far spaceward, he didn't need screen fields against solar particle radiation. So he had had a small hope of rescue. Maybe bigger than small, now.

Unless an enemy craft spotted him first. His scalp crawled with that thought. His right arm, where the thing he might use in the event of capture lay buried, began to itch. But no, he told himself, don't be sillier than regulations require. That scoutboat was positively American. The probability of a hostile vessel being in detection range of his flare and radio – or able to change vectors fast enough – or giving a damn about him in any event – approached so close to zero as made no difference.

'Wish I'd found our bottle in the wreckage,' he said aloud. He was talking to Carl Bailey, who'd helped him smuggle the Scotch aboard at Shepard Field when the fleet was alerted for departure. The steel balls had chewed Carl to pieces, some of which Diaz had seen. 'It gripes me not to empty that bottle. On behalf of us both, I mean. Maybe,' his voice wandered on, 'a million years hence, it'll drift into another planetary system and owl-eyed critters will pick it up in boneless fingers, eh, Carl, and put it in a museum.' He realized what he was doing and snapped his mouth shut. But his mind continued. *The trouble is, those critters won't know about Carl Bailey, who collected antique jazz tapes, and played a rough game of poker, and had a DSM and a gimpy leg from rescuing three boys whose patroller crashed on Venus, and went on the town with Martin Diaz one evening not so long ago when— What did happen that evening, anyhow?*

There was a joint down in the Mexican section of San Diego which Diaz remembered was fun. So they caught a giro outside the Hotel Kennedy, where the spacemen were staying – they could afford swank, and felt they owed it to the Corps – and where they had bought their girls dinner. Diaz punched the cantina's name. The autopilot searched its directory and swung the cab on to the Embarcadero-Balboa skyrail.

Sharon sighed and snuggled into the curve of his arm. 'How beautiful,' she said. 'How nice of you to show me this.' He felt she meant a little more than polite banality. The view through the bubble really was great tonight. The city winked and blazed, a god's hoard of jewels, from horizon to horizon. Only in one direction was there anything but light: westward, where the ocean lay aglow. A nearly full moon stood high in the sky. He pointed out a tiny glitter on its dark edge.

'Vladimir Base.'

'Ugh,' said Sharon. 'Unasians.' She stiffened a trifle.

'Oh, they're decent fellows,' Bailey said from the rear seat.

'How do you know?' asked his own date, Naomi, a serious-looking girl and quick on the uptake.

'I've visited them a time or two,' he shrugged.

'What?' Sharon exclaimed. 'When we're at *war*?'

'Why not?' Diaz said. 'The ambassador of United Asia gave a party for our President just yesterday. I watched on the newscreen. Big social event.'

'But that's different,' Sharon protested. 'The war goes on in space, not on Earth, and—'

'We don't blow up each other's Lunar bases, either,' Bailey said. 'Too close to home. So once in a while we have occasion to, uh, parley is the official word. Actually, the last time I went over – couple years ago now – it was to return a craterbug we'd borrowed and bring some alga-blight antibiotic they needed. They poured me full of excellent vodka.'

'I'm surprised you admit this so openly,' said Naomi.

'No secret, my dear,' purred Diaz in his best grandee manner, twirling an imaginary moustache. 'The newscreens simply don't mention it. Wouldn't be popular, I suppose.'

'Oh, people wouldn't care, seeing it was the Corps,' Sharon said.

'That's right,' Naomi smiled. 'The Corps can do no wrong.'

'Why, thankee kindly.' Diaz grinned at Sharon, chucked her under the chin and kissed her. She held back an instant, having met him only this afternoon. But of course she knew what a date with a Corpsman usually meant, and he knew she knew, and she knew he knew she knew, so before long she relaxed and enjoyed it.

The giro stopped those proceedings by descending to the street and rolling three blocks to the cantina. They entered a low, noisy room hung with bullfight posters and dense with smoke. Diaz threw a glance around and wrinkled his nose. '*Sanamabiche!*' he muttered. 'The tourists have discovered it.'

'Uh-huh,' Bailey answered in the same disappointed *sotto voce*. 'Loud tunics, lard faces, 3V, and a juke wall. But let's have a couple of drinks, at least, seeing we're here.'

'That's the trouble with being in space two or three years at a time,' Diaz said. 'You lose track. Well . . .' They found a booth.

The waiter recognized him, even after so long a lapse, and called the proprietor. The old man bowed nearly to the floor and begged they accept tequila from his private stock. *'No, no, Señor Capitán, conserva el dinero, por favor.'* The girls were delighted – picturesqueness seemed harder to come by each time Diaz made Earthfall – and the evening was off to a good start in spite of everything.

But then someone paid the juke. The wall came awake with a scrawny blonde fourteen-year-old, the latest fashion in sex queens, wearing a grass skirt and three times life size.

> *Bingle-jingle-jungle-bang-POW!*
> *Bingle-jingle-jungle-bang-UGH!*
> *Uh'm uh redhot Congo gal an' Uh'm lookin' fuh a pal*
> *Tuh share muh bingle-jingle-bangle-jungle-ugh-YOW!*

'What did you say?' Sharon called through the saxophones.

'Never mind,' Diaz grunted. 'They wouldn't've included it in your school Spanish anyway.'

'Those things make me almost wish World War Four would start,' Naomi said bitterly.

Bailey's mouth tightened. 'Don't talk like that,' he said. 'Wasn't Number Three a close enough call for the race? Without even accomplishing its aims, for either side. I've seen— Any war is too big.'

Lest they become serious, Diaz said thoughtfully above the racket: 'You know, it should be possible to do something about those Kallikak walls. Like, maybe, an oscillator. They've got oscillators these days which'll even goof a solid-state apparatus at close range.'

'The FCC wouldn't allow that,' Bailey said. 'Especially since it'd interfere with local 3V reception.'

'That's bad? Besides, you could miniaturize the oscillator

so it'd be hard to find. Make it small enough to carry in your pocket. Or in your body, if you could locate a doctor who'd, uh, perform an illegal operation. I've seen uplousing units no bigger than—'

'You could strew 'em around town,' Bailey said, getting interested. 'Hide 'em in obscure corners and—'

Ugga-wugga-wugga, hugga-hugga me, do!

'I *wish* it would stop,' Naomi said. 'I came here to get to know you, Carl, not that thing.'

Bailey sat straight. One hand, lying on the table, shaped a fist. 'Why not?' he said.

'Eh?' Diaz asked.

Bailey rose. 'Excuse me a minute.' He bowed to the girls and made his way through the dancers to the wall control. There he switched the record off.

Silence fell like a meteor. For a moment, voices were stilled, too. Then a large tourist came barrelling off his bar stool and yelled, 'Hey, wha' d'you think you're—'

'I'll refund your money, sir,' Bailey said mildly. 'But the noise bothers the lady I'm with.'

'Huh? Hey, who d'yuh think yuh are, you—'

The proprietor came from around the bar. 'If the lady weeshes it off,' he declared, 'off it stays.'

'What kinda discrimination is this?' roared the tourist. Several other people growled with him.

Diaz prepared to go help, in case things got rough. But his companion pulled up the sleeve of his mufti tunic. The ID bracelet gleamed into view. 'First Lieutenant Carl H. Bailey, United States Astromilitary Corps, at your service,' he said; and a circular wave of quietness expanded around him. 'Please forgive my action. I'll gladly stand the house a round if—'

But that wasn't necessary. The tourist fell all over himself apologizing and begged to buy the drinks. Someone else bought them next, and someone after him. Nobody ventured near the booth, where the spacemen obviously wanted privacy. But from time to time, when Diaz glanced out, he got many smiles and a few shy waves. It was almost embarrassing.

'I was afraid for a minute we'd have a fight,' he said.

'N-no,' Bailey answered. 'I've watched our prestige develop exponentially, being Stateside while my leg healed. I doubt if there's an American alive who'd lift a finger against a Corpsman these days. But I admit I was afraid of a scene. That wouldn't've done the name of the Corps any good. As things worked out, though . . .'

'We came off too bloody well,' Diaz finished. 'Now there's not even any pseudolife in this place. Let's haul mass. We can catch the transpolar shuttle to Paris if we hurry.'

But at that moment the proprietor's friends-and-relations, who also remembered him, began to arrive. They must have been phoned the great news. Pablo was there, Manuel, Carmen with her castanets, Juan with his guitar, Tio Rico waving a bottle in each enormous fist; and they welcomed Diaz back with embraces, and soon there was song and dancing, and the fiesta ended in the rear courtyard watching the moon set before dawn, and everything was like the old days, for Señor Capitán Diaz's sake. That had been a hell of a good furlough.

Another jet splashed fire across the Milky Way. Closer this time, and obviously reducing relative speed. Diaz croaked out a cheer. He had spent weary hours waiting. The hugeness and aloneness had eaten farther into his defences than he wished to realize. He had begun to understand why some people were disturbed to see the stars on a clear mountain night. (Where wind went soughing through Jeffrey pines whose bark smelled like vanilla if you laid your head close, and a river flowed cold and loud over stones – oh, Christ, how beautiful Earth was!) He shoved such matters aside and reactivated his transmitter.

The streak winked out and the stars crowded back into his eyes. But that was all right, it meant the boat had decelerated as much as necessary, and soon a scooter would be homing on his beam, and water and food and sleep, and a new ship and eventually certain letters to write. That would be the worst part – but not for months or years yet, not till one side or the other conceded the present phase of the war. Diaz found himself wishing most for a cigarette.

He hadn't seen the boat's hull this time, of course; no rosy cloud had existed to silhouette its blackness. Nor did he see the scooter until it was almost upon him. That jet was very thin, since it need only drive a few hundred pounds of mass on which two spacesuited men sat. They were little more than a highlight and a shadow. Diaz's pulse filled the silence. 'Hello!' he called in his helmet mike. 'Hello yonder!'

They didn't reply. The scooter matched velocities a few yards off. One man tossed a line with a luminous bulb at the end. Diaz caught it and made fast. The line was drawn taut. Scooter and raft bumped together and began gently rotating.

Diaz recognized those helmets.

He snatched for a sidearm he didn't have. A Unasian sprang to one side, lifeline unreeling. His companion stayed mounted, a chucker gun cradled in his arms. The sun rose blindingly over the raft edge.

There was nothing to be done. Yet. Diaz fought down a physical nausea of defeat, 'raised' his hands and let them hang free. The other man came behind him and deftly wired his wrists together. Both Unasians spent a few minutes inspecting the raft. The man with the gun tuned in on the American band. 'You make very clever salvage, sir,' he said.

'Thank you,' Diaz whispered.

'Come, please.' He was lashed to the carrier rack. Weight tugged at him as the scooter accelerated.

They took an hour or more to rendezvous. Diaz had time to adjust his emotions. The first horror passed into numbness; then he identified a sneaking relief, that he would get a reasonably comfortable vacation from war until the next prisoner exchange; and then he remembered the new doctrine, which applied to all commissioned officers on whom there had been time to operate.

I may never get the chance, he thought frantically. *They*

*told me not to waste myself on anything less than a cruiser;
my chromosomes and several million dollars spent in training me make me that valuable to the country, at least. I may
go straight to Pallas, or wherever their handiest prison base
is, in a lousy scoutboat or cargo ship.*

*But I may get a chance to strike a blow that'll hurt. Have I
got the guts? I hope so. No, I don't even know if I hope it.
This is a cold place to die.*

The feeling passed. Emotional control, drilled into him
at the Academy and practised at every refresher course,
took over. It was essentially psychosomatic, a matter of
using conditioned reflexes to bring muscles and nerves and
glands back towards normal. If the fear symptoms, tension,
tachycardia, sweat, decreased salivation, and the rest, were
alleviated, then fear itself was. Far down under the surface, a
four-year-old named Martin woke from nightmare and
screamed for his mother, who did not come; but Diaz grew
able to ignore him.

The boat became visible, black across star clouds. No, not
a boat. A small ship . . . abnormally large jets and light guns,
a modified Panyushkin . . . what had the enemy been up to in
his asteroid shipyards? Some kind of courier vessel, maybe.
Recognition signals must be flashing back and forth. The
scooter passed smoothly through a lock that closed again
behind it. Air was pumped in, and Diaz went blind as frost
condensed on his helmet. Several men assisted him out of
the armour. They hadn't quite finished when an alarm rang,
engines droned, and weight came back. The ship was start-
ing off at about half a gee.

Short bodies in green uniforms surrounded Diaz. Their
immaculate appearance reminded him of his own unshaven filthiness, how much he ached, and how sandy his
brain felt. 'Well,' he mumbled, 'where's your interrogation
officer?'

'You go more high, Captain,' answered a man with
colonel's insignia. 'Forgive us we do not attend your needs
at once, but he says very important.'

Diaz bowed to the courtesy, remembering what had been

planted in his arm and feeling rather a bastard. Though it looked as if he wouldn't have occasion to use the thing. Dazed by relief and weariness, he let himself be escorted along corridors and tubes until he stood before a door marked with great black Cyrillic warnings and guarded by two soldiers. Which was almost unheard of aboard a space-ship, he thought joltingly.

There was a teleye above the door. Diaz barely glanced at it. Whoever sat within the cabin must be staring through it, at him. He tried to straighten his shoulders. 'Martin Diaz,' he croaked, 'Captain, USAC, serial number—'

Someone yelled from the loudspeaker beside the pickup. Diaz half understood. He whirled about. His will gathered itself and surged. He began to think the impulses that would destroy the ship. A guard tackled him. A rifle butt came down on his head. And that was that.

They told him forty-eight hours passed while he was in sickbay. 'I wouldn't know,' he said dully. 'Nor care.' But he was again in good physical shape. Only a bandage sheathing his lower right arm, beneath the insignialess uniform given him, revealed that surgeons had been at work. His mind was sharply aware of its environment – muscle play beneath his skin, pastel bulkheads and cold fluorescence, faint machine-quiver underfoot, gusts from ventilator grilles, odours of foreign cooking, and always the men, with alien faces and carefully expressionless voices, who had caught him.

At least he suffered no abuse. They might have been justified in resenting his attempt to kill them. Some would call it treacherous. But they gave him the treatment due an officer and, except for supplying his needs, left him alone in his tiny bunk cubicle. Which was worse, in some respects, than punishment. Diaz was actually glad when he was at last summoned for an interview.

They brought him to the guarded door and gestured him through. It closed behind him.

For a moment Diaz noticed only the suite itself. Even a fleet commander didn't get such space and comfort. The ship had long ceased accelerating, but spin provided a reasonable weight. The suite was constructed within a rotatable shell, so that the same deck was 'down' as when the jets were in operation. Diaz stood on a Persian carpet, looking past low-legged furniture to a pair of arched doorways. One revealed a bedroom, lined with microspools – ye gods, there must be ten thousand volumes! The other showed part of an office, a desk, and a great enigmatic control panel and—

The man seated beneath the Monet reproduction got up and made a slight bow. He was tall for a Unasian, with a lean mobile face whose eyes were startlingly blue against a skin as white as a Swedish girl's. His undress uniform was neat but carelessly worn. No rank insignia were visible, for a grey hood, almost a coif, covered his head and fell over the shoulders.

'Good day, Captain Diaz,' he said, speaking English with little accent. 'Permit me to introduce myself: General Leo Ilyitch Rostock, Cosmonautical Service of the People of United Asia.'

Diaz went through the rituals automatically. Most of him was preoccupied with how quiet this place was, how vastly quiet ... But the layout was serene. Rostock must be fantastically important if his comfort rated this much mass. Diaz's gaze flickered to the other man's waist. Rostock bore a sidearm. More to the point, though, one loud holler would doubtless be picked up by the teleye mike and bring in the guards from outside.

Diaz tried to relax. *If they haven't kicked my teeth in so far, they don't plan to. I'm going to live.* But he couldn't believe that. Not here, in the presence of this hooded man. Still more so, in this drawing-room. Its existence beyond Mars was too eerie. 'No, sir, I have no complaints,' he heard himself saying. 'You run a good ship. My compliments.'

'Thank you.' Rostock had a charming, almost boyish smile. 'Although this is not my ship, actually. Colonel Sumoro commands the *Ho Chi Minh*. I shall convey your appreciation to him.'

'You may not be called the captain,' Diaz said bluntly, 'but the vessel is obviously your instrument.'

Rostock shrugged. 'Will you not sit down?' he invited, and resumed his own place on the couch. Diaz took a chair across the table from him, feeling knobby and awkward. Rostock pushed a box forward. 'Cigarette?'

'Thank you.' Diaz struck and inhaled hungrily.

'I hope your arm does not bother you.'

Diaz's belly muscles tightened. 'No. It's all right.'

'The surgeons left the metal ulnar bone in place, as well as its nervous and muscular connections. Complete replacement would have required more hospital equipment than a spaceship can readily carry. We did not want to cripple you by removing the bone. After all, we were only interested in the cartridge.'

Diaz gathered courage and snapped: 'The more I see of you, General, the sorrier I am that it didn't work. You're big game.'

Rostock chuckled. 'Perhaps. I wonder, though, if you are as sorry as you would like to feel you are. You would have died too, you realize.'

'Uh-huh.'

'Do you know what the weapon embedded in you was?'

'Yes. *We* tell our people such things. A charge of isotopic explosive, with a trigger activated by a particular series of motor nerve pulses. Equivalent to about ten tons of TNT.' Diaz gripped the chair arms, leaned forward and said harshly: 'I'm not blabbing anything you don't now know. I daresay you consider it a violation of the customs of war. Not me! I gave no parole—'

'Certainly, certainly.' Rostock waved a deprecating hand. 'We hold . . . what is your idiom? . . . no hard feelings. The device was ingenious. We have already dispatched a warning to our Central, whence the word can go out through the fleet, so your effort, the entire project, has gone for nothing. But it was a rather gallant attempt.'

He leaned back, crossed one long leg over the other, and regarded the American candidly. 'Of course, as you implied, we would have proceeded somewhat differently,' he said. 'Our men would not have known what they carried, and the explosion would have been triggered posthypnotically, by some given class of situations, rather than consciously. In that way, there would be less chance of betrayal.'

'How did you know, anyway?' Diaz sighed.

Rostock gave him an impish grin. 'As the villain of this particular little drama, I shall only say that I have my methods.' Suddenly he was grave. 'One reason we made so great an effort to pick you up before your own rescue party arrived, was to gather data on what you have been doing, you people. You know how comparatively rare it is to get a prisoner in space warfare; and how hard to get spies into an organization of high morale which maintains its own laboratories and factories off Earth. Divergent developments can go far these days, before the other side is aware of them. The miniaturization involved in your own weapon, for example, astonished our engineers.'

'I can't tell you anything else,' Diaz said.

'Oh, you could,' Rostock answered gently. 'You know as well as I what can be done with a shot of babble juice. Not to mention other techniques – nothing melodramatic, nothing painful or disabling, merely applied neurology – in which I believe Unasia is ahead of the Western countries. But don't worry, Captain. I shall not permit any such breach of military custom.

'However, I do want you to understand how much trouble we went to, to get you. When combat began, I reasoned that the ships auxiliary to a dreadnaught would be the likeliest to suffer destruction of the type which leaves a few survivors. From the pattern of action in the first day, I deduced the approximate orbits and positions of several American capital ships. Unasian tactics throughout the second day were developed with two purposes: to inflict damage, of course, but also to get the *Ho* so placed that we could be likely to detect any distress signals. This cost us the *Genghis* – a calculated risk that did not pay off – I am not omniscient. But we did hear your call.

'You are quite right about the importance of this ship here. My superiors will be horrified at my action. But of necessity, they have given me *carte blanche*. And since the *Ho* itself takes no direct part in any engagement if we can avoid it, the probability of our being detected and attacked was small.'

Rostock's eyes held Diaz's. He tapped the table, softly and repeatedly, with one fingernail. 'Do you appreciate what all this means, Captain?' he asked. 'Do you see how badly you were wanted?'

Diaz could only wet his lips and nod.

'Partly,' Rostock said, smiling again, 'there was the desire I have mentioned, to . . . er . . . check up on American activities during the last cease-fire period. But partly, too, there was a wish to bring you up to date on what we have been doing.'

'Huh?' Diaz half scrambled from his chair, sagged back and gaped.

'The choice is yours, Captain,' Rostock said. 'You can be transferred to a cargo ship when we can arrange it, and so to an asteroid camp, and in general receive the normal treatment of a war prisoner. Or you may elect to hear what I would like to discuss with you. In the latter event, I can guarantee nothing. Obviously I can't let you go home in a routine prisoner exchange with a prime military secret of ours. You will have to wait until it is no longer a secret – until American intelligence has learned the truth, and we know that they have. That may take years. It may take forever, because I have some hope that the knowledge will change certain of your own attitudes.

'No, no, don't answer now. Think it over. I will see you again tomorrow. In twenty-four hours, that is to say.'

Rostock's eyes shifted past Diaz, as if to look through the bulkheads. His tone dropped to a whisper. 'Have you ever wondered, like me, why we carry Earth's rotation period to space with us? Habit; practicality; but is there not also an element of magical thinking? A hope that somehow we can create our own sunrises? The sky is very black out there. We need all the magic we can invent. Do we not?'

Several hours later, alarms sounded, voices barked over the intercoms, spin was halted but weight came quickly back as the ship accelerated. Diaz knew just enough Mandarin to understand from what he overheard that radar contact had been made with American units and combat would soon resume. The guard who brought him dinner in his cubicle confirmed it, with many a bow and hissing smile. Diaz had gained enormous face by his audience with the man in the suite.

He couldn't sleep, though the racket soon settled down to a purposeful murmur with few loud interruptions. Restless in his bunk harness, he tried to reconstruct a total picture from the clues he had. The primary American objective was the asteroid base system of the enemy. But astromilitary tactics were too complicated for one brain to grasp. A battle might go on for months, flaring up whenever hostile units came near enough in their enormous orbitings to exchange fire. Eventually, Diaz knew, if everything went well – that is, didn't go too badly haywire – Americans would land on the Unasian worldlets. That would be the rough part. He remembered ground operations on Mars and Ganymede far too well.

As for the immediate situation, though, he could only make an educated guess. The leisurely pace at which the engagement was developing indicated that ships of dread-naught mass were involved. Therefore no mere squadron was out there, but an important segment of the American fleet, perhaps the task force headed by the *Alaska*. But if this was true, then the *Ho Chi Minh* must be directing a flotilla of comparable size.

Which wasn't possible! Flotillas and subfleets were bossed from dreadnaughts. A combat computer and its human staff were too big and delicate to be housed in anything less. And the *Ho* was not even as large as the *Argonne* had been.

Yet what the hell was this but a command ship? Rostock had hinted as much. The activity aboard was characteristic: the repeated sound of courier boats coming and going, intercom calls, technicians hurrying along the corridors, but no shooting.

Nevertheless . . .

Voices jabbered beyond the cell door. Their note was triumphant. Probably they related a hit on an American vessel. Diaz recalled brushing aside chunks of space-frozen meat that had been his Corps brothers. Sammy Yoshida was in the *Utah Beach*, which was with the *Alaska* – Sammy who'd covered for him back at the Academy when he crawled in dead drunk hours after taps, and some years later had dragged him from a shell-struck foxhole on Mars and shared oxygen till a rescue squad happened by. Had the *Utah Beach* been hit? Was that what they were giggling about out there?

Prisoner exchange, in a year or two or three, will get me back for the next round of the war, Diaz thought in darkness. *But I'm only one man. And I've goofed somehow, spilled a scheme which might've cost the Unies several ships before they tumbled. It's hardly conceivable I could smuggle out whatever information Rostock wants to give me. But there'd be some tiny probability that I could, somehow, sometime. Wouldn't there?*

I don't want to. Dios mio, how I don't want to! Let me rest a while, and then be swapped, and go back for a long furlough on Earth, where anything I ask for is mine and mainly I ask for sunlight and ocean and flowering trees. But Carl liked those things too, didn't he?

A lull came in the battle. The fleets had passed each other, decelerating as they fired. They would take many hours to turn around and get back within combat range. A great quietness descended on the *Ho*. Walking down the passageways, which thrummed with rocketblast, Diaz saw how the technicians slumped at their posts. The demands on them were as hard as those on a pilot or gunner or missile chief. Evolution designed men to fight with their hands, not with computations and pushbuttons. Maybe ground combat wasn't the worst kind at that.

The sentries admitted Diaz through the door of the warning. Rostock sat at the table again. His coiffed features looked equally drained, and his smile was automatic. A samovar and two teacups stood before him.

'Be seated, Captain,' he said tonelessly. 'Pardon me if I do not rise. This has been an exhausting time.'

Diaz accepted a chair and a cup. Rostock drank noisily, eyes closed and forehead puckered. There might have been an extra stimulant in his tea, for before long he appeared more human. He refilled the cups, passed out cigarettes, and leaned back on his couch with a sigh.

'You may be pleased to know,' he said, 'that the third pass will be the final one. We shall refuse further combat and proceed instead to join forces with another flotilla near Pallas.'

'Because that suits your purposes better,' Diaz said.

'Well, naturally. I compute a higher likelihood of ultimate success if we follow a strategy of . . . no matter now.'

Diaz leaned forward. His heart slammed. 'So this *is* a command ship,' he exclaimed. 'I thought so.'

The blue eyes weighed him with care. 'If I give you any further information,' Rostock said – softly, but the muscles tightened along his jaw – 'you must accept the conditions I set forth.'

'I do,' Diaz got out.

'I realize that you do so in the hope of passing on the secret to your countrymen,' Rostock said. 'You may as well forget about that. You won't get the chance.'

'Then why do you want to tell me? You won't make a Unie out of me, General.' The words sounded too stuck up, Diaz decided. 'That is, I respect your people and so forth, but . . . uh . . . my loyalties lie elsewhere.'

'Agreed. I don't hope or plan to change them. At least, not in an easterly direction.' Rostock drew hard on his cigarette, let smoke stream from his nostrils, and squinted through it. 'The microphone is turned down,' he remarked.

'We cannot be overheard unless we shout. I must warn you, if you make any attempt to reveal what I am about to say to you to any of my own people I shall not merely deny it but order you sent out the airlock. It is that important.'

Diaz rubbed his hands on his trousers. The palms were wet. 'Okay,' he said.

'Not that I mean to browbeat you, Captain,' said Rostock hastily. 'What I offer is friendship. In the end, maybe, peace.' He sat a while longer, looking at the wall, before his glance shifted back to Diaz. 'Suppose you begin the discussion. Ask me what you like.'

'Uh . . .' Diaz floundered about, as if he'd been leaning on a door that was thrown open. 'Uh . . . well, was I right? Is this a command ship?'

'Yes. It performs every function of a flag dreadnaught, except that it seldom engages in direct combat. The tactical advantages are obvious. A smaller, lighter vessel can get about much more readily, hence be a correspondingly more effective directrix. Furthermore, if due caution is exercised, we are not likely to be detected and fired at. The massive armament of a dreadnaught is chiefly to stave off the missiles that can annihilate the command post within. Ships of this class avoid that whole problem by avoiding attack in the first place.'

'But your computer! You, you must have developed a combat computer as . . . small and rugged as an autopilot . . . I thought miniaturization was our speciality.'

Rostock laughed

'And you'd still need a large human staff,' Diaz protested. 'Bigger than the whole crew of this ship!

'Wouldn't you?' he finished weakly.

Rostock shook his head. 'No.' His smile faded. 'Not under this new system. I am the computer.'

'What?'

'Look.' Rostock pulled off his hood.

The head beneath was hairless, not shaved but depilated. A dozen silvery plates were set into it, flush with the scalp; in them were plug outlets. Rostock pointed towards the office. 'The rest of me is in there,' he said. 'I need only set the jacks into the appropriate points of myself, and I become . . . no, not part of the computer. It becomes part of me.'

He fell silent again, gazing now at the floor. Diaz hardly dared move, until his cigarette burned his fingers and he had to stub it out. The ship pulsed around them. Monet's picture of sunlight caught in young leaves was like something seen at the far end of a tunnel.

'Consider the problem,' Rostock said at last, low. 'In spite of much loose talk about giant brains, computers do not think, except perhaps on an idiot level. They simply perform logical operations, symbol-shuffling, according to instructions given them. It was shown long ago that there are infinite classes of problems that no computer can solve: the classes dealt with in Gödel's theorem, that can only be solved by the nonlogical process of creating a metalanguage. Creativity is not logical and computers do not create.

'In addition, as you know, the larger a computer becomes, the more staff it requires, to perform such operations as data coding, programming, retranslation of the solutions into practical terms, and adjustment of the artificial answer to the actual problems. Yet your own brain does this sort of thing constantly . . . because it is creative. Moreover, the advanced computers are heavy, bulky, fragile things. They use cryogenics and all the other tricks, but that involves elaborate ancillary apparatus. Your brain weighs a kilogram or so, is quite adequately protected in the skull, and needs less than a hundred kilos of outside equipment – your body.

'I am not being mystical. There is no reason why creativity cannot someday be duplicated in an artificial structure. But I think that structure will look very much like a living organism; will, indeed, be one. Life has had a billion years to develop these techniques.

'Now if the brain has so many advantages, why use a computer at all? Obviously, to do the uncreative work, for which the brain is not specifically designed. The brain visualizes a problem of, say, orbits, masses, and tactics and formulates it as a set of matrix equations; then the computer

goes swiftly through the millions of idiot counting operations needed to produce a numerical solution. What we
have developed here, we Unasians, is nothing but a direct
approach. We eliminate the middle man, as you Americans
would say.

'In yonder office is a highly specialized computer. It is
built from solid-state units, analogous to neurons, but in spite
of being able to treat astromilitary problems, it is a comparatively small, simple, and sturdy device. Why? Because it
is used in connection with my brain, which directs it. The
normal computer must have its operational patterns built in.
Mine develops synapse pathways as needed, just as a man's
lower brain can develop skills under the direction of the
cerebral cortex. And these pathways are modifiable by experience; the system is continually restructuring itself. The
normal computer must have elaborate failure detection
systems and arrangements for rerouting. I in the hookup
here sense any trouble directly, and am no more disturbed
by the temporary disability of some region than you are
disturbed by the fact that most of your brain cells at any
given time are resting.

'The human staff becomes superfluous here. My technicians bring me the data, which need not be reduced to
standardized format. I link myself to the machine and . . .
think about it . . . there are no words. The answer is worked
out in no more time than any other computer would require.
But it comes to my consciousness not as a set of figures, but
in practical terms, decisions about what to do. Furthermore,
the solution is modified by my human awareness of those
factors too complex to go into mathematical form – like the
physical condition of men and equipment, morale, long-
range questions of logistics and strategy and ultimate goals.
You might say this is a computer system with common sense.
Do you understand, Captain?'

Diaz sat still for a long time before he said, 'Yes. I think I
do.'

Rostock had got a little hoarse. He poured himself a fresh
cup of tea and drank half, struck another cigarette and said

earnestly: 'The military value is obvious. Were that all, I would never have revealed this to you. But something else developed as I practised and increased my command of the system. Something quite unforeseen. I wonder if you will comprehend.' He finished his cup. 'The repeated experience has . . . changed me. I am no longer human. Not really.'

The ship whispered, driving through darkness.

'I suppose a hookup like that would affect the emotions,' Diaz ventured. 'How does it feel?'

'There are no words,' Rostock repeated, 'except those I have made for myself.' He rose and walked restlessly across the subdued rainbows in the carpet, hands behind his back, eyes focused on nothing Diaz could see. 'As a matter of fact, the emotional effect may be a simple intensification. Although . . . there are myths about mortals who became gods. How did it feel to them? I think they hardly noticed the palaces and music and feasting on Olympus. What mattered was how, piece by piece, as he mastered his new capacities, the new god won a god's understanding. His perception, involvement, detachment, totalness . . . there *are* no words.'

Back and forth he paced, feet noiseless but metal and energies humming beneath his low and somehow troubled voice. 'My cerebrum directs the computer,' he said, 'and the relationship becomes reciprocal. True, the computer part has no creativity of its own; but it endows mine with a speed and sureness you cannot imagine. After all, a great part of original thought consists merely in proposing trial solutions – the scientist hypothesizes, the artist draws a charcoal line, the poet scribbles a phrase – and testing them to see if they work. By now, to me, this mechanical aspect of imagination is back down on the subconscious level where it belongs. What my awareness senses is the final answer, springing to life almost simultaneously with the question, and yet with a felt reality to it such as comes only from having pondered and tested the issue thousands of times.

'Also, the amount of sense data I can handle is fantastic. Oh, I am blind and deaf and numb away from my machine half! So you will realize that over the months I have tended to spend more and more time in the linked state. When there was no immediate command problem to solve, I would sit and savour total awareness. Or I would think.'

In a practical tone: 'That is how I perceived that you were about to sabotage us, Captain. Your posture alone betrayed you. I guessed the means at once and ordered the guards to knock you unconscious. I think, also, that I detected in you the potential I need. But that demands closer examination. Which is easily given. When I am linked, you cannot lie to me. The least insincerity is written across your whole organism.'

He paused, to stand a little slumped, looking at the bulkhead. For a moment Diaz's legs tensed. *Three jumps and I can be there and get his gun!* But no, Rostock wasn't any brain-heavy dwarf. The body in that green uniform was young and trained. Diaz took another cigarette. 'Okay,' he said. 'What do you propose?'

'First,' Rostock said, turning about – and his eyes kindled – 'I want you to understand what you and I are. What the spacemen of both factions are.'

'Professional soldiers,' Diaz grunted uneasily. Rostock waited. Diaz puffed hard and ploughed on, since he was plainly expected to. 'The last soldiers left. You can't count those ornamental regiments on Earth, nor the guys sitting by the big missiles. Those missiles will never be fired. World War Three was a large enough dose of nucleonics. Civilization was lucky to survive. Terrestrial life would be lucky to survive, next time around. So war has moved into space. Uh ... professionalism ... the old traditions of mutual respect and so forth have naturally revived.' He made himself look up. 'What more clichés need I repeat?'

'Suppose your side completely annihilated our ships,' Rostock said. 'What would happen?'

'Why ... that's been discussed theoretically ... by damn near every political scientist, hasn't it? The total command of space would not mean total command of Earth. We could destroy the whole Eastern Hemisphere without being

touched. But we wouldn't, because Unasia would fire its
cobalt weapons while dying, and we'd have no Western
Hemisphere to come home to, either. Not that that situation
will ever arise. Space is too big; there are too many ships and
fortresses scattered around; combat is too slow a process.
Neither fleet can wipe out the other.'

'Since we have this perpetual stalemate, then,' Rostock
pursued, 'why do we have perpetual war?'

'Um . . . well, not really. Cease-fires—'

'Breathing spells! Come now, Captain, you are too intelligent to believe that rigmarole. If victory cannot be achieved,
why fight?'

'Well, uh, partial victories are possible. Like our capture
of Mars, or your destruction of three dreadnaughts in one
month, on different occasions. The balance of power shifts.
Rather than let its strength continue being whittled down,
the side which is losing asks for a parley. Negotiations
follow, which end to the relative advantage of the stronger
side. Meanwhile the arms race continues. Pretty soon a new
dispute arises, the cease-fire ends, and maybe the other side
is lucky that time.'

'Is this situation expected to be eternal?'

'No!' Diaz stopped, thought a minute, and grinned
with one corner of his mouth. 'That is, they keep talking
about an effective international organization. Trouble is,
the two cultures are too far apart by now. They can't live
together.'

'I used to believe that myself,' Rostock said. 'Lately I
have not been sure. A world federalism could be devised
which would let both civilizations keep their identities.
Many such proposals have in fact been made, as you know.
None has got beyond the talking stage. None ever will. Because you see, what maintains the war is not the difference
between our two cultures, but their similarity.'

'Whoa, there!' Diaz bristled. 'I resent that.'

'Please,' Rostock said. 'I pass no moral judgments. For
the sake of argument, at least, I can concede you the moral
superiority, remarking only in parenthesis that Earth holds

billions of people who not only fail to comprehend what you mean by freedom but would not like it if you gave it to them. The similarity I am talking about is technological. Both civilizations are based on the machine, with all the high organization and dynamism which this implies.'

'So?'

'So war is a necessity— Wait! I am not talking about "merchants of death", or "dictators needing an outside enemy", or whatever the current propaganda lines are. I mean that conflict is built into the culture. There *must* be an outlet for the destructive emotions generated in the mass of the people by the type of life they lead. A type of life for which evolution never designed them.

'Have you ever heard about L. F. Richardson? No? He was an Englishman in the last century, a Quaker, who hated war but, being a scientist, realized the phenomenon must be understood clinically before it can be eliminated. He performed some brilliant theoretical and statistical analyses which showed, for example, that the rate of deadly quarrels was nearly constant over the decades. There could be many small clashes or a few major ones, but the result was the same. Why were the United States and the Chinese Empire so peaceful during the nineteenth century? The answer is that they were not; they had their Civil War and Taiping Rebellion, which devastated them as much as required. I need not multiply examples. We can discuss this later in detail. I have carried Richardson's work a good deal further and more rigorously. I say to you now only that civilized societies must have a certain rate of immolations.'

Diaz listened to silence for a minute before he said: 'Well, I've sometimes thought the same. I suppose you mean we spacemen are the goats these days?'

'Exactly. War fought out here does not menace the planet. By our deaths we keep Earth alive.'

Rostock sighed. His mouth drooped. 'Magic works, you know,' he said, 'works on the emotions of the people who practise it. If a primitive witch doctor told a storm to go away, the storm did not hear, but the tribe did and took heart. The ancient analogy to us, though, is the sacrificial king in the early agricultural societies; a god in mortal form, who was regularly slain so that the fields might bear fruit. This was not mere superstition. You must realize that. It worked – on the people. The rite was essential to the operation of their culture, to their sanity and hence to their survival.

'Today the machine age has developed its own sacrificial kings. We are the chosen of the race, the best it can offer. None gainsays us. We may have what we choose, pleasure, luxury, women, adulation – only not the simple pleasures of wife and child and hope, for we must die that the people may live.'

Again silence, until: 'Do you seriously mean that's why the war goes on?' Diaz breathed.

Rostock nodded.

'But nobody . . . I mean, people wouldn't—'

'They do not reason these things out, of course. Traditions develop blindly. The ancient peasant did not elaborate logical reasons why the king must die. He merely knew this was so, and left the syllogism for modern anthropologists to expound. I did not see the process going on today until I had had the chance to . . . to become more perceptive than I had been,' Rostock said humbly.

Diaz couldn't endure sitting any longer. He jumped to his feet. 'Assuming you're right,' he snapped, 'and you may be, what of it? What can be done?'

'Much,' Rostock said. Calm descended on his face like a mask. 'I am not being mystical about this, either. The sacrificial king has reappeared as the end product of a long chain of cause and effect. There is no reason inherent in natural law why this must be. Richardson was right in his basic hope, that when war becomes understood, as a phenomenon, it can be eliminated. This would naturally involve restructuring the entire terrestrial culture – gradually, subtly. Remember—' His hand shot out, seized Diaz's shoulder and gripped painfully hard. 'There is a new element in history today. Us. The kings. We are not like those who spend their lives under Earth's sky. In some ways we are more, in other ways less, but always we are different. You and I are more akin to each other than to our planet-dwelling countrymen. Are we not?

'In the time and loneliness granted me, I have used all my new powers to think about this. Not only think; this is so much more than cold reason. I have tried to feel. To love what is, as the Buddhists say. I believe a nucleus of spacemen like us, slowly and secretly gathered, wishing the good of everyone on Earth and the harm of none, gifted with powers and insights they cannot really imagine at home – I believe we may accomplish something. If not us, then our sons. Men ought not to kill each other, when the stars are waiting.'

He let go, turned away and looked at the deck. 'Of course,' he mumbled, 'I, in my peculiar situation, must first destroy a number of your brothers.'

They had given Diaz a whole pack of cigarettes, an enormous treasure out here, before they locked him into his cubicle for the duration of the second engagement. He lay in harness, hearing clang and shout and engine roar through the vibrating bulkheads, stared at blackness, and smoked until his tongue was foul. Sometimes the *Ho* accelerated, mostly it ran free and he floated. Once a tremor went through the entire hull, near miss by a shaped charge. Doubtless gamma rays, ignoring the magnetic force screens, sleeted through the men and knocked another several months off their life expectancies. Not that that mattered; spacemen rarely lived long enough to worry about degenerative diseases. Diaz hardly noticed.

Rostock's not lying. Why should he? What could he gain? He may be a nut, of course. But he doesn't act like a nut either. He wants me to study his statistics and equations, satisfy myself that he's right. And he must be damn sure I will be convinced, to tell me what he has.

How many are there like him? Few, I'm sure. The man-machine symbiosis is obviously new, or we'd've had some inkling ourselves. This is the first field trial of the system. I wonder if the others have reached the same conclusions as Rostock. No, he said he doubts that; their minds impressed him as being more deeply channelled than his. He's a lucky accident.

Lucky? Now how can I tell? I'm only a man. I've never experienced an IQ of a thousand, or whatever the figure may be. A god's purposes aren't necessarily what a man would elect.

An eventual end to war? Well, other institutions had been ended, at least in the Western countries: judicial torture, chattel slavery, human sacrifice – no, wait, according to Rostock human sacrifice had been revived.

'But is our casualty rate high enough to fit your equations?' Diaz had argued. 'Space forces aren't as big as old-time armies. No country could afford that.'

'Other elements than death must be taken into account,' Rostock answered. 'The enormous expense is one factor. Taxpaying is a form of symbolic self-mutilation. It also tends to direct civilian resentments and aggressions against their own governments, thus taking some pressure off international relations.

'Chiefly, though, there is the matter of emotional intensity. A spaceman does not simply die, he usually dies horribly and that moment is the culmination of a long period under grisly conditions. His groundling brothers, administrative and service personnel, suffer vicariously: "sweat it out", as your idiom so well expresses the feeling. His kinfolk, friends, women, are likewise racked. When Adonis dies – or Osiris, Tammuz, Baldur, Christ, Tlaloc, whichever of his hundred names you choose – the people must in some degree share his agony. That is part of the sacrifice.'

Diaz had never thought about it in quite that way. Like most Corpsmen, he had held the average civilian in thinly disguised contempt. But ... from time to time, he remembered, he'd been glad his mother died before he enlisted.

And why did his sister hit the bottle so hard? Then there had been Lois, she of the fire-coloured hair and violet eyes, who wept as if she would never stop weeping when he left for duty. He'd promised to get in touch with her on his return, but of course he knew better.

Which did not erase memories of men whose breath and blood came exploding from burst helmets; who shuddered and vomited and defecated in the last stages of radiation sickness; who stared without immediate comprehension at a red spurt which a second ago had been an arm or a leg; who went insane and must be gassed because psychoneurosis is catching on a six months' orbit beyond Saturn; who – Yeah, Carl had been lucky.

You could talk as much as you wished about Corps brotherhood, honour, tradition, and gallantry. It remained sentimental guff ... No, that was unjust. The Corps had saved the people, their lives and liberties. There could be no higher achievement – for the Corps. But knighthood had once been a noble thing, too; then, lingering after its day, it became a yoke and eventually a farce. The warrior virtues were not ends in themselves. If the warrior could be made obsolete ...

Could he? How much could one man, even powered by a machine, hope to do? How much could he even hope to understand?

The moment came upon Diaz. He lay as if blinded by shellburst radiance.

As consciousness returned, he knew first, irrelevantly, what it meant to get religion.

'By God,' he told the universe, 'we're going to try!'

The battle would resume shortly. At any moment, in fact, some scoutship leading the American force might fire a missile. But when Diaz told his guard he wanted to speak with General Rostock, he was taken there within minutes.

The door closed behind him. The living-room lay empty, altogether still except for the machine throb, which was not loud since the *Ho* was running free. Because acceleration might be needful on short notice, there was no spin. Diaz hung weightless as fog. And the Monet flung into his eyes all Earth's sunlight and summer forests.

'Rostock?' he called uncertainly.

'Come,' said a voice, almost too low to hear. Diaz gave a shove with his foot and flew towards the office.

He stopped himself by grasping the doorjamb. A semi-circular room lay before him, the entire side taken up by controls and meters. Lights blinked, needles wavered on dials, buttons and switches and knobs reached across the black panelling. But none of that was important. Only the man at the desk mattered, who free-sat with wires running from his head to the wall.

Rostock seemed to have lost weight. Or was that an illusion? The skin was drawn taut across his high cheekbones and gone a dead, glistening white. His nostrils were flared and the colourless lips held tense. Diaz looked into his eyes, once, and away again. He could not meet them. He could not even think about them. He drew a shaken breath and waited.

'You made your decision quickly,' Rostock whispered. 'I had not awaited you until after the engagement.'

'I . . . I didn't think you would see me till then.'

'This is more important.' Diaz felt as if he were being probed with knives. He could not altogether believe it was his imagination. He stared desperately at panelled instruments. Their nonhumanness was like a comforting hand. *They must be for the benefit of maintenance techs*, he thought in a distant part of himself. *The brain doesn't need them.* 'You are convinced,' Rostock said in frank surprise.

'Yes,' Diaz answered.

'I had not expected that. I hoped for little more than your reluctant agreement to study my work.' Rostock regarded him for a still century. 'You were ripe for a new faith,' he decided. 'I had not taken you for the type. But then, the mind can only use what data are given it, and I have hitherto had small opportunity to meet Americans. Never since I became what I am. You have another psyche from ours.'

'I need to understand your findings, sir,' Diaz said. 'Right now I can only believe. That isn't enough, is it?'

Slowly, Rostock's mouth drew into a smile of quite human warmth. 'Correct. But given the faith, intellectual comprehension should be swift.'

'I ... I shouldn't be taking your time .. now, sir,' Diaz stammered. 'How should I begin? Should I take some books back with me?'

'No.' Acceptance had been reached; Rostock spoke resonantly, a master to his trusted servant. 'I need your help here. Strap into yonder harness. Our first necessity is to survive the battle upon us. You realize that this means sacrificing many of your comrades. I know how that will hurt you. Afterwards we shall spend our lives repaying our people ... both our peoples. But today I shall ask you questions about your fleet. Any information is valuable, especially details of construction and armament which our intelligence has not been able to learn.'

Doña mía. Diaz let go the door, covered his face and fell free, endlessly. *Help me.*

'It is not betrayal,' said the superman. 'It is the ultimate loyalty you can offer.'

Diaz made himself look at the cabin again. He shoved against the bulkhead and stopped by the harness near the desk.

'You cannot lie to me,' said Rostock. 'Do not deny the pain I am giving you.' Diaz glimpsed his fists clamping together. 'Each time I look at you, I share what you feel.'

Diaz clung to his harness. There went an explosion through him.

NO, BY GOD!

Rostock screamed.

'Don't,' Diaz sobbed. 'I don't want—' But wave after wave ripped outward. Rostock flopped about in his harness and shrieked. The scene came back, ramming home like a bayonet.

'We like to put an extra string on our bow,' the psych officer said. Lunar sunlight, scarcely softened by the dome, blazed off his bronze eagles, wings and beaks. 'You know that your right ulna will be replaced with a metal section which contains a nerve-triggered nuclear cartridge. But that may not be all, gentlemen.'

He bridged his fingers. The young men seated on the other side of his desk stirred uneasily. 'In this country,' the psych officer said, 'we don't believe humans should be turned into puppets. Therefore you will have voluntary control of your bombs; no posthypnosis, Pavlov reflex, or any such insult. However, those of you who are willing will receive a rather special extra treatment, and that fact will be buried from the consciousness of every one of you.

'Our reasoning is that if and when the Unasians learn about the prisoner weapon, they'll remove the cartridge by surgery but leave the prosthetic bone in place. And they will, we hope, not examine it in microscopic detail. Therefore they won't know that it holds an oscillator, integrated with the crystal structure. Nor will you; because what you don't know, you can't babble under anaesthesia.

'The opportunity may come, if you are captured and lose your bomb, to inflict damage by this reserve means. You may find yourself near a crucial electronic device, for example a spaceship's autopilot. At short range, the oscillator will do an excellent job of bollixing it. Which will at least discomfit the enemy, and may give you a chance to escape.

'The posthypnotic command will be such that you'll remember about this oscillator when conditions seem right for using it. Not before. Of course, the human mind is a damned queer thing; it twists and turns and bites its own tail. In order to make an opportunity to strike this blow, your subconscious may lead you down strange paths – may even have you seriously contemplating treason, if treason seems the only way of getting access to what you can wreck. Don't let that bother you afterwards, gentlemen. Your superiors will know what happened.

'Nevertheless, the experience may be painful. And post-hypnosis is, at best, humiliating to a free man. So this aspect of the programme is strictly volunteer. Does anybody want to go for broke?'

The door flung open. The guards burst in. Diaz was already behind the desk, next to Rostock. He yanked out the general's sidearm and fired at the soldiers. Free-fall recoil sent him back against the computer panel. He braced himself, fired again, and used his left elbow to smash the nearest meter face.

Rostock clawed at the wires in his head. For a moment Diaz guessed what it must be like to have random oscillations in your brain, amplified by an electronic engine that was part of you. He laid the pistol to the screaming man's temple and fired once more.

Now to get out! He shoved hard, arrowing past the sentries, who rolled through the air in a crimson galaxy of blood globules. Confusion boiled in the corridor beyond. Someone snatched at him. He knocked the fellow aside and dived along a tubeway. Somewhere hereabouts should be a scooter locker – there, and nobody around!

He didn't have time to get on a spacesuit, even if a Unasian one would have fitted, but he slipped an air dome over the scooter. That, with the heater unit and oxy reclaim, would serve. He didn't want to get off anywhere en route; not before he'd steered the machine through an American hatch.

With luck, he'd do that. Their command computer gone, the enemy were going to get smeared. American ships would close in as the slaughter progressed. Eventually one should come within range of the scooter's little radio.

He set the minilock controls, mounted the saddle, dogged the air dome, and waited for ejection. It came none too soon. Three soldiers had just appeared down the passageway. Diaz applied full thrust and jetted away from the *Ho*. Its blackness was soon lost among the star clouds.

Battle commenced. The first Unasian ship to be destroyed must have been less than fifty miles distant. Luckily, Diaz was facing the other way when the missile exploded.

Wildcat

*Every new capability that man gains is, sooner
rather than later, turned against his fellow man.
The use is often indirect, sometimes very subtle
indeed; but it is not the less significant for that, nor
necessarily less dangerous.*

It was raining again, hot and heavy out of a hidden sky, and
the air stank with swamp. Herries could just see the tall
derricks a mile away, under a floodlight glare, and hear their
engines mutter. Farther away, a bull brontosaur cried and
thunder went through the night.

Herries' boots resounded hollowly on the dock. Beneath
the slicker, his clothes lay sweat-soggy, the rain spilled off his
hat and down his collar. He swore in a tired voice and
stepped onto his gangplank.

Light from the shack on the barge glimmered off
drenched wood. He saw the snaky neck just in time, as it
reared over the gangplank rail and struck at him. He sprang
back, grabbing for the Magnum carbine slung over one
shoulder. The plesiosaur hissed monstrously and flipper-
slapped the water. It was like a cannon going off.

Herries threw the gun to his shoulder and fired. The long
sleek form took the bullet – somewhere – and screamed. The
raw noise hurt the man's eardrums.

Feet thudded over the wharf. Two guards reached Herries and began to shoot into the dark water. The door
of the shack opened and a figure stood black against its
yellow oblong, a tommy-gun stammering idiotically in its
hands.

'Cut it out!' bawled Herries. 'That's enough! Hold your
fire!'

Silence fell. For a moment only the ponderous rainfall
had voice. Then the brontosaur bellowed again, remotely,
and there were seethings and croakings in the water.

'He got away,' said Herries. 'Or more likely his pals are now stripping him clean. Blood smell.' A dull anger lifted in him. He turned and grabbed the lapel of the nearest guard. 'How often do I have to tell you characters, every gangway has to have a man near it with grenades?'

'Yes, sir. Sorry, sir.' Herries was a large man, and the other face looked up at him, white and scared in the wan electric radiance. 'I just went off to the head—'

'You'll stay here,' said Herries. 'I don't care if you explode. Our presence draws these critters, and you ought to know that by now. They've already snatched two men off this dock. They nearly got a third tonight – me. At the first suspicion of anything out there, you're to pull the pin on a grenade and drop it in the water, understand? One more dereliction like this, and you're fired— No.' He stopped, grinning humourlessly. 'That's not much of a punishment, is it? A week in hack on bread.'

The other guard bristled. 'Look here, Mr Herries, we got our rights. The union—'

'Your precious union is a hundred million years in the future,' snapped the engineer. 'It was understood that this is a dangerous job, that we're subject to martial law, and that I can discipline anyone who steps out of line. Okay – remember.'

He turned his back and tramped across the gangplank to the barge deck. It boomed underfoot. With the excitement over, the shack had been closed again. He opened the door and stepped through, peeling off his slicker.

Four men were playing poker beneath an unshaded bulb. The room was small and cluttered, hazy with tobacco smoke and the Jurassic mist. A fifth man lay on one of the bunks, reading. The walls were gaudy with pinups.

Olson riffled the cards and looked up. 'Close call, Boss,' he remarked, almost casually. 'Want to sit in?'

'Not now,' said Herries. He felt his big square face sagging with weariness. 'I'm bushed.' He nodded at Carver, who had just returned from a prospecting trip farther north. 'We lost one more derrick today.'

'Huh?' said Carver. 'What happened this time?'

'It turns out this is the mating season.' Herries found a chair, sat down, and began to pull off his boots. 'How they tell one season from another, I don't know . . . length of day, maybe . . . but anyhow the brontosaurs aren't shy of us any more – they're going nuts. Now they go gallyhooting around and trample down charged fences or anything else that happens to be in the way. They've smashed three rigs to date, and one man.'

Carver raised an eyebrow in his chocolate-coloured face. It was a rather sour standing joke here, how much better the Negroes looked than anyone else. A white man could be outdoors all his life in this clouded age and remain pasty. 'Haven't you tried shooting them?' he asked.

'Ever try to kill a brontosaur with a rifle?' snorted Herries. 'We can mess 'em up a little with .50-calibre machine-guns or a bazooka – just enough so they decide to get out of the neighbourhood – but being less intelligent than a chicken, they take off in any old direction. Makes as much havoc as the original rampage.' His left boot hit the floor with a sullen thud. 'I've been begging for a couple of atomic howitzers, but it has to go through channels . . . Channels!' Fury spurted in him. 'Five hundred human beings stuck in this nightmare world, and our requisitions have to go through channels!'

Olson began to deal the cards. Polansky gave the man in the bunk a chill glance. 'You're the wheel, Symonds,' he said. 'Why the devil don't you goose the great Trans-temporal Oil Company?'

'Nuts,' said Carver. 'The great benevolent all-wise United States Government is what counts. How about it, Symonds?'

You never got a rise out of Symonds, the human tape recorder, just a playback of the latest official line. Now he laid his book aside and sat up in his bunk. Herries noticed that the volume was Marcus Aurelius, in Latin yet.

Symonds looked at Carver through steel-rimmed glasses and said in a dusty tone: 'I am only the comptroller and supply supervisor. In effect, a chief clerk. Mr Herries is in charge of operations.'

He was a small shrivelled man, with thin grey hair above a thin grey face. Even here, he wore stiff-collared shirt and sober tie. One of the hardest things to take about him was the way his long nose waggled when he talked.

'In charge!' Herries spat expertly into a gobboon. 'Sure, I direct the prospectors and the drillers and everybody else on down through the bull cook. But who handles the paper-work – all our reports and receipts and requests? You.' He tossed his right boot on the floor. 'I don't want the name of boss if I can't get the stuff to defend my own men.'

Something bumped against the supervisors' barge; it quivered and the chips on the table rattled. Since there was no outcry from the dock guards, Herries ignored the matter. Some swimming giant. And except for the plesiosaurs and the nonmalicious bumbling bronties, all the big dinosaurs encountered so far were fairly safe. They might step on you in an absent-minded way, but most of them were peaceful and you could outrun those that weren't. It was the smaller carnivores, about the size of a man, leaping out of brush or muck with a skullful of teeth, that had taken most of the personnel lost. Their reptile life was too diffuse: even mor-tally wounded by elephant gun or grenade launcher, they could rave about for hours. They were the reasons for sleep-ing on the barges tied up by this sodden coast, along the gulf that would some day be Oklahoma.

Symonds spoke in his tight little voice: 'I send your recommendations in, of course. The project office passes on them.'

'I'll say it does,' muttered young Greenstein irreverently.

'Please do not blame me,' insisted Symonds.

I wonder. Herries glowered at him. Symonds had an in of some kind. That was obvious. A man who was simply a glorified clerk would not be called to Washington for un-specified conferences with unspecified people as often as this one was. But what was he, then?

A favourite relative? No ... in spite of high pay, this operation was no political plum. FBI? Scarcely ... the security checks were all run in the future. A hack in the bureaucracy? That was more probable. Symonds was here to see that oil was pumped and dinosaurs chased away and the hideously fecund jungle kept beyond the fence according to the least comma in the latest directive from headquarters.

The small man continued: 'It has been explained to you officially that the heavier weapons are all needed at home. The international situation is critical. You ought to be thankful you are safely back in the past.'

'Heat, large economy-size alligators, and not a woman for a hundred million years,' grunted Olson. 'I'd rather be blown up. Who dealt this mess?'

'You did,' said Polansky. 'Gimme two, and make 'em good.'

Herries stripped the clothes off his thick hairy body, went to the rear of the cabin, and entered the shower cubby. He left the door open, to listen in. A boss was always lonely. Maybe he should have married when he had the chance. But then he wouldn't be here. Except for Symonds, who was a widower and in any case more a government than company man, Transoco had been hiring only young bachelors for operations in the field.

'It seems kinda funny to talk about the international situation,' remarked Carver. 'Hell, there won't be any international situation for several geological periods.'

'The inertial effect makes simultaneity a valid approximational concept,' declared Symonds pedantically. His habit of lecturing scientists and engineers on their professions had not endeared him to them. 'If we spend a year in the past, we must necessarily return to our own era to find a year gone, since the main projector operates only at the point of its own existence which—'

'Oh, stow it,' said Greenstein. 'I read the orientation manual too.' He waited until everyone had cards, then shoved a few chips forward and added: ''Druther spend my time a little nearer home. Say with Cleopatra.'

'Impossible,' Symonds told him. 'Inertial effect again. In

order to send a body into the past at all, the projector must energize it so much that the minimal time-distance we can cover becomes precisely the one we have covered to arrive here, one hundred and one million, three hundred twenty-seven thousand, et cetera, years.'

'But why not time-hop into the future? You don't buck entropy in that direction. I mean, I suppose there is an inertial effect there, too, but it would be much smaller, so you could go into the future—'

'—about a hundred years at a hop, according to the handbook,' supplied Polansky.

'So why don't they look at the twenty-first century?' asked Greenstein.

'I understand that that is classified information,' Symonds said. His tone implied that Greenstein had skirted some unimaginably gross obscenity.

Herries put his head out of the shower. 'Sure it's classified,' he said. 'They'd classify the wheel if they could. But use your reason and you'll see why travel into the future isn't practical. Suppose you jump a hundred years ahead. How do you get home to report what you've seen? The projector will yank you a hundred million years into the past, less the distance you went forward.'

Symonds dived back into his book. Somehow he gave an impression of lying there rigid with shock that men dared think after he had spoken the phrase of taboo.

'Uh ... yes. I get it.' Greenstein nodded. He had been recruited only a month ago, to replace a man drowned in a moss-veiled bog. Before then, like nearly all the world, he had had no idea time travel existed. So far he had been too busy to examine its implications.

To Herries it was an old, worn-thin story.

'I daresay they did send an expedition a hundred million years up, so it could come back to the same week as it left,' he said. 'Don't ask me what was found. Classified: Tip-top Secret, Burn Before Reading.'

'You know, though,' said Polansky in a reflective tone, 'I been thinking some myself. Why are we here at all? I mean, oil is necessary to defence and so forth, but it seems to me it'd make more sense for the US Army to come through, cross the ocean, and establish itself where the enemy nations are going to be. Then we'd have a gun pointed at their heads!'

'Nice theory,' said Herries. 'I've daydreamed myself. But there's only one main projector, to energize all the subsidiary ones. Building it took almost the whole world supply of certain rare earths. Its capacity is limited. If we started sending military units into the past, it'd be a slow and cumbersome operation – and not being a security officer, I'm not required to kid myself that Moscow doesn't know we have time travel. They've probably even given Washington a secret ultimatum: "Start sending back war material in any quantity, and we'll hit you with everything we've got." But evidently they don't feel strongly enough about our pumping oil on our own territory – or what will one day be our own territory – to make it a, uh, *casus belli*.'

'Just as we don't feel their satellite base in the twentieth century is dangerous enough for us to fight about,' said Greenstein. 'But I suspect we're the reason they agreed to make the moon a neutral zone. Same old standoff.'

'I wonder how long it can last?' murmured Polansky.

'Not much longer,' said Olson. 'Read your history. I'll see you, Greenstein, boy, and raise you two.'

Herries let the shower run about him. At least there was no shortage of hot water. Transoco had sent back a complete nuclear reactor. But civilization and war still ran on oil, he thought, and oil was desperately short up there.

Time, he reflected, was a paradoxical thing. The scientists had told him it was utterly rigid. Perhaps, though of course it would be a graveyard secret, the cloak-and-dagger boys had tested that theory the hard way, going back into the historical past (it could be done after all, Herries suspected, by a round-about route that consumed fabulous amounts of energy) in an attempt to head off the Bolshevik revolution. It would have failed. Neither past nor future could be changed; they could only be discovered. Some of Transoco's

men had discovered death, an eon before they were born . . .
But there would not be such a shortage of oil in the future if
Transoco had not gone back and drained it in the past. A
self-causing future . . .

Primordial stuff, petroleum. Hoyle's idea seemed to be
right, it had not been formed by rotting dinosaurs but was
present from the beginning. It was the stuff that had stuck
the planets together.

And, Herries thought, was sticking to him now. He
reached for the soap.

Earth spun gloomily through hours, and morning crept
over wide brown water. There was no real day as men understood day; the heavens were a leaden sheet with dirty black
rain-clouds scudding below the permanent fog layers.

Herries was up early, for a shipment was scheduled. He
came out of the bosses' messhall and stood for a moment
looking over the mud beach and the few square miles of
cleared land, sleazy buildings, and gaunt derricks inside an
electric mesh fence. Automation replaced thousands of
workers, so that five hundred men were enough to handle
everything, but still the compound was the merest scratch,
and the jungle remained a terrifying black wall. Not that the
trees were so utterly alien. Besides the archaic grotesqueries,
like ferns and mosses of gruesome size, he saw cycad, red-
wood, and gingko, scattered prototypes of oak and willow
and birch. But Herries missed wild flowers.

A working party with its machines was repairing the fence
the brontosaur had smashed through yesterday, the well it
had wrecked, the inroads of brush and vine. A caterpillar
tractor hauled a string of loaded wagons across raw red
earth. A helicopter buzzed overhead, on watch for dinosaurs. It was the only flying thing. There had been a nearby
pterodactyl rookery, but the men had cleaned that out
months ago. When you got right down to facts, the most
sinister animal of all was man.

Greenstein joined Herries. The new assistant was tall,
slender, with curly brown hair and the defenceless face of

youth. Above boots and dungarees he wore a blue sports shirt; it offered a kind of defiance to this sullen world. 'Smoke?' he invited.

'Thanks.' Herries accepted the cigarette. His eyes still dwelt on the drills. Their walking beams went up and down, up and down, like a joyless copulation. Perhaps a man could get used to the Jurassic rain forest and eventually see some dark beauty there, for it was at least life: but this field would always remain hideous, being dead and pumping up the death of men.

'How's it going, Sam?' he asked when the tobacco had soothed his palate.

'All right,' said Greenstein. 'I'm shaking down. But God, it's good to know today is mail call!'

They stepped off the porch and walked towards the transceiving station. Mud squelched under their feet. A tuft of something, too pale and fleshy to be grass, stood near Herries' path. The yard crew had better uproot that soon, or in a week it might claim the entire compound.

'Girl friend, I suppose,' said the chief. 'That does make a month into a hell of a long drought between letters.'

Greenstein flushed and nodded earnestly. 'We're going to get married when my two years here are up,' he said.

'That's what most of 'em plan on. A lot of saved-up pay and valuable experience – sure, you're fixed for life.' It was on Herries' tongue to add that the life might be a short one, but he suppressed the impulse.

Loneliness dragged at his nerves. No one waited in the future for him. It was just as well, he told himself during the endless nights. Hard enough to sleep without worrying about some woman in the same age as the cobalt bomb.

'I've got her picture here, if you'd like to see it,' offered Greenstein shyly.

His hand was already on his wallet. A tired grin slid up Herries' mouth. 'Right next to your ... er .. heart, eh?' he murmured

Greenstein blinked, threw back his head, and laughed.

The field had not heard so merry a sound in a long while. Nevertheless, he showed the other man a pleasant-faced, unspectacular girl.

Out in the swamp, something hooted and threshed about.

Impulsively, Herries asked: 'How do you feel about this operation, Sam?'

'Huh? Why, it's . . . interesting work. And a good bunch of guys.'

'Even Symonds?'

'Oh, he means well.'

'We could have more fun if he didn't bunk with us.'

'He can't help being . . . old,' said Greenstein.

Herries glanced at the boy. 'You know,' he said, 'you're the first man in the Jurassic Period who's had a good word for Ephraim Symonds. I appreciate that. I'd better not say whether or not I share the sentiment, but I appreciate it.'

His boots sludged ahead, growing heavier with each step. 'You still haven't answered my first question,' he resumed after a while. 'I didn't ask if you enjoyed the work, I asked how you feel about it. Its purpose. We have the answers here to questions which science has been asking – will be asking – for centuries. And yet, except for a couple of underequipped palaeobiologists, who aren't allowed to publish their findings, we're doing nothing but rape the Earth in an age before it has ever conceived us.'

Greenstein hesitated. Then, with a surprise dryness: 'You're getting too psychoanalytic for me, I'm afreud.'

Herries chuckled. The day seemed a little more alive, all at once. '*Touché!* Well, I'll rephrase Joe Polansky's question of last night. Do you think the atomic standoff in our home era – to which this operation is potentially rather important – is stable?'

Greenstein considered for a moment. 'No,' he admitted. 'Deterrence is a stopgap till something better can be worked out.'

'They've said as much since it first began. Nothing has been done. It's improbable that anything will be. Ole Olson describes the international situation as a case of the irresistibly evil force colliding with the immovably stupid object.'

'Ole likes to use extreme language,' said Greenstein. 'So tell me, what else could our side do?'

'I wish to God I had an answer.' Herries sighed. 'Pardon me. We avoid politics here as much as possible; we're escapists in several senses of the word. But frankly, I sound out new men. I was doing it to you. Because in spite of what Washington thinks, a Q clearance isn't all that a man needs to work here.'

'Did I pass?' asked Greenstein, a bit too lightly.

'Sure. So far. You may wish you hadn't. The burning issue today is not whether to tolerate "priviliged neutralism", or whatever the latest catchword is up there. It's: Did I get the armament I've been asking for?'

The transceiving station bulked ahead. It was a long corrugated-iron shed, but dwarfed by the tanks that gleamed behind it. Every one of those was filled, Herries knew. Today they would pump their crude oil into the future. Or rather, if you wanted to be exact, their small temporal unit would establish a contact and the gigantic main projector in the twentieth century would then 'suck' the liquid towards itself. And in return the compound would get food, tools, weapons, supplies, and mail. Herries prayed for at least one howitzer ... and no VIP's. That senator a few months ago!

For a moment, contemplating the naked ugliness of tanks and pumps and shed, Herries had a vision of this one place stretching through time. It would be abandoned some day, when the wells were exhausted, and rain and jungle would rapidly eat the last thin traces of man. Later would come the sea, and then it would be dry land again, a cold prairie scoured by glacial winds, and then it would grow warm and ... on and on, a waste of years until the time projector was invented and the great machine stood on this spot. And afterwards? Herries didn't like to think what might be here after that.

Symonds was already present. He popped rabbit-like out

of the building, a coded manifest in one hand, a pencil behind his ear. 'Good morning, Mr Herries,' he said. His tone gave its usual impression of stiff self-importance.

'Morning. All set in there?' Herries went in to see for himself. A spatter of rain began to fall, noisy on the metal roof. The technicians were at their posts and reported clear. Outside, one by one, the rest of the men were drifting up. This was mail day, and little work would be done for the remainder of it.

Herries laid the sack of letters to the future inside the shed in its proper spot. His chronometer said one minute to go. 'Stand by!' At the precise time, there was a dim whistle in the air and an obscure pulsing glow. Meters came to life. The pumps began to throb, driving crude oil through a pipe that faced open-ended into the shed. Nothing emerged that Herries could see. Good. Everything in order. The other end of the pipe was a hundred million years in the future. The mail sack vanished with a small puff, as air rushed in where it had waited. Herries went back outside.

'Ah ... excuse me.'

He turned around, with a jerkiness that told him his nerves were half unravelled. 'Yes?' he snapped.

'May I see you a moment?' asked Symonds. 'Alone?' and the pale eyes behind the glasses said it was not a request but an order.

Herries nodded curtly, swore at the men for hanging around idle when the return shipment wasn't due for hours, and led the way to a porch tacked on to one side of the transceiving station. There were some camp stools beneath it. Symonds hitched up his khakis as if they were a business suit and sat primly down, his hands flat on his knees.

'A special shipment is due today,' he said. 'I was not permitted to discuss it until the last moment.'

Herries curled his mouth. 'Go tell Security that the Kremlin won't be built for a hundred million years. Maybe they haven't heard.'

'What no one knew, no one could put into a letter home.'

'The mail is censored anyway. Our friends and relatives

think we're working somewhere in Asia.' Herries spat into the mud and said: 'And in another year the first lot of recruits are due home. Plan to shoot them as they emerge, so they can't possibly talk in their sleep?'

Symonds seemed too humourless even to recognize sarcasm. He pursed his lips and declared: 'Some secrets need be kept for a few months only; but within that period, they *must* be kept.'

'Okay, okay. Let's hear what's coming today.'

'I am not allowed to tell you that. But about half the total tonnage will be crates marked top secret. These are to remain in the shed, guarded night and day by armed men.' Symonds pulled a slip of paper from his jacket. 'These men will be assigned to that duty, each one taking eight hours a week.'

Herries glanced at the names. He did not know everyone here by sight, though he came close, but he recognized several of these. 'Brave, discreet, and charter subscribers to *National Review*,' he murmured. 'Teacher's pets. All right. Though I'll have to curtail exploration correspondingly – either that, or else cut down on escorts and sacrifice a few extra lives.'

'I think not. Let me continue. You will get these orders in the mail today, but I will prepare you for them now. A special house must be built for the crates, as rapidly as possible, and they must be moved there immediately upon its completion. I have the specifications in my office safe; essentially, it must be air-conditioned, burglar-proof, and strong enough to withstand all natural hazards.'

'Whoa, there!' Herries stepped forward. 'That's going to take reinforced concrete and—'

'Materials will be made available,' said Symonds. He did not look at the other man but stared straight ahead of him, across the rain-smoky compound to the jungle. He had no expression on his pinched face, and the reflection of light off his glasses gave him a strangely blind look.

'But – Judas priest!' Herries threw his cigarette to the ground; it was swallowed in mud and running water. He felt the heat enfold him like a blanket. 'There's the labour too, the machinery, and— How the devil am I expected to expand this operation if—'

'Expansion will be temporarily halted,' cut in Symonds. 'You will simply maintain current operations with skeleton crews. The majority of the labour force is to be reassigned to construction.'

'*What?*'

'The compound fence must be extended and reinforced. A number of new storehouses are to be erected to hold certain supplies which will presently be sent to us. Bunkhouse barges for an additional five hundred are required. This, of course, entails more sickbay, recreational, mess, laundry, and other facilities.'

Herries stood dumbly, staring at him. Pale lightning flickered in the sky.

The worst of it was, Symonds didn't even bother to be arrogant. He spoke like a schoolmaster.

'Oh, no!' whispered Herries after a long while. 'They're not going to try to establish that Jurassic military base after all!'

'The purpose is classified.'

'Yeah. Sure. Classified. Arise, ye duly cleared citizens of democracy, and cast your ballot on issues whose nature is classified, that your leaders whose names and duties are classified may— Great. Hopping. Balls. Of. Muck.' Herries swallowed. Vaguely, through his pulse, he felt his fingers tighten into fists.

'I'm going up,' he said 'I'm going to protest personally in Washington.'

'That is not permitted,' Symonds said in a dry, clipped tone. 'Read your contract. You are under martial law. Of course,' and his tone was neither softer nor harder, 'you may file a written recommendation.'

Herries stood for a while. Out beyond the fence stood a bulldozer, wrecked and abandoned. The vines had almost buried it and a few scuttering little marsupials lived there. Perhaps they were his own remote ancestors. He could take a .22 and go potshooting at them some day.

'I'm not permitted to know anything,' he said at last. 'But is curiosity allowed? An extra five hundred men aren't much. I suppose, given a few airplanes and so on, a thousand of us could plant atomic bombs where enemy cities will be. Or could we? Can't locate them without astronomical studies first, and it's always clouded here. So it would be practical to boobytrap only with mass action weapons. A few husky cobalt bombs, say. But there are missiles available to deliver those in the twentieth century. So . . . what is the purpose?'

'You will learn the facts in due course,' answered Symonds. 'At present, the government has certain military necessities.'

'Haw!' said Herries. He folded his arms and leaned against the roofpost. It sagged a bit . . . shoddy work, shoddy world, shoddy destiny. 'Military horses' necks! I'd like to get one of those prawn-eyed brass hats down here, just for a week, to run his precious security check on a lovesick brontosaur. But I'll probably get another visit from Senator Lardhead, the one who took up two days of my time walking around asking about the possibilities of farming. *Farming!*'

'Senator Wien is from an agricultural state. Naturally he would be interested—'

'—in making sure that nobody here starts raising food and shipping it back home to bring grocery prices down to where people can afford an occasional steak. Sure. I'll bet it cost us a thousand man-hours to make his soil tests and tell him, yes, given the proper machinery this land could be farmed. Of course, maybe I do him an injustice. Senator Wien is also on the Military Affairs Committee, isn't he? He may have visited us in that capacity, and soon we'll get a directive to start our own little victory gardens.'

'Your language is close to being subversive,' declared Symonds out of prune-wrinkled lips. 'Senator Wien is a famous statesman.'

For a moment the legislator's face rose in Herries' memory; it had been the oldest and most weary face he had ever known. Something had burned out in the man who fought a decade for honourable peace; the knowledge that there was no peace and could be none became a kind of death, and Senator Wien dropped out of his Free World Union organization to arm his land for Ragnarok. Briefly, his anger fading, Herries pitied Senator Wien. And the President, and the Chief of Staff, and the Secretary of State, for their work must be like a nightmare where you strangled your mother and could not stop your hands. It was easier to fight dinosaurs.

He even pitied Symonds, until he asked if his request for an atomic weapon had finally been okayed, and Symonds replied, 'Certainly not.' Then he spat at the clerk's feet and walked out into the rain.

After the shipment and guards were seen to, Herries dismissed his men. There was an uneasy buzz among them at the abnormality of what had arrived; but today was mail day, after all, and they did not ponder it long. He would not make the announcement about the new orders until tomorrow. He got the magazines and newspapers to which he subscribed (no one up there 'now' cared enough to write to him, though his parents had existed in a section of space-time that ended only a year before he took this job) and wandered off to the boss' barge to read a little.

The twentieth century looked still uglier than it had last month. The nations felt their pride and saw no way of retreat. The Middle Eastern war was taking a decisive turn which none of the great powers could afford. Herries wondered if he might not be cut off in the Jurassic. A single explosion could destroy the main projector. Five hundred womanless men in a world of reptiles— He'd take the future, cobalt bomb and all.

After lunch there fell a quiet, Sunday kind of atmosphere. Men lay on their bunks reading their letters over and over. Herries made his rounds, machines and kitchen and sickbay, inspecting.

'I guess we'll discharge O'Connor tomorrow,' said D

Yamaguchi. 'He can do light work with that Stader on his arm. Next time tell him to duck when a power shovel comes down.'

'What kind of sick calls have you been getting?' asked the chief.

Yamaguchi shrugged. 'Usual things, very minor. I'd never have thought this swamp country could be so healthful. I guess disease germs that can live on placental mammals haven't evolved yet.'

Father Gonzales, one of the camp's three chaplains, buttonholed Herries as he came out. 'Can you spare me a minute?' he said.

'Sure, padre. What is it?'

'About organizing some baseball teams. We need more recreation. This is not a good place for men to live.'

'Sawbones was just telling me—'

'I know. No flu, no malaria, oh, yes. But man is more than a body.'

'Sometimes I wonder,' said Herries. 'I've seen the latest headlines. The dinosaurs have more sense than we do.'

'We have the capacity to do nearly all things,' said Father Gonzales. 'At present, I mean in the twentieth century, we seem to do evil very well. We can do as much good, given the chance.'

'Who's denying us the chance?' asked Herries. 'Just ourselves, H. Sapiens. Therefore I wonder if we really are able to do good.'

'Don't confuse sinfulness with damnation,' said the priest. 'We have perhaps been unfortunate in our successes. And yet even our most menacing accomplishments have a kind of sublimity. The time projector, for example. If the minds able to shape such a thing in metal were only turned towards human problems, what could we not hope to do?'

'But that's my point,' said Herries. 'We don't do the high things. We do what's trivial and evil so consistently that I wonder if it isn't in our nature. Even this time travel business ... more and more I'm coming to think there's something fundamentally unhealthy about it. As if it's an invention that only an ingrown mind would have made first.'

'First?'

Herries looked up into the steaming sky. A foul wind met his face. 'There are stars above those clouds,' he said, 'and most stars must have planets. I've not been told how the time projector works, but elementary differential calculus will show that travel into the past is equivalent to attaining, momentarily, an infinite velocity. In other words, the basic natural law that the projector uses is one that somehow goes beyond relativity theory. If a time projector is possible, so is a spaceship that can reach the stars in a matter of days, maybe of minutes or seconds. If we were sane, padre, we wouldn't have been so anxious for a little organic grease and the little military advantage involved that the first thing we did was go back into the dead past after it. No, we'd have invented that spaceship first, and gone out to the stars where there's room to be free and to grow. The time projector would have come afterwards, as a scientific research tool.'

He stopped, embarrassed at himself and trying awkwardly to grin. 'Excuse me. Sermons are more your province than mine.'

'It was interesting,' said Father Gonzales. 'But you brood too much. So do a number of men. Even if they have no close ties at home – it was wise to pick them for that – they are all of above-average intelligence, and aware of what the future is becoming. I'd like to shake them out of their depression. If we could get some more sports equipment . . .'

'Sure. I'll see what I can do.'

'Of course,' said the priest, 'the problem is basically philosophical. Don't laugh. You too were indulging in philosophy, and doubtless you think of yourself as an ordinary, unimaginative man. Your wildcatters may not have heard of Aristotle, but they are also thinking men in their way. My personal belief is that this heresy of a fixed, rigid time line lies at the root of their growing sorrowfulness whether they know it or not.'

'Heresy?' The engineer lifted thick sandy brows. 'It's been proved. It's the basis of the theory which showed how to build a projector; that much I do know. How could we be here, if the Mesozoic were not just as real as the Cenozoic? But if all time is coexistent, then all time must be fixed – unalterable – because every instant is the unchanging past of some other instant.'

'Perhaps so, from God's viewpoint,' said Father Gonzales. 'But we are mortal men. And we have free will. The fixed-time concept need not, logically, produce fatalism. Remember, Herries, man's will is an important reason why twentieth-century civilization is approaching suicide. If we think we know our future is unchangeable, if our every action is fore-ordained, if we are doomed already, what's the use of trying? Why go through the pain of thought, of seeking an answer and struggling to make others accept it? But if we really believed in ourselves, we would look for a solution, and find one.'

'Maybe,' said Herries uncomfortably. 'Well, give me a list of the equipment you want, and I'll put in an order for it the next time the mail goes out.'

As he walked off, he wondered if the mail would ever go out again.

Passing the rec hall, he noticed a small crowd before it and veered to see what was happening. He could not let men gather to trade doubts and terrors, or the entire operation was threatened. *In plain English*, he told himself with a growing bitter honesty, *I can't permit them to think*.

But the sounds which met him, under the subtly alien rustle of forest leaves and the distant bawl of a thunder lizard, was only a guitar. Chords danced forth beneath expert fingers, and a young voice lilted:

> . . . I travelled this wide world over,
> A hundred miles or more,
> But a saddle on a milk cow,
> I never seen before! . . .

Looking over shoulders, Herries made out Greenstein, sprawled on a bench and singing. He heard chuckles from the listeners. Well deserved: the kid was good; Herries wished he could relax and simply enjoy the performance. Instead, he must note that they were finding it pleasant, and that swamp and war were alike forgotten for a valuable few minutes.

The song ended. Greenstein stood up and stretched. 'Hi, Boss,' he said.

Hard, wind-beaten faces turned to Herries and a mumble of greeting went around the circle. He was well enough liked, he knew, insofar as a chief can be liked. But that is not much. A leader can inspire trust, loyalty, what have you, but he cannot be humanly liked, or he is no leader.

'That was good,' said Herries. 'I didn't know you played.'

'I didn't bring this whangbox with me, since I had no idea where I was going till I got here,' answered Greenstein. 'Wrote home for it and it arrived today.'

A heavy-muscled crewcut man said, 'You ought to be on the entertainment committee.' Herries recognized Worth, one of the professional patriots who would be standing guard on Symonds' crates; but not a bad sort, really, after you learned to ignore his rather tedious opinions.

Greenstein said an indelicate word. 'I'm sick of committees,' he went on. 'We've got so much into the habit of being herded around – everybody in the twentieth century has – that we can't even have a little fun without first setting up a committee.'

Worth looked offended but made no answer. It began to rain again, just a little.

'Go on now, anyway,' said Joe Eagle Wing. 'Let's not take ourselves so goddam serious. How about another song?'

'Not in the wet.' Greenstein returned his guitar to its case. The group began to break up, some to the hall and some back towards their barges.

Herries lingered, unwilling to be left alone with himself. 'About that committee,' he said. 'You might reconsider. It's probably true what you claim, but we're stuck with a situ ation. We've simply got to tell most of the boys, "Now is the time to be happy", or they never will be.'

Greenstein frowned. 'Maybe so. But hasn't anyone ever thought of making a fresh start? Of unlearning those bad habits?'

'You can't do that within the context of an entire society's vices,' said Herries. 'And how're you going to get away?'

Greenstein gave him a long look. 'How the devil did you ever get this job?' he asked. 'You don't sound like a man who'd be cleared for a dishwashing assistantship.'

Herries shrugged. 'All my life I've liked totalitarianism even less than what passes for democracy. I served in a couple of the minor wars and— No matter. Possibly I might not be given the post if I applied now. I've been here more than a year, and it's changed me some.'

'It must,' said Greenstein, flickering a glance at the jungle.

'How's things at home?' asked Herries, anxious for another subject.

The boy kindled, 'Oh, terrific!' he said eagerly. 'Miriam, my girl, you know, she's an artist, and she's got a commission to—'

The loudspeaker coughed and blared across the compound, into the strengthening rain: 'Attention! Copter to ground, attention! Large biped dinosaur, about two miles away north-northeast, coming fast.'

Herries cursed and broke into a run.

Greenstein paced him. Water sheeted where their boots struck. 'What is it?' he called.

'I don't know . . . yet . . . but it might be . . . a really big . . . carnivore.' Herries reached the headquarters shack and flung the door open. A panel of levers was set near his personal desk. He slapped one down and the 'combat stations' siren skirled above the field. Herries went on, 'I don't know why anything biped should make a beeline for us unless the smell of blood from the critter we drove off yesterday is attracting it. The smaller carnivores are sure as hell drawn. The charged fence keeps them away, but I doubt if it would do much more than enrage a dinosaur— Follow me!'

Jeeps were already leaving their garage when Herries and Greenstein came out. Mud leaped up from their wheels and dripped back off the fenders. The rain fell harder, until the forest beyond the fence blurred and the earth smoked with vapours. The helicopter hung above the derricks, like a skeleton vulture watching a skeleton army, and the alarm sirens filled the brown air with screaming.

'Can you drive one of these buggies?' asked Herries.

'I did in the Army,' said Greenstein.

'Okay, we'll take the lead one. The main thing is to stop that beast before it gets in among the wells.' Herries vaulted the right-hand door and planted himself on sopping plastic cushions. A ·50-calibre machine-gun was mounted on the hood before him, and the microphone of a police car radio hung at the dash. Five jeeps followed as Greenstein swung into motion. The rest of the crew, ludicrous ants across these wide wet distances, went scurrying to defend the most vital installations.

The north gate opened and the cars splashed out beyond the fence. There was a strip several yards across, also kept cleared; then the jungle wall rose, black, brown, dull red and green and yellow. Here and there along the fence an occasional bone gleamed up out of the muck, some animal shot by a guard or killed by the voltage. Oddly enough, Herries irrelevantly remembered, such a corpse drew enough scavenging insects to clean it in a day, but it was usually ignored by the nasty man-sized hunter dinosaurs that still slunk and hopped and slithered in this neighbourhood. Reptiles just did not go in for carrion. However, they followed the odour of blood ...

'Farther east,' said the helicopter pilot's radio voice. 'There. Stop. Face the woods. He's coming out in a minute. Good luck, Boss. Next time gimme some bombs and I'll handle the bugger myself.'

'We haven't been granted any heavy weapons.' Herries licked lips that seemed rough. His pulse was thick. No one had ever faced a tyrannosaur before.

The jeeps drew into line, and for a moment only their

windshield wipers had motion. Then undergrowth crashed, and the monster was upon them.

It was indeed a tyrannosaur, thought Herries in a blurred way. A close relative, at least. It blundered ahead with the overweighted, underwitted stiffness which palaeontologists had predicted, and which had led some of them to believe that it must have been a gigantic, carrion-eating hyena. They forgot that, like the Cenozoic snake or crocodile, it was too dull to recognize dead meat as food; that the brontosaurs it preyed on were even more clumsy; and that sheer length of stride would carry it over the earth at a respectable rate.

Herries saw a blunt head three man-heights above ground, and a tail ending fifteen yards away. Scales of an unfairly beautiful steel grey shimmered in the rain, which made small waterfalls off flanks and wrinkled neck and tiny useless forepaws. Teeth clashed in a mindless reflex, the ponderous belly wagged with each step, and Herries felt the vibration of tons coming down claw-footed. The beast paid no attention to the jeeps, but moved jerkily towards the fence. Sheer weight would drive it through the mesh.

'Get in front of him, Sam!' yelled the engineer.

He gripped the machine-gun. It snarled on his behalf, and a sleet of bullets stitched a bloody seam across the white stomach. The tyrannosaur halted, weaving its head about. It made a hollow, coughing roar. Greenstein edged the jeep closer.

The others attacked from the sides. Tracer streams hosed across alligator tail and bird legs. A launched grenade burst with a little puff on the right thigh. It opened a red ulcer-like crater. The tyrannosaur swung slowly about towards one of the cars.

That jeep dodged aside. 'Get in on him!' shouted Herries. Greenstein shifted gears and darted through a fountain of mud. Herries stole a glance. The boy was grinning. Well, it would be something to tell the grandchildren, all right!

His jeep fled past the tyrannosaur, whipped about on two wheels, and crouched under a hammer of rain. The reptile halted. Herries cut loose with his machine-gun. The monster standing there, swaying a little, roaring and bleeding, was not entirely real. This had happened a hundred million years ago. Rain struck the hot gun barrel and sizzled off.

'From the sides again,' rapped Herries into his microphone. 'Two and Three on his right. Four and Five on his left. Six, go behind him and lob a grenade at the base of his tail.'

The tyrannosaur began another awkward about face. The water in which it stood was tinged red.

'Aim for his eyes!' yelled Greenstein, and dashed recklessly towards the profile now presented him.

The grenade from behind exploded. With a sudden incredible speed, the tyrannosaur turned clear around. Herries had an instant's glimpse of the tail like a snake before him, then it struck.

He threw up an arm and felt glass bounce off it as the windshield shattered. The noise when metal gave way did not seem loud, but it went through his entire body. The jeep reeled on ahead. Instinct sent Herries to the floorboards. He felt a brutal impact as his car struck the dinosaur's left leg. It hooted far above him. He looked up and saw a foot with talons, raised and filling the sky. It came down. The hood crumpled at his back and the engine was ripped from the frame.

Then the tyrannosaur had gone on. Herries crawled up into the bucket seat. It was canted at a lunatic angle. 'Sam,' he croaked. 'Sam, Sam.'

Greenstein's head was brains and splinters, with half the lower jaw on his lap and a burst-out eyeball staring up from the seat beside him.

Herries climbed erect. He saw his torn-off machine-gun lying in the mud. A hundred yards off, at the jungle edge, the tyrannosaur fought the jeeps. It made clumsy rushes, which they sideswerved, and they spat at it and gnawed at it. Herries thought in a dull, remote fashion: *This can go on forever. A man is easy to kill, one swipe of a tail and all his songs are a red smear in the rain. But a reptile dies hard, being less alive to start with. I can't see an end to this fight.*

The Number Four jeep rushed in. A man sprang from it and it darted back in reverse from the monster's charge. The man— 'Stop that, you idiot,' whispered Herries into a dead microphone, 'stop it, you fool' – plunged between the huge legs. He moved sluggishly enough with clay on his boots, but he was impossibly fleet and beautiful under that jerking bulk. Herries recognized Worth. He carried a grenade in his hand. He pulled the pin and dodged claws for a moment. The flabby, bleeding stomach made a roof over his head. Jaws searched blindly above him. He hurled the grenade and ran. It exploded against the tyrannosaur's belly. The monster screamed. One foot rose and came down. The talons merely clipped Worth, but he went spinning, fell in the gumbo ten feet away and tried weakly to rise but couldn't.

The tyrannosaur staggered in the other direction, spilling its entrails. Its screams took on a ghastly human note. Somebody stopped and picked up Worth. Somebody else came to Herries and gabbled at him. The tyrannosaur stumbled in yards of gut, fell slowly, and struggled, entangling itself.

Even so, it was hard to kill. The cars battered it for half an hour as it lay there, and it hissed at them and beat the ground with its tail. Herries was not sure it had died when he and his men finally left. But the insects had long been busy, and a few of the bones already stood forth clean white.

The phone jangled on Herries' desk. He picked it up. 'Yeah?'

'Yamaguchi in sickbay,' said the voice. 'Thought you'd want to know about Worth.'

'Well?'

'Broken lumbar vertebrae. He'll live, possibly without permanent paralysis, but he'll have to go back for treatment.'

'And be held incommunicado a year, till his contract's up. I wonder how much of a patriot he'll be by that time.'

'What?'

'Nothing. Can it wait till tomorrow? Everything's so disorganized right now, I'd hate to activate the projector.'

'Oh, yes. He's under sedation anyway.' Yamaguchi paused. 'And the man who died—'

'Sure. We'll ship him back too. The government will even supply a nice coffin. I'm sure his girlfriend will appreciate that.'

'Do you feel well?' asked Yamaguchi sharply.

'They were going to be married,' said Herries. He took another pull from the fifth of bourbon on his desk. It was getting almost too dark to see the bottle. 'Since patriotism nowadays ... in the future, I mean ... in our own home, sweet home ... since patriotism is necessarily equated with necrophilia, in that the loyal citizen is expected to rejoice every time his government comes up with a newer gadget for mass-producing corpses ... I am sure the young lady will just love to have a pretty coffin. So much nicer than a mere husband. I'm sure the coffin will be chrome plated.'

'Wait a minute—'

'With tail fins.'

'Look here,' said the doctor, 'you're acting like a case of combat fatigue. I know you've had a shock today. Come see me and I'll give you a tranquillizer.'

'Thanks,' said Herries, 'I've got one.' He took another swig and forced briskness into his tone. 'We'll send 'em back tomorrow morning, then. Now don't bother me. I'm composing a letter to explain to the great white father that this wouldn't have happened if we'd been allowed one stinking little atomic howitzer. Not that I expect to get any results. It's policy that we aren't allowed heavy weapons down here, and who ever heard of facts affecting a policy? Why, facts might be un-American.'

He hung up, put the bottle on his lap and his feet on the desk, lit a cigarette and stared out the window. Darkness came sneaking across the compound like smoke. The rain had stopped for a while, and lamps and windows threw broken yellow gleams off puddles, but somehow the gathering night was so thick that each light seemed quite alone. There was no one else in the headquarters shack at this hour. Herries had not turned on his own lights.

To hell with it, he thought. *To hell with it.*

His cigarette tip waxed and waned as he puffed, like a small dying star. But the smoke didn't taste right when invisible. Or had he put away so many toasts to dead men that his tongue was numbed? He wasn't sure. It hardly mattered.

The phone shrilled again. He picked it up, fumble-handed in the murk. 'Chief of operations,' he said pleasantly. 'To hell with you.'

'What?' Symonds' voice rattled a bare bit. Then: 'I have been trying to find you. What are you doing there this late?'

'I'll give you three guesses. Playing pinochle? No. Carrying on a sordid affair with a lady iguanodon? No. None of your business? Right! *Give* that gentleman a box of seegars.'

'Look here, Mr Herries,' stated Symonds, 'this is no time for levity. I understand that Matthew Worth was seriously injured today. He was supposed to be on guard duty tonight – the secret shipment. This has disarranged all my plans.'

'Tsk-tsk-tsk. My nose bleeds for you.'

'The schedule of duties must be revised. According to my notes, Worth would have been on guard from midnight until 4 a.m. Since I do not know precisely what other jobs his fellows are assigned to, I cannot single any one of them out to replace him. Will you do so? Select a man who can then sleep later tomorrow morning?'

'Why?' asked Herries.

'Why? Because . . . because—'

'I know. Because Washington said so. Washington is afraid some nasty dinosaur from what is going to be Russia will sneak in and look at an unguarded crate and hurry home with the information. Sure, I'll do it. I just wanted to hear you sputter.'

Herries thought he made out an indignant breath sucked past an upper plate. 'Very good,' said the clerk. 'Make the necessary arrangements for tonight, and we will work out a new rotation of watches tomorrow.'

Herries put the receiver back.

The list of tight-lipped, tight-minded types was somewhere in his desk, he knew vaguely. A copy, rather. Symonds had a copy, and no doubt copies would be going to the Pentagon and the FBI and the Transoco personnel office and— Well, look at the list, compare it with the work schedule, see who wouldn't be doing anything of critical importance tomorrow forenoon, and put him on a bit of sentry-go. Simple.

Herries took another swig. He could resign, he thought. He could back out of the whole fantastically stupid, fantastically meaningless operation. He wasn't compelled to work. Of course, they could hold him for the rest of his contract. It would be a lonesome year. Or maybe not; maybe a few others would trickle in to keep him company. To be sure, he'd then be under surveillance the rest of his life. But who wasn't, in a century divided between two garrisons?

The trouble was, he thought, there was nothing a man could do about the situation. You could become a peace-at-any-cost pacifist and thereby, effectively, league yourself with the enemy; and the enemy had carried out too many cold massacres for any half-way sane man to stomach. Or you could fight back (thus becoming more and more like what you fought) and hazard planetary incineration against the possibility of a tolerable outcome. It only took one to make a quarrel, and the enemy had long ago elected himself that one. Now, it was probably too late to patch up the quarrel. Even if important men on both sides wished for a disengagement, what could they do against their own fanatics, vested interests, terrified common people ... against the whole momentum of history?

Hell take it, thought Herries, *we may be damned but why must we be fools into the bargain?*

Somewhere a brontosaur hooted, witlessly ploughing through a night swamp.

Well, I'd better— No!

Herries stared at the end of his cigarette. It was almost scorching his fingers. At least, he thought, at least he could find out what he was supposed to condone. A look into those crates, which should have held the guns he had begged for, and perhaps some orchestral and scientific instruments ... and instead held God knew what piece of Pentagonal-brained idiocy ... a look would be more than a blow in Symonds' smug eye. It would be an assertion that he was Herries, a free man, whose existence had not yet been point-lessly spilled from a splintered skull. He, the individual, would know what the Team planned; and if it turned out to be a crime against reason, he could at the very least resign and sit out whatever followed.

Yes. By the dubious existence of divine mercy, yes.

Again a bit of rain, a small warm touch on his face, like tears. Herries splashed to the transceiver building and stood quietly in the sudden flashlight glare. At last, out of black-ness, the sentry's voice came: 'Oh, it's you, sir.'

'U-huh. You know Worth got hurt today? I'm taking his watch.'

'What? But I thought—'

'Policy,' said Herries.

The incantation seemed to suffice. The other man shuffled forth and laid his rifle in the engineer's hands. 'And here's the glim,' he added. 'Nobody came by while I was on duty.'

'What would you have done if somebody'd tried to get in?'

'Why, stopped them, of course.'

'And if they didn't stop?'

The dim face under the dripping hat turned puzzledly towards Herries. The engineer sighed. 'I'm sorry, Thornton. It's too late to raise philosophical questions. Run along to bed.'

He stood in front of the door, smoking a damp cigarette, and watched the man trudge away. All the lights were out now, except overhead lamps here and there. They were brilliant, but remote; he stood in a pit of shadow and won-dered what the phase of the moon was and what kind of constellations the stars made nowadays.

He waited. There was time enough for his rebellion. Too

much time, really. A man stood in rain, fog about his feet and a reptile smell in his nose, and he remembered anemones in springtime, strewn under trees still cold and leafless, with here and there a little snow between the roots. Or he remembered drinking beer in a New England country inn one fall day, when the door stood open to red sumac and yellow beech and a far blue wandering sky. Or he remembered a man snatched under black Jurassic quagmires, a man stepped into red ruin, a man sitting in a jeep and bleeding brains down on to the picture of the girl he had planned to marry. And then he started wondering what the point of it all was, and decided that it was either without any point whatsoever or else had the purpose of obliterating anemones and quiet country inns, and he was forced to dissent somehow.

When Thornton's wet footsteps were lost in the dark, Herries unlocked the shed door and went through. It was smotheringly hot inside. Sweat sprang forth under his raincoat as he closed the door again and turned on his flashlight. Rain tapped loudly on the roof. The crates loomed over him, box upon box, many of them large enough to hold a dinosaur. It had taken a lot of power to ship that tonnage into the past. No wonder taxes were high. And what might the stuff be? A herd of tanks, possibly ... some knocked-down bombers ... Lord knew what concept the men who lived in offices, insulated from the sky, would come up with. And Symonds had implied it was a mere beginning; more shipments would come when this had been stored out of the way, and more, and more.

Herries found a workbench and helped himself to tools. He would have to be careful; no sense in going to jail. He laid the flashlight on a handy barrel and stooped down by one of the crates. It was of strong wood, securely screwed together. But while that would make it harder to dismantle, it could be reassembled without leaving a trace. Maybe. Of course, it might be booby trapped. No telling how far the religion of secrecy could lead the office men.

Oh, well, if I'm blown up I haven't lost much. Herries

peeled off his slicker. His shirt clung to his body. He squatted and began to work.

It went slowly. After taking off several boards, he saw a regular manufacturer's crate, open-slatted. Something within was wrapped in burlap. A single curved metal surface projected slightly. What the devil? Herries got a crowbar and prised one slat loose. The nails shrieked. He stooped rigid for a while, listening, but heard only the rain, grown more noisy. He reached in and fumbled with the padding . . . God, it was hot!

Only when he had freed the entire blade did he recognize what it was. And then his mind would not quite function; he gaped a long while before the word registered.

A ploughshare.

'But they don't know what to do with the farm surpluses at home,' he said aloud, inanely.

Like a stranger's, his hands began to repair what he had torn apart. He couldn't understand it. Nothing seemed altogether real any more. Of course, he thought in a dim way, theoretically anything might be in the other boxes, but he suspected more ploughs, tractors, discs, combines . . . why not bags of seeds . . .? *What were they planning to do?*

'Ah.'

Herries whirled. The flashlight beam caught him like a spear.

He grabbed blindly for his rifle. A dry little voice behind the blaze said: 'I would not recommend violence.' Herries let the rifle fall. It thudded.

Symonds closed the shed door behind him and stepped forward in his mincing fashion, another shadow among bobbing misshapen shadows. He had simply flung on shirt and pants, but bands of night across them suggested necktie, vest, and coat.

'You see,' he explained without passion, 'all the guards were instructed *sub rosa* to notify me of anything unusual, even when it did not seem to warrant action on their part.' He gestured at the crate. 'Please continue reassembling it.'

Herries crouched down again. Hollowness filled him; his sole wonder was how best to die. For if he were sent back to the twentieth century, surely, surely they would lock him up and lose the key, and the sunlessness of death was better than that. It was strange, he thought, how his fingers used the tools with untrembling skill.

Symonds stood behind him and held his light on the work. At last he asked primly, 'Why did you break in like this?'

I could kill him, thought Herries. *He's unarmed. I could wring his scrawny neck between these two hands, and take a gun, and go into the swamp to live a few days. . . . But it might be easier just to turn the rifle on myself.*

He sought words with care, for he must decide what to do, though it seemed remote and scarcely important. 'That's not an easy question to answer,' he said.

'The significant ones never are.'

Astonished, Herries jerked a glance upwards and back. (And was the more surprised that he could still know surprise.) But the litle man's face was in darkness. Herries saw a blank glitter off the glasses.

He said, 'Let's put it this way. There are limits even to the right of self-defence. If a killer attacked me, I can fight back with anything I've got. But I wouldn't be justified in grabbing some passing child for a shield.'

'So you wished to make sure that nothing you would consider illegitimate was in those boxes?' asked Symonds academically.

'I don't know. What is illegitimate, these days? I was . . . I was disgusted. I liked Greenstein, and he died because Washington had decided we couldn't have bombs or atomic shells. I didn't know how much more I could consent to. I had to find out.'

'I see.' The clerk nodded. 'For your information, it is agricultural equipment. Later shipments will include industrial and scientific material, a large reserve of canned food, and as much of the world's culture as it proves possible to microfilm.'

Herries stopped working, turned around and rose. His knees would not hold him. He leaned against the crate and it was a minute before he could get out: 'Why?'

Symonds did not respond at once. He reached forth a precise hand and took up the flashlight Herries had left on the barrel. Then he sat down there himself, with the two glowing tubes in his lap. The light from below ridged his face in shadows, and his glasses made blind circles. He said, as if ticking off the points of an agenda:

'You would have been informed of the facts in due course, when the next five hundred people arrive. Now you have brought on yourself the burden of knowing what you would otherwise have been ignorant of for months yet. I think it may safely be assumed that you will keep the secret and not be broken by it. At least, the assumption is necessary.'

Herries heard his own breath harsh in his throat. 'Who are these people?'

The papery half-seen countenance did not look at him, but into the pit-like reaches of the shed. 'You have committed a common error,' said Symonds, as if to a student. 'You have assumed that because men are constrained by circumstances to act in certain ways, they must be evil or stupid. I assure you, Senator Wien and the few others responsible for this are neither. They must keep the truth even from those officials within the project whose reaction would be rage or panic instead of a sober attempt at salvage. Nor do they have unlimited powers. Therefore, rather than indulge in tantrums about the existing situation, they use it. The very compartmentalization of effort and knowledge enforced by Security helps conceal their purposes and mislead those who must be given some information.'

Symonds paused. A slight frown crossed his forehead, and he tapped an impatient fingernail on a flashlight casing. 'Do not misunderstand,' he went on. 'Senator Wien and his associates have not forgotten their oaths of office, nor are they trying to play God. Their primary effort goes, as it must, to a straightforward dealing with the problems of the twentieth century. It is not they who are withholding the one significant datum – a datum which, incidentally, any informed person could reason out for himself if he cared to. It is properly constituted authority, using powers legally granted to stamp certain reports top secret. Of course, the senator has used his considerable influence to bring about the present eventuality, but that is normal politics.'

Herries growled: 'Get to the point, damn you! What are you talking about?'

Symonds shook his thin grey head. 'You are afraid to know, are you not?' he asked quietly.

'I—' Herries turned about, faced the crate and beat it with his fist. The parched voice in the night continued to punish him:

'You know that a time-projector can go into the future about a hundred years at a jump, but can only go pastwards in jumps of approximately one hundred megayears. We all realize there is a way to explore certain sections of the historical past, in spite of this handicap, by making enough century hops forward before the one long hop backwards. But can you tell me how to predict the historical future? Say, a century hence? Come, come, you are an intelligent man. Answer me.'

'Yeah,' said Herries. 'I get the idea. Leave me alone.'

'Team A, a group of well-equipped volunteers, went into the twenty-first century,' pursued Symonds. 'They recorded what they observed and placed the data in a chemically inert box within a large block of reinforced concrete erected at an agreed-on location: one which a previous expedition to circa one hundred million A.D. had confirmed would remain stable. I presume they also mixed radioactive materials of long half-life into the concrete, to aid in finding the site. Of course, the bracketing of time jumps is such that they cannot now get back to the twentieth century. But Team B went a full hundred-megayear jump into the future, excavated the data, and returned home.'

Herries squared his body and faced back to the other man. He was drained, so weary that it was all he could do to keep on his feet. 'What did they find?' he asked. There was no tone in his voice or in him.

'Actually, several expeditions have been made to the year

one hundred million,' said Symonds. 'Energy requirements for a visit to two hundred millon – A.D. or B.C. – were considered prohibitive. In one hundred million, life is re-evolving on Earth. However, as yet the plants have not liberated sufficient oxygen for the atmosphere to be breathable. You see, oxygen reacts with exposed rock, so that if no biological processes exist to replace it continuously— But you have a better technical education than I.'

'Okay,' said Herries, flat and hard. 'Earth was sterile for a long time in the future. Including the twenty-first century?'

'Yes. The radioactivity had died down enough so that Team A reported no danger to itself, but some of the longer-lived isotopes were still measurably present. By making differential measurements of abundance, Team A was able to estimate rather closely when the bombs had gone off.'

'And?'

'Approximately one year from the twentieth-century base date we are presently using.'

'One year ... from now.' Herries stared upward. Blackness met him. He heard the Jurassic rain on the iron roof, like drums.

'Possibly less,' Symonds told him. 'There is a factor of uncertainty. This project must be completed well within the safety margin before the war comes.'

'The war comes,' Herries repeated. 'Does it have to come? Fixed time line or not, does it have to come? Couldn't the enemy leaders be shown the facts ... couldn't our side, even, capitulate—'

'Every effort is being made,' said Symonds like a machine. 'Quite apart from the theory of rigid time, it seems unlikely that they will succeed. The situation is too unstable. One man, losing his head and pressing the wrong button, can write the end; and there are so many buttons. The very revelation of the truth, to a few chosen leaders or to the world public, would make some of them panicky. Who can tell what a man in panic will do? That is what I meant when I said that Senator Wien and his co-workers have not forgotten their oaths of office. They have no thought of taking refuge, they know they are old men. To the end, they will try to save the twentieth century. But they do not expect it; so they are also trying to save the human race.'

Herries pushed up from the crate he had been leaning against. 'Those five hundred who're coming,' he whispered. 'Women?'

'Yes. If time remains to rescue a few more, after the ones you are preparing for have gone through, it will be done. But there will be at least a thousand young, healthy adults here, in the Jurassic. You face a difficult time, when the truth must be told them; you can see why the secret must be kept until then. It is quite possible that someone here will lose his head. That is why no heavy weapons have been sent: a single deranged person must not be able to destroy everyone. But you will recover. You must.'

Herries jerked the door open and stared out into the roaring darkness. 'No traces of us . . . in the future,' he said, hearing his voice high and hurt like a child's.

'How much trace do you expect would remain after geological eras?' answered Symonds. He was still the reproving schoolmaster; but he sat on the barrel and faced the great moving shadows in a corner. 'It is assumed that you will remain here for several generations, until your numbers and resources have been expanded sufficiently. The Team A I spoke of will join you a century hence. It is also, I might add, composed of young men and women in equal numbers. But this planet in this age is not a good home. We trust that your descendants will perfect the spaceships we know to be possible, and take possession of the stars instead.'

Herries leaned in the doorway, sagging with tiredness and the monstrous duty to survive. A gust of wind threw rain into his eyes. He heard dragons calling in the night.

'And you?' he said, for no good reason.

'I shall convey any final messages you may wish to send home,' said the dried-out voice.

Neat little footsteps clicked across the floor until the clerk paused beside the engineer. Silence followed, except for the rain.

'Surely I will deserve to go home,' said Symonds.

And the breath whistled inwards between teeth which had snapped together. He raised his hands, claw-fingered, and screamed aloud: 'You can let me go home *then*!'

He began running towards the supervisors' barge. The sound of him was soon lost. Herries stood for a time yet in the door.

Cold Victory

*In many respects, revolution is a separate phenom-
enon from regular military conflict—until it brings
on the latter in the form of civil war.*

It was the old argument, Historical Necessity versus the
Man of Destiny. When I heard them talking, three together,
my heart twisted within me and I knew that once more I
must lay down the burden of which I can never be rid.

This was in the Battle Rock House, which is a quiet
tavern on the edge of Syrtis Town. I come there whenever I
am on Mars. It is friendly and unpretentious: shabby,
comfortable loungers scattered about under the massive
sandwood rafters, honest liquor and competent chess and
the talk of one's peers.

As I entered, a final shaft of thin hard sunlight stabbed in
through the window, dazzling me, and then night fell like a
thunderclap over the ocherous land and the fluoros snapped
on. I got a mug of porter and strolled across to the table
about which the three people sat.

The stiff little bald man was obviously from the college;
he wore his academics even here, but Martians are like that.
'No, no,' he was saying. 'These movements are too great for
any one man to change them appreciably. Humanism, for
example, was not the political engine of Carnarvon; rather,
he was the puppet of Humanism, and danced as the blind
brainless puppeteer made him.'

'I'm not so sure,' answered the man in grey, undress uniform of the Order of Planetary Engineers. 'If he and his
cohorts had been less doctrinaire, the government of Earth
might still be Humanist.'

'But being born of a time of trouble, Humanism was inevitably fanatical,' said the professor.

The big, kilted Venusian woman shifted impatiently. She
was packing a gun and her helmet was on the floor beside

her. Lucifer Clan, I saw from the tartan. 'If there are folk around at a crisis time with enough force, they'll shape the way things turn out,' she declared. 'Otherwise things will drift.'

I rolled up a lounger and set my mug on the table. Conversational kibitzing is accepted in the Battle Rock. 'Pardon me, gentles,' I said. 'Maybe I can contribute.'

'By all means, Captain,' said the Martian, his eyes flickering over my Solar Guard uniform and insignia. 'Permit me: I am Professor Freylinghausen – Engineer Buwono; Freelady Nielsen-Singh.'

'Captain Crane.' I lifted my mug in a formal toast. 'Mars, Luna, Venus, and Earth in my case ... highly representative, are we not? Between us, we should be able to reach a conclusion.'

'To a discussion in a vacuum!' snorted the amazon.

'Not quite,' said the engineer. 'What did you wish to suggest, Captain?'

I got out my pipe and began stuffing it. 'There's a case from recent history – the anti-Humanist counterrevolution, in fact – in which I had a part myself. Offhand, at least, it seems a perfect example of sheer accident determining the whole future of the human race. It makes me think we must be more the pawns of chance than of law.'

'Well, Captain,' said Freylinghausen testily, 'let us hear your story and then pass judgment.'

'I'll have to fill you in on some background.' I lit my pipe and took a comforting drag. I needed comfort just then. It was not to settle an argument that I was telling this, but to reopen an old hurt which would never let itself be forgotten. 'This happened during the final attack on the Humanists—'

'A perfect case of inevitability, sir,' interrupted Freylinghausen. 'May I explain? Thank you. Forgive me if I repeat obvious facts. Their arrangement and interpretation are perhaps not so obvious.

'Psychotechnic government had failed to solve the problems of Earth's adjustment to living on a high technological level. Conditions worsened until all too many people were

ready to try desperation measures. The Humanist revolution
was the desperation measure that succeeded in being tried. A
typical reaction movement, offering a return to a less intellec-
tualized existence; the saviour with the time machine, as
Toynbee once phrased it. So naturally its leader, Carnarvon,
got to be dictator of the planet.

'But with equal force it was true that Earth could no
longer *afford* to cut back her technology. Too many people,
too few resources. In the several years of their rule, the
Humanists failed to keep their promises; their attempts led
only to famine, social disruption, breakdown. Losing
popular support, they had to become increasingly arbitrary,
thus alienating the people still more.

'At last the oppression of Earth became so brutal that the
democratic governments of Mars and Venus brought pressure to bear. But the Humanists had gone too far to back
down. Their only possible reaction was to pull Earth–Luna
out of the Solar Union.

'We could not see that happen, sir. The lesson of history is
too plain. Without a Union council to arbitrate between
planets and a Solar Guard to enforce its decisions – there
will be war until man is extinct. Earth could not be allowed
to secede. Therefore, Mars and Venus aided the counter-
revolutionary, anti-Humanist cabal that wanted to restore
liberty and Union membership to the mother planet. Therefore, too, a space fleet was raised to support the uprising
when it came.

'Don't you see? Every step was an unavoidable conse-
quence, by the logic of survival, of all that had gone before.'

'Correct so far, Professor,' I nodded. 'But the success of
the counterrevolution and the Mars–Venus intervention was
by no means guaranteed. Mars and Venus were still frontiers, thinly populated, only recently made habitable. They
didn't have the military potential of Earth.

'The cabal was well organized. Its well-timed mutinies
swept Earth's newly created pro-Humanist ground and air
forces before it. The countryside, the ocean, even the cities
were soon cleared of Humanist troops.

'But Dictator Carnarvon and the men still loyal to him were holed up in a score of fortresses. Oh, it would have been easy enough to dig them out or blast them out – except that the navy of sovereign Earth, organized from seized units of the Solar Guard, had also remained loyal to Humanism. Its C.-in-C. Admiral K'ung, had acted promptly when the revolt began, jailing all personnel he wasn't sure of ... or shooting them. Only a few got away.

'So there the pro-Union revolutionaries were, in possession of Earth but with a good five hundred enemy warships orbiting above them. K'ung's strategy was simple. He broadcast that unless the rebels surrendered inside one week – or if meanwhile they made any attempt on Carnarvon's remaining strongholds – he'd start bombarding with nuclear weapons. That, of course, would kill perhaps a hundred million civilians, flatten the factories, poison the sea ranches ... he'd turn the planet into a butcher shop.

'Under such a threat, the general population was no longer backing the Union cause. They clamoured for surrender; they began raising armies. Suddenly the victorious rebels had enemies not merely in front and above them, but behind ... everywhere!

'Meanwhile, as you all know, the Unionist fleet under Dushanovitch-Alvarez had rendezvoused off Luna; as mixed a bunch of Martians, Venusians, and freedom-minded Earthmen as history ever saw. They were much inferior both in strength and organization; it was impossible for them to charge in and give battle with any hope of winning ... but Dushanovitch-Alvarez had a plan. It depended on luring the Humanist fleet out to engage him.

'Only Admiral K'ung wasn't having any. The Unionist command knew, from deserters, that most of his captains wanted to go out and annihilate the invaders, returning to deal with Earth at their leisure. It was a costly nuisance, the Unionists sneaking in, firing and retreating, blowing up ship after ship of the Humanist forces. But K'ung had the final word, and he would not accept the challenge until the rebels on the ground had capitulated. He was negotiating with them now, and it looked very much as if they would give in.

'So there it was, the entire outcome of the war – the whole history of man, for if you will pardon my saying so, gentles, Earth is still the key planet – everything hanging on this one officer, Grand Admiral K'ung Li-Po, a grim man who had given his oath and had a damnably good grasp of the military facts of life.'

I took a long draught from my mug and began the story, using the third-person form which is customary on Mars.

The speedster blasted at four gees till she was a bare five hundred kilometres from the closest enemy vessels. Her radar screens jittered with their nearness and in the thunder of abused hearts her crew sat waiting for the doomsday of a homing missile. Then she was at the calculated point, she spat her cargo out the main lock and leaped ahead still more furiously. In moments the thin glare of her jets was lost among crowding stars.

The cargo was three spacesuited men, linked to a giant air tank and burdened with a variety of tools. The orbit into which they had been flung was aligned with that of the Humanist fleet so that relative velocity was low.

In cosmic terms, that is. It still amounted to nearly a thousand kilometres per hour and was enough, unchecked, to spatter the men against an armoured hull.

Lieutenant Robert Crane pulled himself along the light cable that bound him, up to the tank. His hands groped in the pitchy gloom of shadowside. Then all at once rotation had brought him into the moonlight and he could see. He found the rungs and went hand over hand along the curve of the barrel, centrifugal force streaming his body outwards. Damn the clumsiness of space armour! Awkwardly, he got one foot into a stirrup-like arrangement and scrambled around until he was in the 'saddle' with both boots firmly locked; then he unclipped the line from his waist.

The stars turned about him in a cold majestic wheel. Luna was nearly at the full, ashen pale, scored and pocked and filling his helmet with icy luminescence. Earth was an enormous greyness in the sky, a half ring of blinding light from the hidden sun along one side.

Twisting a head made giddy by the spinning, he saw the other two mounted behind him. García was in the middle – you could always tell a Venusian; he painted his clan markings on his suit – and the Martian Wolf at the end. 'Okay,' he said, incongruously aware that the throat mike pinched his Adam's apple, 'let's stop this merry-go-round.'

His hands moved across a simple control panel. A tangentially mounted nozzle opened, emitting an invisible stream of air. The stars slowed their lunatic dance, steadied . . . hell and sunfire, now he'd overcompensated, give it a blast from the other side . . . the tank was no longer in rotation. He was not hanging head downward, but falling, a long weightless tumble through a sterile infinity.

Three men rode a barrel of compressed air towards the massed fleet of Earth.

'Any radar reading?' García's voice was tinny in the earphones.

'A moment, if you please, till I have it set up.' Wolf extended a telescoping mast, switched on the portable 'scope, and began sweeping the sky. 'Nearest indication . . . um . . . one o'clock, five degrees low, four hundred twenty-two kilometres distant.' He added radial and linear velocity and García worked an astrogator's slide rule, swearing at the tricky light.

The base line was not the tank, but its velocity, which could be assumed straight-line for so short a distance. Actually, the weird horse had its nose pointed a full thirty degrees off the direction of movement. 'High' and 'low', in weightlessness, were simply determined by the plane bisecting the tank, with the men's heads arbitrarily designated as 'aimed up'.

The airbarrel had jets aligned in three planes, as well as the rotation-controlling tangential nozzles. With Wolf and García to correct him, Crane blended vectors until they were on a course that would nearly intercept the ship. Gas was released from the forward jet at a rate calculated to match velocity.

Crane had nothing but the gauges to tell him that he was braking. Carefully dehydrated air emerges quite invisibly, and its ionization is negligible; there was no converter to radiate, and all equipment was painted a dead nonreflecting black.

Soundless and invisible – too small and fast for a chance eye to see in the uncertain moonlight, for a chance radar beam to register as anything worth buzzing an alarm about. Not enough infrared for detection, not enough mass, no trail of ions – the machinists on the *Thor* had wrought well, the astrogators had figured as closely as men and computers are able. But in the end it was only a tank of compressed air, a bomb, a few tools, and three men frightened and lonely.

'How long will it take us to get there?' asked Crane. His throat was dry and he swallowed hard.

'About forty-five minutes to that ship we're zeroed in on,' García told him. 'After that, *¿quien sabe?* We'll have to locate the *Monitor*.'

'Be most economical with the air, if you please,' said Wolf. 'We also have to get back.'

'Tell me more,' snorted Crane.

'If this works,' remarked García, 'we'll have added a new weapon to the System's arsenals. That's why I volunteered. If Antonio García of Hesperus gets his name in the history books, my whole clan will contribute to give me the biggest ranch on Venus.'

They were an anachronism, thought Crane, a resurrection from old days when war was a wilder business. The psychotechs had not picked a team for compatibility, nor welded them into an unbreakable brotherhood. They had merely grabbed the first three willing to try an untested scheme. There wasn't time for anything else. In another forty hours, the pro-Union armies on Earth would either have surrendered or the bombardment would begin.

'Why are you lads here?' went on the Venusian. 'We might as well get acquainted.'

'I took an oath,' said Wolf. There was nothing priggish about it; Martians thought that way.

'What of you, Crane?'

'I . . . it looked like fun,' said the Earthman lamely. 'And it might end this damned war.'

He lied and he knew so, but how do you explain? Do you admit it was an escape from your shipmates' eyes?

Not that his going over to the rebels had shamed him. Everyone aboard the *Marduk* had done so, except for a couple of CPO's who were now under guard in Aphrodite. The cruiser had been on patrol off Venus when word of Earth's secession had flashed. Her captain had declared for the Union and the Guard to which he belonged, and the crew cheered him for it.

For two years, while Dushanovitch-Alvarez, half idealist and half buccaneer, was assembling the Unionist fleet, intelligence reports trickled in from Earth. Mutiny was being organized, and men escaped from those Guard vessels – the bulk of the old space service – that had been at the mother planet and were seized to make a navy. Just before the Unionists accelerated for rendezvous, a list of the new captains appointed by K'ung had been received. And the skipper of the *Huitzilopochtli* was named Benjamin Crane.

Ben . . . what did you do when your brother was on the enemy side? Dushanovitch-Alvarez had let the System know that a bombardment of Earth would be regarded as genocide and all officers partaking in it would be punished under Union law. It seemed unlikely that there would be any Union to try the case, but Lieutenant Robert Crane of the *Marduk* had protested: this was not a normal police operation, it was war, and executing men who merely obeyed the government they had pledged to uphold was opening the gates to a darker barbarism than the fighting itself. The Unionist force was too shorthanded, it could not give Lieutenant Crane more than a public reproof for insubordination, but his messmates had tended to grow silent when he entered the wardroom.

If the superdreadnaught *Monitor* could be destroyed, and

K'ung with it, Earth might not be bombarded. Then if the Unionists won, Ben would go free, or he would die cleanly in battle – reason enough to ride this thing into the Humanist fleet!

Silence was cold in their helmets.

'I've been thinking,' said García. 'Suppose we do carry this off, but they decide to blast Earth anyway before dealing with our boats. What then?'

'Then they blast Earth,' said Wolf. 'Though most likely they won't have to. Last I heard, the threat alone was making folk rise against our friends on the ground there.' Moonlight shimmered along his arm as he pointed at the darkened planet-shield before them. 'So the Humanists will be back in power, and even if we chop up their navy, we won't win unless we do some bombarding of our own.'

'*¡Madre de Dios!*' García crossed himself, a barely visible gesture in the unreal flood of undiffused light. 'I'll mutiny before I give my name to such a thing.'

'And I,' said Wolf shortly. 'And most of us, I think.'

It was not that the Union fleet was crewed by saints, thought Crane. Most of its personnel had signed on for booty; the System knew how much treasure was locked in the vaults of Earth's dictators. But the horror of nuclear war had been too deeply graven for anyone but a fanatic at the point of desperation to think of using it.

Even in K'ung's command, there must be talk of revolt. Since his ultimatum, deserters in lifeboats had brought Dushanovitch-Alvarez a mountain of precise information. But the Humanists had had ten years in which to build a hard cadre of hard young officers to keep the men obedient.

Strange to know that Ben was with them – *why*?

I haven't seen you in more than two years now, Ben – nor my own wife and children, but tonight it is you who dwell in me, and I have not felt such pain for many years. Not since that time we were boys together, and you were sick one day and I went alone down the steep bluffs above the Mississippi. There I found the old man denned up under the trees, a tramp, one of many millions for whom there was no place in this new world of shining machines – but he was not embittered, he drew his citizen's allowance and tramped the planet and he had stories to tell me which our world of bright hard metal had forgotten. He told me about Br'er Rabbit and the briar patch; never had I heard such a story, it was the first time I knew the rich dark humour of the earth itself. And you got well, Ben, and I took you down to his camp, but he was gone and you never heard the story of Br'er Rabbit. On that day, Ben, I was as close to weeping as I am this night of murder.

The minutes dragged past. Only numbers went between the three men on the tank, astrogational corrections. They sat, each in his own skull with his own thoughts.

The vessel on which they had zeroed came into plain view, a long black shark swimming against the Milky Way. They passed within two kilometres of her. Wolf was busy now, flicking his radar around the sky, telling off ships. It was mostly seat-of-the-pants piloting, low relative velocities and small distances, edging into the mass of Earth's fleet. That was not a very dense mass; kilometres gaped between each unit. The *Monitor* was in the inner ring; a deserter had given them the approximate orbit.

'You're pretty good at this, boy,' said García.

'I rode a scooter in the asteroids for a couple of years,' answered Crane. 'Patrol and rescue duty.'

That was when there had still been only the Guard, one fleet and one flag. Crane had never liked the revolutionary government of Earth, but while the Union remained and the only navy was the Guard and its only task to help any and all men, he had been reasonably content. Please God, that day would come again.

Slowly, over the minutes, the *Monitor* grew before him, a giant spheroid never meant to land on a planet. He could see gun turrets scrawled black across remote star-clouds. There was more reason for destroying her than basic strategy – luring the Humanists out to do battle; more than good tactics – built only last year, she was the most formidable

engine of war in the Solar System. It would be the annihil-
ation of a symbol. The *Monitor*, alone among ships that
rode the sky, was designed with no other purpose than killing.

Slow, now, easy, gauge the speeds by eye, remember how
much inertia you've got ... Edge up, brake, throw out a
magnetic anchor and grapple fast. Crane turned a small
winch, the cable tautened and he bumped against the hull.

Nobody spoke. They had work to do, and their short-
range radio might have been detected. García unshipped
the bomb. Crane held it while the Venusian scrambled from
the saddle and got a firm boot-grip on the dreadnaught. The
bomb didn't have a large mass. Crane handed it over, and
García slapped it on to the hull, gripped by a magnetic
plate. Stooping, he wound a spring and jerked a lever. Then,
with spaceman's finicking care, he returned to the saddle.
Crane paid out the cable till it ran off the drum; they were
free of their grapple.

In twenty minutes, the clockwork was to set off the bomb.
It was a little one, plutonium fission, and most of its energy
would be wasted on vacuum. Enough would remain to
smash the *Monitor* into a hundred fragments.

Crane worked the airjets, forcing himself to be calm and
deliberate. The barrel swung about to point at Luna, and he
opened the rear throttle wide. Acceleration tugged at him,
he braced his feet in the stirrups and hung on with both
hands. Behind them, the *Monitor* receded, borne on her own
orbit around a planet where terror walked.

When they were a good fifteen kilometres away, he asked
for a course. His voice felt remote, as if it came from outside
his prickling skin. Most of him wondered just how many
men were aboard the dreadnaught and how many wives and
children they had to weep for them. Wolf squinted through a
sextant and gave his readings to García. Corrections made,
they rode towards the point of rendezvous: a point so tricky
to compute, in this Solar System where the planets were never
still, that they would doubtless not come within a hundred
kilometres of the speedster that was to pick them up. But

they had a hand-cranked radio that would broadcast a signal for the boat to get a fix on them.

How many minutes had they been going? Ten . . .? Crane looked at the clock in the control panel. Yes, ten. Another five or so, at this acceleration, ought to see them beyond the outermost orbit of the Humanist ships—

He did not hear the explosion. A swift and terrible glare opened inside his helmet, enough light reflected off the inner surface for his eyes to swim in white-hot blindness. He clung to his seat, nerves and muscles tensed against the hammer blow that never came. The haze parted raggedly, and he turned his head back towards Earth. A wan nimbus of incandescent gas hung there. A few tattered stars glowed blue as they fled from it.

Wolf's voice whispered in his ears: 'She's gone already. The bomb went off ahead of schedule. Something in the clockwork—'

'But she's gone!' García let out a rattling whoop. 'No more flagship. We got her, lads, we got the stinking can!'

Not far away was a shadow visible only where it blocked off the stars. A ship . . . light cruiser – 'Cram on the air!' said Wolf roughly. 'Let's get the devil out of here.'

'I can't.' Crane snarled it, still dazed, wanting only to rest and forget every war that ever was. 'We've only got so much pressure left, and none to spare for manoeuvring if we get off course.'

'All right . . .' They lapsed into silence. That which had been the *Monitor,* gas and shrapnel, dissipated. The enemy cruiser fell behind them, and Luna filled their eyes with barren radiance

They were not aware of pursuit until the squad was almost on them. There were a dozen men in combat armour, driven by individual jet-units and carrying rifles. They over-hauled the tank and edged in – less gracefully than fish, for they had no friction to kill forward velocity, but they moved in.

After the first leap of his heart, Crane felt cold and numb. None of his party bore arms: they themselves had

been the weapon, and now it was discharged. In a mechanical fashion, he turned his headset to the standard band.

'Rebels ahoy!' The voice was strained close to breaking,
an American voice. . . . For a moment such a wave of home-
sickness for the green dales of Wisconsin went over Crane
that he could not move nor realize he had been captured.
'Stop that thing and come with us!'

In sheer reflex, Crane opened the rear throttles full. The
barrel jumped ahead, almost ripping him from the saddle.
Ions flared behind as the enemy followed. Their units were
beam-powered from the ship's nuclear engines, and they had
plenty of reaction mass in their tanks. It was only a moment
before they were alongside again.

Arms closed around Crane, dragging him from his seat.
As the universe tilted about his head, he saw Wolf likewise
caught. García sprang to meet an Earthman, hit him and
bounced away but got his rifle. A score of bullets must have
spat. Suddenly the Venusian's armour blew white clouds of
freezing water vapour and he drifted dead.

Wolf wrestled in vacuum and tore one hand free. Crane
heard him croak over the radio: 'They'll find out—' Another
frosty geyser erupted; Wolf had opened his own air-tubes.

Men closed in on either side of Crane, pinioning his arms.
He could not have suicided even if he chose to. The rest
flitted near, guns ready. He relaxed, too weary and dazed to
fight, and let them face him around and kill forward speed,
then accelerate towards the cruiser.

The airlock was opening for him before he had his voice
back. 'What ship is this?' he asked, not caring much, only
filling in an emptiness.

'*Huitzilopochtli*. Get in there with you.'

Crane floated weightless in the wardroom, his left ankle
manacled to a stanchion. They had removed his armour,
leaving the thick grey coverall which was the underpadding,
and given him a stimpill. A young officer guarded him, sidearm holstered; no reason to fear a fettered captive. The
officer did not speak, though horror lay on his lips.

The pill had revived Crane, his body felt supple and he sensed every detail of the room with an unnatural clarity. But his heart had a thick beat and his mouth felt cottony.

This was Ben's ship.

García and Wolf were dead.

None of it was believable.

Captain Benjamin Crane of the Space Navy, Federation of Earth and the Free Cities of Luna, drifted in through a ghostly quiet. It was a small shock to see him again . . . when had the last time been, three years ago? They had met in Mexico City, by arrangement, when their leaves coincided, and had a hell of a good time. Then they went up to their father's house in Wisconsin, and that had somehow not been quite as good, for the old man was dead and the house had stood long empty. But it had been a fine pheasant shoot, on a certain cool and smoky-clear fall morning. Robert Crane remembered how the first dead leaves crackled underfoot, and how the bird dog stiffened into a point that was flowing line and deep curves, and the thin high wedge of wild geese, southward bound.

That was the first thing he thought of, and next he thought that Ben had put on a good deal of weight and looked much older, and finally he recalled that he himself had changed towards gauntness and must seem to have more than the two-year edge on Ben he really did.

The captain stiffened as he came through the air. He grabbed a handhold barely in time, and stopped his flight ungracefully. The quietness lengthened. There was little to see on Ben's heavy face, unless you knew him as well – inside and out – as his own brother did.

He spoke finally, a whisper: 'I never looked for this.'

Crane of the *Marduk* tried to smile. 'What are the mathematical odds against it?' he wondered. 'That I, of all people, should be on this mission, and that your ship of all Earth's fleet should have captured me. How did you detect us?'

'That bomb . . . you touched it off too soon. The initial flare brought us to the ports, and the gas glow afterwards, added to the moonlight, was enough to reveal a peculiar object. We locked a radar on it and I sent men out.'

'Accident,' said Robert Crane. 'Some little flaw in the mechanism. It wasn't supposed to detonate till we were well away.'

'I knew you were on ... the other side,' said Ben with great slowness. 'That's a wild chance in itself, you realize. I happened to know the *Marduk* was assigned to Venus patrol only because the *Ares* suffered meteoroid damage at the last moment. Consider how unlikely it is that a rock will ever disable a ship. If it hadn't been for that, the *Marduk* would probably have been right here when the ... trouble began, and you'd have had no choice but to remain loyal.'

'Like you, Ben?'

The young officer of Earth floated 'upright', at attention, but his eyes were not still. Ben nodded sardonically at him. 'Mr Nicholson, this prisoner happens to be my brother.'

No change appeared in the correct face.

Ben sighed. 'I suppose you know what you did, Lieutenant Crane.'

'Yes,' said Robert. 'We blew up your flagship.'

'It was a brilliant operation,' said Ben dully. 'I've had a verbal report on your ... vessel. I imagine you planted an atomic bomb on the *Monitor*'s hull. If we knew just where your fleet is and how it's arrayed, as you seem to know everything about us, I'd like to try the same thing on you.'

Robert floated, waiting. A thickening grew in his throat. He felt sweat form under his arms and along his ribs, soaking into the coverall. He could smell his own stink.

'But I wonder why that one man of yours suicided,' went on Ben. He frowned, abstractedly, and Robert knew he would not willingly let the riddle go till he had solved it. 'Perhaps your mission was more than striking a hard blow at us. Perhaps he didn't want us to know its real purpose.'

Ben, you're no fool. You were always a suspicious son-of-a-gun, always probing, never quite believing what you were told. I know you, Ben.

What had Wolf's religion been? Crane didn't know. He

hoped it wasn't one which promised hellfire to suicides. Wolf had died to protect a secret which the drugs of Earth's psychotechs – nothing so crude as torture – would have dissolved out of him.

If they had not been captured ... the natural reaction would have been for Earth's fleet to rush forth seeking revenge before the Unionists attacked them. They did not know, they must not know, that Dushanovitch-Alvarez lacked the ships to win an open battle except on his own ground and under his own terms; that the loyalists need only remain where they were, renew the threat of bombardment, carry it out if necessary, and the Union men would be forced to slink home without offering a shot.

'Sir ...'

Ben's head turned, and Robert saw, with an odd little sadness, grey streaks at the temples. What was his age – thirty-one? *My kid brother is growing old already.*

'Yes, Mr Nicholson?'

The officer cleared his throat. 'Sir, shouldn't the prisoner be interrogated in the regular way? He must know a good deal about—'

'I assure you, not about our orbits and dispositions,' said Robert Crane with what coolness he could summon. 'We change them quite often.'

'Obviously,' agreed Ben. 'They don't want us to raid them as they've been raiding us. We have to stay in orbit because of our strategy. They don't, and they'd be fools if they did.'

'Still ...' began Nicholson.

'Oh, yes, Intelligence will be happy to pump him,' said Ben. 'Though I suspect this show will be over before they've got much information of value. Vice Admiral Hokusai of the *Krishna* has succeeded to command. Get on the radio, Mr Nicholson, and report what has happened. In the meantime, I'll question the prisoner myself. Privately.'

'Yes, sir.' The officer saluted and went out. There was compassion in his eyes.

Ben closed the door behind him. Then he turned around and floated, crossing his legs, one hand on a stanchion and

the other rubbing his forehead. His brother had known he
would do exactly that. *But how accurately can he read me?*

'Well, Bob.' Ben's tone was gentle.

Robert Crane shifted, feeling the link about his ankle.
'How are Mary and the kids?' he asked.

'Oh . . . quite well, thank you. I'm afraid I can't tell you
much about your own family. Last I heard, they were living
in Manitowoc Unit, but in the confusion since . . .' Ben
looked away. 'They were never bothered by our police,
though. I have some little influence.'

'Thanks,' said Robert. Bitterness broke forth: 'Yours are
safe in Luna City. Mine will get the fallout when you bom-
bard, or they'll starve in the famine to follow.'

The captain's mouth wrenched. 'Don't say that!' After a
moment: 'Do you think I like the idea of shooting at Earth?
If your so-called liberators really give a curse in hell about
the people their hearts bleed for so loudly, they'll surrender
first. We're offering terms. They'll be allowed to go to Mars
or Venus.'

'I'm afraid you misjudge us, Ben,' said Robert. 'Do you
know why I'm here? It wasn't simply a matter of being on
the *Marduk* when she elected to stay with the Union. I believed in the liberation.'

'Believe in those pirates out there?' Ben's finger stabbed
at the wall, as if to pierce it and show the stars and the
hostile ships swimming between.

'Oh, sure, they've been promised the treasure vaults. We
had to raise men and ships somehow. What good was that
money doing, locked away by Carnarvon and his gang?'
Robert shrugged. 'Look, I was born and raised in America.
We were always a free people. The Bill of Rights was mod-
elled on our own old Ten Amendments. From the moment
the Humanists seized power, I had to start watching what I
said, who I associated with, what tapes I got from the
library. My kids were growing up into perfect little parrots.
It was too much. When the purges began, when the police
fired on crowds rioting because they were starving – and they
were starving because this quasi-religious creed cannot

accept the realities and organize things rationally – I was only waiting for my chance.

'Ben, be honest. Wouldn't you have signed on with us if you'd been on the *Marduk*?'

The face before him was grey. 'Don't ask me that! No!'

'I can tell you exactly why not, Ben.' Robert folded his arms and would not let his brother's eyes go. 'I know you well enough. We're different in one respect. To you, no principle can be as important as your wife and children – and they're hostages for your good behaviour. Oh, yes, K'ung's psychotechs evaluated you very carefully. Probably half their captains are held by just such chains.'

Ben laughed, a loud bleak noise above the murmur of the ventilators. 'Have it your way. And don't forget that your family is alive, too, because I stayed with the government. I'm not going to change, either. A government, even the most arbitrary one, can perhaps be altered in time. But the dead never come back to life.'

He leaned forward, suddenly shuddering. 'Bob, I don't want you sent Earthside for interrogation. They'll not only drug you, they'll set about changing your whole viewpoint. Surgery, shock, a rebuilt personality – you won't be the same man when they've finished.

'I can wangle something else. I have enough pull, especially now in the confusion after your raid, to keep you here. When the war is settled, I'll arrange for your escape. There's going to be so much hullaballoo on Earth that nobody will notice. But you'll have to help me, in turn.

'*What was the real purpose of your raid? What plans does your high command have?*'

For a time which seemed to become very long, Robert Crane waited. He was being asked to betray his side voluntarily; the alternative was to do it anyway, after the psychmen got through with him. Ben had no authority to make the decision. It would mean court-martial later, and punishment visited on his family as well, unless he could justify it by claiming quicker results than the long-drawn process of narcosynthesis.

The captain's hands twisted together, big knobby hands, and he stared at them. 'This is a hell of a choice for you, I know,' he mumbled. 'But there's Mary and . . . the kids, and men here who trust me. Good decent men. We aren't fiends, believe me. But I can't deny my own shipmates a fighting chance to get home alive.'

Robert Crane wet his lips. 'How do you know I'll tell the truth?' he asked.

Ben looked up again, crinkling his eyes. 'We had a formula once,' he said. 'Remember? "Cross my heart and hope to die, spit in my eye if I tell a lie." I don't think either of us ever lied when we took that oath.'

'And— Ben, the whole war hangs on this, maybe. Do you seriously think I'd keep my word for a kid's chant if it could decide the war?'

'Oh, no.' A smile ghosted across the captain's mouth. 'But there's going to be a meeting of skippers, if I know Hokusai. He'll want the opinions of us all as to what we should do next. Having heard them, he'll make his own decision. I'll be one voice among a lot of others.

'But if I can speak with whatever information you've given me . . . do you understand? The council will meet long before you could be sent Earthside and quizzed. I need your knowledge *now*. I'll listen to whatever you have to say. I may or may not believe you . . . I'll make my own decision as to what to recommend . . . but it's the only way I can save you, and myself, and everything else I care about.'

He waited then, patiently as the circling ships. They must have come around the planet by now, thought Robert Crane. The sun would be drowning many stars, and Earth would be daylit if you looked out.

Captains' council . . . It sounded awkward and slow, when at any moment, as far as they knew, Dushanovitch-Alvarez might come in at the head of his fleet. But after all, the navy would remain on general alert, second officers would be left in charge. They had time.

And they would want time. Nearly every one of them had kin on Earth. None wished to explode radioactive death across the world they loved. K'ung's will had been like steel, but now they would – subconsciously, and the more powerfully for that – be looking for any way out of the frightful necessity. A respected officer, giving good logical reasons for postponing the bombardment, would be listened to by the keenest ears.

Robert Crane shivered. It was a heartless load to put on a man. The dice of future history . . . he could load the dice, because he knew Ben as any man knows a dear brother, but maybe his hand would slip while he loaded them.

'Well?' It was a grating in the captain's throat.

Robert drew a long breath. 'All right,' he said.

'Yes?' A high, cracked note; Ben must be near breaking, too.

'I'm not in command, you realize.' Robert's words were blurred with haste. 'I can't tell for sure what— But I do know we've got fewer ships. A lot fewer.'

'I suspected that.'

'We have some plan – I haven't been told what – it depends on making you leave this orbit and come out and fight us where we are. If you stay home, we can't do a damn thing. This raid of mine . . . we'd hope that with your admiral dead, you'd join battle out towards Luna.'

Robert Crane hung in the air, twisting in its currents, the breath gasping in and out of him. Ben looked dim, across the room, as if his eyes were failing.

'Is that the truth, Bob?' The question seemed to come from light-years away.

'Yes. Yes. I can't let you go and get killed and— Cross my heart and hope to die, spit in my eye if I tell a lie!'

I set down my mug, empty, and signalled for another. The bartender glided across the floor with it and I drank thirstily, remembering how my throat had felt mummified long ago on the *Huitzilopochtli*, remembering much else.

'Very well, sir.' Freylinghausen's testy voice broke a stillness. 'What happened?'

'You ought to know that, Professor,' I replied. 'It's in the history tapes. The Humanist fleet decided to go out at once and dispose of its inferior opponent. Their idea – correct, I suppose – was that a space victory would be so demoralizing that the rebels on the ground would capitulate immediately after. It would have destroyed the last hope of re-inforcements, you see.'

'And the Union fleet won,' said Nielsen-Singh. 'They chopped the Humanist navy into fishbait. I know. My father was there. We bought a dozen new reclamation units with his share of the loot, afterwards.'

'Naval history is out of my line, Captain Crane,' said the engineer, Buwono. 'How did Dushanovitch-Alvarez win?'

'Oh ... by a combination of things. Chiefly, he disposed his ships and gave them such velocities that the enemy, fol-lowing the usual principles of tactics, moved at high acceler-ations to close in. And at a point where they would have built up a good big speed, he had a lot of stuff planted, rocks and ball bearings and scrap iron ... an artificial meteoroid swarm, moving in an opposed orbit. After that had done its work, the two forces were of very nearly equal strength, and it became a battle of standard weapons. Which Dushano-vitch-Alvarez knew how to use! A more brilliant naval mind hasn't existed since Lord Nelson.'

'Yes, yes,' said Freylinghausen impatiently. 'But what has this to do with the subject under discussion?'

'Don't you see, Professor? It was chance right down the line – chance which was skilfully exploited when it arose to be sure, but nevertheless a set of unpredictable accidents. The *Monitor* blew up ten minutes ahead of schedule; as a result, the commando that did it was captured. Normally, this would have meant that the whole plan would have been given away. I can't emphasize too strongly that the Human-ists would have won if they'd only stayed where they were.'

I tossed off a long gulp of porter, knocked the dottle from my pipe, and began refilling it. My hands weren't quite steady. 'But chance entered here, too, making Robert Crane's brother the man to capture him. And Robert knew how to manipulate Ben. At the captains' council, the *Huit-*

zilopochtli's skipper spoke the most strongly in favour of going out to do battle. His arguments, especially when everyone knew they were based on information obtained from a prisoner, convinced the others.'

'But you said . . .' Nielsen-Singh looked confused.

'Yes, I did.' I smiled at her, though my thoughts were entirely in the past. 'But it wasn't till years later that Ben heard the story of Br'er Rabbit and the briar patch; he came across it in his brother's boyhood diary. Robert Crane told the truth, swore to it by a boyhood oath – but his brother could not believe he'd yield so easily. Robert was almost begging him to stay with K'ung's original plan. Ben was sure that was an outright lie . . . that Dushanovitch-Alvarez must actually be planning to attack the navy in its orbit and could not possibly survive a battle in open space. So that, of course, was what he argued for at the council.

'It took nerve, though,' said Nielsen-Singh. 'Knowing what the *Huitzilopochtli* would have to face . . . knowing you'd be aboard, too . . .'

'She was a wreck by the time the battle was over,' I said. 'Not many in her survived.'

After a moment, Buwono nodded thoughtfully. 'I see your point, Captain. The accident of the bomb's going off too soon almost wrecked the Union plan. The accident of that brotherhood saved it. A thread of coincidences . . . yes, I think you've proved your case.'

'I'm afraid not, gentles.' Freylinghausen darted birdlike eyes around the table. 'You misunderstand me. I was not speaking of minor ripples in the mainstream of history. Certainly those are ruled by chance. But the broad current moves quite inexorably, I assure you. *Vide*: Earth and Luna are back in the Union under a more or less democratic government, but no solution has yet been found to the problem which brought forth the Humanists. They will come again; under one name or another they will return. The war was merely a ripple.'

'Maybe.' I spoke with inurbane curtness, not liking the thought. 'We'll see.'

'If nothing else,' said Nielsen-Singh, 'you people bought for Earth a few more decades of freedom. They can't take that away from you.'

I looked at her with sudden respect. It was true. Men died and civilizations died, but before they died they lived. No effort was altogether futile.

I could not remain here, though. I had told the story, as I must always tell it, and now I needed aloneness.

'Excuse me.' I finished my drink and stood up. 'I have an appointment . . . just dropped in . . very happy to have met you, gentles.'

Buwono rose with the others and bowed formally. 'I trust we shall have the pleasure of your company again, Captain Robert Crane.'

'Robert—? Oh.' I stopped. I had told what I must in third person, but everything had seemed so obvious. 'I'm sorry. Robert Crane was killed in the battle. I am Captain Benjamin Crane, at your service, gentles.'

I bowed to them and went out the door. The night was lonesome in the streets and across the desert.

Inside Straight

One reason for the persistence of war is that it has frequently been the only means that anyone could see for the preservation or establishment of certain values more dear than life. When this happens, whether pacifists like it or not, those who fight will be proud to do so, and they will glory in their victories.

In the main, sociodynamic theory predicted quite accurately the effects of the secondary drive. It foresaw that once a cheap interstellar transportation was available, there would be considerable emigration from the Solar System – men looking for a fresh start, malcontents of all kinds, 'peculiar people' desiring to maintain their way of life without interference. It also predicted that these colonies would in turn spawn colonies, until this part of the galaxy was sprinkled with human-settled planets, and that in their relative isolation, these politically independent worlds would develop some very odd societies.

However, the economic bias of the Renaissance period, and the fact that war was a discarded institution in the Solar System, led these same predictors into errors of detail. It was felt that, since planets useful to man are normally separated by scores of light-years, and since any planet colonized on a high technological level would be quite self-sufficient, there would be little intercourse and no strife between these settlements. In their own reasonableness, the Renaissance intellectuals overlooked the fact that man as a whole is not a rational animal, and that exploration and war do not always have economic causes.

– Simon Vardis, *A Short History of Pre-Commonwealth Politics*, Reel I, Frame 617

They did not build high on New Hermes. Plenty of space was available, and the few cities sprawled across many square kilometres in a complex of low, softly tinted domes and cylindroids. Parks spread green wherever you looked, each breeze woke a thousand bell-trees into a rush of chiming; flowers and the bright-winged summerflits ran wildly coloured beneath a serene blue sky. The planetary capital, Arkinshaw, had the same leisurely old-fashioned look as the other towns Ganch had seen; only down by the docks were energy and haste to be found.

The restaurant Wayland had taken him to was incredibly archaic; it even had live service. When they had finished a subtly prepared lunch, the waiter strolled to their table. 'Was there anything else, sir?' he asked.

'I thank you, no,' said Wayland. He was a small, lithe man with close-cropped grey hair and a brown nutcracker face in which lay startlingly bright blue eyes. On him, the local dress – a knee-length plaid tunic, green buskins, and yellow mantle – looked good ... which was more than you could say for most of them, reflected Ganch.

The waiter produced a tray. No bill lay on it, as Ganch had expected, but a pair of dice. *Oh, no!* he thought. *By the Principle, no! Not this again!*

Wayland rattled the cubes in his hand, muttering an incantation. They flipped on the table. Eight spots looked up. 'Fortune seems to favour you, sir,' said the waiter.

'May she smile on a more worthy son,' replied Wayland. Ganch noted with disgust that the planet's urbanity-imperative extended even to servants. The waiter shook the dice and threw.

'Snake eyes,' he smiled. 'Congratulations, sir. I trust you enjoyed the meal.'

'Yes, indeed,' said Wayland, rising. 'My compliments to the chef, and you and he are invited to my next poker game. I'll have an announcement about it on the telescreens.'

He and the waiter exchanged bows and compliments. Wayland left, ushering Ganch through the door and out on to the slidewalk. They found seats and let it carry them towards the waterfront, which Ganch had expressed a desire to see.

'Ah . . .' Ganch cleared his throat. 'How was that done?'

'Eh?' Wayland blinked. 'Don't you have dice on Dromm?'

'Oh, yes. But I mean the principle of payment for the meal.'

'I shook him. Double or nothing. I won.'

Ganch shook his head. He was a tall, muscular man in a skintight black uniform. That and the scarlet eyes in his long bony face (not albinism, but healthy mutation) marked him as belonging to the Great Cadre of Dromm.

'But then the restaurant loses money,' he said.

'This time, yes,' nodded Wayland. 'It evens out in the course of a day, just as all our commerce evens out, so that in the long run everybody earns his rightful wage or profits.'

'But suppose one – ah – cheats?'

Surprisingly, Wayland reddened, and looked around. When he spoke again, it was in a low voice: 'Don't ever use that word, sir, I beg of you. I realize the mores are different on your planet, but here there is one unforgivable, utterly obscene sin, and it's the one you just mentioned.' He sat back, breathing heavily for a while, before he cooled off and proffered cigars. Ganch declined – tobacco did not grow on Dromm – but Wayland puffed his own into lighting with obvious enjoyment.

'As a matter of fact,' he said presently, 'our whole social conditioning is such as to preclude the possibility of . . . unfairness. You realize how thoroughly an imperative can be inculcated with modern psychopediatrics. It is a matter of course that all equipment, from dice and coins to the most elaborate stellarium set, is periodically checked by a games engineer.'

'I see,' said Ganch doubtfully.

He looked around as the slidewalk carried him on. It was a pleasant, sunny day, like most on New Hermes. Only to be expected on a world with two small continents, the rest of the land split into a multitude of islands. The people he saw had a relaxed appearance, the men in their tunics and mantles, the women in their loose filmy gowns, the children in little or nothing. A race of sybarites; they had had it too easy here, and degenerated.

Sharply he remembered Dromm, gaunt glacial peaks and windscoured deserts, storm and darkness galloping down from the poles, the iron cubicles of cities and the obedient grey-clad masses that filled them. That world had brought forth the Great Cadre, and tempered them in struggle and heartbreak, and given them power first over a people and then over a planet and then over two systems.

Eventually ... who knew? The galaxy?

'I am interested in your history,' he said, recalling himself. 'Just how was New Hermes settled?'

'The usual process,' shrugged Wayland. 'Our folk came from Caledonia, which had been settled from Old Hermes, whose people were from Earth. A puritanical gang got into control and started making all kinds of senseless restrictions on natural impulses. Finally a small group, our ancestors, could take no more, and went off looking for a planet of their own. That was about three hundred years ago. They went far, into this spiral arm which was then completely unexplored, in the hope of being left alone; and that hope has been realized. To this day, except for a couple of minor wars, we've simply had casual visitors like yourself.'

Casual! A grim amusement twisted Ganch's mouth upwards.

To cover it, he asked: 'But surely you've had your difficulties? It cannot have been a mere matter of landing here and founding your cities.'

'Oh, no, of course not. The usual pioneer troubles – unknown diseases, wild animals, storms, a strange ecology. They endured some hard times before the machines were constructed. Now, of course, we have it pretty good. There are fifty million of us, and space for many more; but we're in no hurry to expand the population. We like elbow room.'

Ganch frowned until he had deduced the meaning of that

last phrase. They spoke Anglic here, as on Dromm and most colonies, but naturally an individual dialect had evolved.

Excitement gripped him. Fifty million! There were two hundred million people on Dromm, and conquered Thanit added half again as many.

Of course, said his military training, sheer numbers meant little. Automatized equipment made all but the most highly skilled officers and technicians irrelevant. War between systems involved sending a space fleet that met and beat the enemy fleet in a series of engagements: bases on planets had to be manned, and sometimes taken by ground forces, but the fighting was normally remote from the worlds concerned. Once the enemy navy was broken, its home had to capitulate or be sterilized by bombardment from the skies.

Still ... New Hermes should be an even easier prey than Thanit had been.

'Haven't you taken any precautions against ... hostiles?' he asked, mostly because the question fitted his assumed character

'Oh, yes, to be sure,' said Wayland. 'We maintain a navy and marine corps; matter of fact, I'm in the Naval Intelligence Reserve myself, captain's rank. We had to fight a couple of small wars in the previous century, once with the Corridans – nonhumans out for loot – and once with Oberkassel, whose people were on a religious-fanatic kick. We won them both without much trouble.' He added modestly: 'But of course, sir, neither planet was very intelligently guided.'

Ganch suppressed a desire to ask for figures on naval strength. This guileless dice-thrower might well spout them on request, but ...

The slidewalk reached the waterfront and they got off. Here the sea glistened blue, streaked with white foam, and the harbour was crowded with shipping. Not only flying boats, but big watercraft were moored to the ferroconcrete piers. Machines were loading and unloading in a whirl of bright steel arms, warehouses gaped for the planet's wealth, the air was rich with oil and spices. A babbling surfed around Ganch and broke on his eardrums.

Wayland pointed unobtrusively around, his voice almost lost in the din: 'See, we have quite a cultural variety of our own. That tall blond man in the fur coat is from Norrin, he must have brought in a load of pelts. The little dark fellow in the sarong is a spice trader from the Radiant Islands. The Mongoloid wearing a robe is clear from the Ivory Gate, probably with handicrafts to exchange for our timber. And—'

They were interrupted by a young woman, good-looking, with long black hair and a tilt-nosed freckled face. She wore a light blue uniform jacket, a lieutenant's twin comets on the shoulders, as well as a short loose-woven skirt revealing slim brown legs. 'Will! Where have you been?'

'Showing the distinguished guest of our government around,' said Wayland formally. 'The Prime Selector himself appointed me to that pleasant task. Ganch, may I have the honour of presenting my niece, Lieutenant Christabel Hesty of the New Hermesian Navy? Lieutenant Hesty, this gentleman hight Ganch, from Dromm. It's a planet lying about fifty light-years from us, a fine place I'm sure. They are making a much overdue ethnographic survey of this galactic region, and Ganch is taking notes on us.'

'Honoured, sir.' She bowed and shook hands with herself in the manner of Arkinshaw. 'We've heard of Dromm. Visitors have come thence in the past several years. I trust you are enjoying your stay?'

Ganch saluted stiffly, as was prescribed for the Great Cadre. 'Thank you, very much.' He was a little shocked at such blatant sexual egalitarianism, but reflected that it might be turned to advantage.

'Will, you're just the man I want to see.' Lieutenant Hesty's voice bubbled over. 'I came down to wager on a cargo from Thorncroft and you—'

'Ah, yes. I'll be glad to help you, though of course the requirements of my guild are—'

'You'll get your commission.' She made a face at him and

turned laughing to Ganch. 'Perhaps you didn't know, sir, my uncle is a tipster?'

'No, I didn't,' said the Dromman. 'What profession is that?'

'Probability analyst. It takes years and years of training. When you want to make an important wager, you call in a tipster.' She tugged at Wayland's sleeve. 'Come on, the trading will start any minute.'

'Do you mind, sir?' asked Wayland.

'Not at all,' said Ganch. 'I would be very interested. Your economic system is unique.' *And*, he added to himself, *the most inefficient I have yet heard of.*

They entered a building which proved to be a single great room. In the centre was a long table, around which crowded a colourful throng of men and women. An outsize electronic device of some kind stood at the end, with a tall rangy man in kilt and beryllium-copper breastplate at the controls. Wayland stepped aside, his face taking on an odd withdrawn look.

'How does this work?' asked Ganch – *sotto voce*, for the crowd did not look as if it wanted its concentration disturbed.

'The croupier there is a trader from Thorncroft,' whispered Christabel Hesty. This close, with her head beneath his chin, Ganch could smell the faint sun-warmed perfume of her hair. It stirred a wistfulness in him, buried ancestral memories of summer meadows on Earth. He choked off the emotion and listened to her words.

'He's brought in a load of refined thorium, immensely valuable. He puts that up as his share, and those who wish to trade get into the game with shares of what they have – they cover him, as in craps, though they're playing Orthotron now. The game is a complex one, I see a lot of tipsters around ... yes, and the man in the green robe is a games engineer, umpire and technician. I'm afraid you wouldn't understand the rules at once, but perhaps you would like to make side bets?'

'No, thank you,' said Ganch. 'I am content to observe.'

He soon found out that Lieutenant Hesty had not exaggerated the complications. Orthotron seemed to be a remote descendant of roulette such as they had played on Thanit before the war, but the random-pulse tubes shifted the probabilities continuously, and the rules themselves changed as the game went on. When the scoreboard on the machine flashed, chips to the tune of millions of credits clattered from hand to hand. Ganch found it hard to believe that anyone could ever learn the system, let alone become so expert in it as to make a profession of giving advice. A tipster would have to allow for the presence of other tipsters, and . . .

His respect for Wayland went up. The little man must have put a lightning-fast mind through years of the most rigorous training; and there must be a highly developed paramathematical theory behind it all. If that intelligence and energy had gone into something useful, military technique, for instance . . .

But it hadn't, and New Hermes lay green and sunny, wide open for the first determined foe.

Ganch grew aware of tension. It was not overtly expressed, but faces tightened, changed colour, pupils narrowed and pulses beat in temples until he could almost feel the emotion, crackling like lightning in the room. Now and then Wayland spoke quietly to his niece, and she laid her bets accordingly.

It was with an effort that she pulled herself away, with two hours lost and a few hundred credits gained. Nothing but courtesy to the guest made her do it. Her hair was plastered to her forehead, and she went out with a stiff-legged gait that only slowly loosened.

Wayland accepted his commission and laughed a trifle shakily. 'I earn my living, sir!' he said. 'It's brutal on the nerves.'

'How long will they play?' asked Ganch.

'Till the trader is cleaned out or has won so much that no one can match him. In this case, I'd estimate about thirty hours.'

'Continuous? How can the nervous system endure it, not to mention the feet?'

'It's hard,' admitted Christabel Hesty. Her eyes burned. 'But exciting! There's nothing in the galaxy quite like that suspense. You lose yourself in it.'

'And, of course,' said Wayland mildly, 'man adapts to any cultural pattern. We'd find it difficult to live as you do on Dromm.'

No doubt, thought Ganch sardonically. *But you are going to learn how.*

On an isolated planet like this, an outworlder was always a figure of romance. In spite of manners, which must seem crude here, Ganch had only to suggest an evening out for Christabel Hesty to leap at the offer.

He simply changed to another uniform, but she appeared in a topless gown of deep-blue silkite, her dark hair sprinkled with tiny points of light, and made his heart stumble. He reminded himself that women were breeders, nothing else. But Principle! How dull they were on Dromm!

His object was to gain information, but he decided he might as well enjoy his work.

They took an elevated way to the Stellar House, Arkinshaw's single skyscraper, and had cocktails in a clear-domed roof garden with sunset rioting around them. A gentle music, some ancient waltz from Earth herself, lilted in the air, and the gaily clad diners talked in low voices and clinked glasses and laughed softly.

. Lieutenant Hesty raised her glass to his. 'Your luck, sir,' she pledged him. Then, smiling: 'Shall we lower guard?'

'I beg your pardon?'

'My apologies. I forgot you are a stranger, sir. The proposal was to relax formality for this evening.'

'By all means,' said Ganch. He tried to smile in turn. 'Though I fear my class is always rather stiff.'

Her long, soot-black eyelashes fluttered. 'Then I hight Chris tonight,' she said. 'And your first name . . .?'

'My class does not use them. I am Ganch, with various identifying symbols attached.'

'We meet some strange outworlders,' she said frankly, 'but in truth, you Drommans seem the most exotic yet.'

'And New Hermes gives us that impression,' he chuckled.

'We know so little about you—a few explorers and traders, and now you. Is your mission official?'

'Everything on Dromm is official,' said Ganch, veraciously enough. 'I am an ethnographer making a detailed study of your folkways.' And that was a lie.

'Excuse my saying so, I shouldn't criticize another civilization, but isn't it terribly drab having one's entire life regulated by the State?'

'It is . . .' Ganch hunted for words. 'Secure,' he finished earnestly. 'Ordered. One knows where one stands.'

'A pity you had that war with Thanit. They seemed such nice people, those who visited here.'

'We had no choice,' answered Ganch with the smoothness of rote. 'An irresponsible, aggressive government attacked us.' She did not ask for details, and he supposed it was the usual thing: interest in other people's fate obeys an inverse-square law, and fifty light-years is a gulf of distance no man can really imagine.

In point of fact, he told himself with the bitter honesty of his race, Thanit had sought peace up to the last moment; Dromm's ultimatum had demanded impossible concessions, and Thanit had had no choice but to fight a hopeless battle. Her conquests had been well-planned, the armoured legions of Dromm had romped over her and now she was being digested by the State.

Chris frowned, a shadow on the wide clear brow. 'I find it hard to see why they would make a war . . . why anyone would,' she murmured. 'Isn't there enough on any planet to content its people? And if by chance they should be unhappy, there are always new worlds.'

'Well,' shrugged Ganch, 'you should know why. You're in the navy yourself, aren't you, and New Hermes has fought a couple of times.'

'Strictly in self-defence,' she said. 'Naturally, we now mount guard on our defeated enemies, even seventy years later, to be sure they don't try again. As for me, I have a peaceful desk job in the statistics branch, correlating data.'

Ganch felt a thrumming within himself. He could hardly have asked for better luck. Precise information on the armament of New Hermes was just what Dromm lacked. If he could bring it back to old wan Halsker it would mean a directorship, at least!

And afterwards, when a new conquest was to be administered and made over . . . His ruby eyes studied Chris from beneath drooping lids. A territorial governor had certain perquisites of office.

'I suppose there are many poor twisted people in the universe,' went on the girl. 'Like those Oberkassel priests, with their weird doctrine they wanted to force on everybody. It's hard to believe intolerance exists, but alien planets have done strange things to human minds.'

A veiling was on her violet gaze as she looked at him. She must want to know his soul, what it was that drove the Great Cadre and why anyone should enjoy having power over other men. He could have told her a great deal – the cruel wintry planet, the generations-long war against the unhuman Ixlatt who made sport of torturing prisoners, then war between factions that split men, war against the red-eyed mutants, whipped-up xenophobia, pogroms, concentration camps . . . Ganch's grandfather had died in one.

But the mutation was more than an accidental mark; it was in the nervous system, answer to a pitiless environment. A man of the Great Cadre did not know fear on the conscious level. Danger lashed him to alertness, but there was no fright to cloud his thoughts. And, by genetics or merely as the result of persecution, he had a will to power which only death could stop. The Great Cadre had subdued a hundred times their numbers, and made them into brain-channelled tools of the State, simply by being braver and more able in war. And Dromm was not enough, not when each darkness brought unconquered stars out overhead.

A philosopher from distant Archbishop, where they went in for imaginative speculation, had visited Dromm a decade ago. His remark still lay in Ganch's mind, and stung: 'Unjust treatment is apt to produce paranoia in the victim. Your race has outlived its oppressors, but not the reflexes they built into your society. You'll never rest till the whole universe is enslaved, for your canalized nervous systems make you incapable of regarding anyone else as anything but a dangerous enemy.'

The philosopher had not gone home alive, but his words remained; Ganch had tried to forget them, and could not.

Enough! His mind had completed its tack in the blink of an eye, and now he remembered that the girl expected an answer. He sipped his cocktail and spoke thoughtfully:

'Yes, these special groups, isolated on their special planets, have developed in many peculiar ways. New Hermes, for instance, if you will pardon my saying so.'

Chris raised her brows. 'Of course, this is my home and I'm used to it, Ganch,' she replied, 'but I fail to see anything which would surprise an outsider very much. We live quietly for the most part, with a loose parliamentary government to run planetary affairs. The necessities of life are produced free for all by the automatic factories; to avoid the annoyance of regulations, we leave everything else to private enterprise, subject only to the reasonable restrictions of the Conservation Authority and a fair-practices act. We don't need more government than that, because the educational system instills respect for the rights and dignity of others and we have no ambitious public-works projects.

'You might say our whole culture is founded on a principle of live and let live.'

She stroked her chin, man-fashion. 'Of course, we have police and courts. And we discourage a concentration of power, political or economic, but that's simply to preserve individual liberty. Our economic system helps; it's hard to build up a gigantic business when one game may wipe it out.'

'Now there,' said Ganch, 'you strike the oddity. This passion for gambling. How does it arise?'

'Oh . . . I wouldn't call it a passion. It's merely one way of pricing goods and services, just as haggling is on Kwan-Yin, and socialism on Arjay, and supply-demand on Alexander.'

'But how did it originate?'

Chris lifted smooth bare shoulders and smiled. 'Ask the historians, not me. I suppose our ancestors, reacting from the Caledonian puritanism, were apt to glorify vices and practise them to excess. Gambling was the only one that didn't taper off as a more balanced society evolved. It came to be a custom. Gradually it superseded the traditional methods of exchange.

'It doesn't make any difference, you see; being honest gambling, it comes out even. Win one, lose one . . . that's almost the motto of our folk. To be sure, in games of skill like poker, a good player will come out ahead in the long run; but any society gives an advantage to certain talents. On Alexander, most of the money and prestige flow to the successful entrepreneur. On Einstein, the scientists are the rich and honoured leaders. On Hellas, it's male prowess and female beauty. On Arjay, it's the political spellbinder. On Dromm, I suppose, the soldier is on top. With us, it's the shrewd gambler.

'The important thing,' she finished gravely, 'is not who gets the most, but whether everyone gets enough.'

'But that is what makes me wonder,' said Ganch. 'This trader we saw today, for instance. Suppose he loses everything?'

'It would be a blow, of course. But he wouldn't starve, because the necessities are free anyway; and he'll have the sense – he'll have learned in the primaries – to keep a reserve to start over with. We have few paupers.'

'Your financial structure must be most complicated.'

'It is,' she said wryly. 'We've had to develop a tremendous theoretical science and a great number of highly trained men to handle it. That game today was childish compared with what goes on in, say, the securities exchange. I don't pretend to understand what happens there. I'm content to turn a wheel for my monthly pay, and if I win to go out and see if I can't make a little more.'

'And you *enjoy* this . . . insecurity?'

'Why, yes. As I imagine you enjoy war, and an engineer enjoys building a spaceship, and— ' Chris looked at the table. 'It's always hard and risky settling a new planet, even one as Earth-like as ours. Our ancestors got a taste for excitement. When no more was to be had in subduing nature, they transferred the desire to— Ah, here come the hors d'oeuvres.'

Ganch ate a stately succession of courses with pleasure. He was not good at small talk, but Chris made such eager conversation that it was simple to lead her: the details of her life and work, insignificant items but they clicked together. By the coffee and liqueur, Ganch knew where the military microfiles of New Hermes were kept and was fairly sure he knew how to get at them.

Afterwards they danced. Ganch had never done it before, but his natural co-ordination soon fitted him into the rhythm. There was a curious bittersweet savour to holding the girl in his arms . . . dearest enemy. He wondered if he should try to make love to her. An infatuated female officer would be useful . . .

No. In such matters, she was the sophisticate and he the bumbling yokel. Coldly, though not without regret, he dismissed the idea.

They sat at a poker table for a while, where the management put up chips to the value of their bill. Ganch was completely outclassed; he learned the game readily, but his excellent analytical mind could not match the Hermesians. It was almost as if they knew what cards he held. He lost heavily, but Chris made up for it and when they quit they only had to pay half of what they owed.

They hired an aircar, and for a while its gravity drive lifted them noiselessly into a night-blue sky, under a flooding moon and myriad stars and the great milky sprawl of the galaxy. Beneath them a broken bridge of moonlight shuddered across the darkened sea, and they heard the far, faint crying of birds.

When he let Chris off at her apartment, Ganch wanted to stay. It was a wrenching to say good night and turn back to his own hotel. He stamped out the wish and bent his mind elsewhere. There was work to do.

Dromm was nothing if not thorough. Her agents had been on New Hermes for ten years now, mostly posing as natives of unsuspicious planets like Guise and Anubis. Enough had been learned to earmark this world for conquest after Thanit, and to lay out the basic military campaign.

The Hermesians were not really naïve. They had their own spies and counterspies. Customs inspection was careful. But each Dromman visitor had brought a few plausible objects with him – a personal teleset, a depilator, a sample of nuclear-powered tools for sale – nothing to cause remark; and those objects had stayed behind, in care of a supposed immigrant from Kwan-Yin who lived in Arkinshaw. This man had re-fashioned them into as efficient a set of machinery for breaking and entering as existed anywhere in the known galaxy.

Ganch was quite sure Wayland had a tail on him. It was an elementary precaution. But a field intelligence officer of Dromm had ways to shake a tail off without its appearing more than accidental. Ganch went out the following afternoon, having notified Wayland that he did not need a guide: he just wanted to stroll around and look at things for himself. After wandering a bit, he went into a pleasure house. It was a holiday, Discovery Day, and Arkinshaw swarmed with a merry crowd; in the jam-packed building Ganch slipped quietly into a washroom cubicle.

His shadows would most likely watch all exits; and they wouldn't be surprised if he stayed inside for many hours. The hetaerae of New Hermes were famous.

Alone, Ganch slipped out of his uniform and stuffed it down the rubbish disintegrator. Beneath it he wore the loose blue coat and trousers of a Kwan-Yin colonist. A life-mask over his head, a complete alteration of posture and gait . . . it was another man who stepped into the hall and sauntered out the main door as if his amusements were completed. He went quite openly to Fraybiner's house; what was more natural than that some home-planet relative of Tao Chung should pay a call?

When they were alone, Fraybiner let out a long breath. 'By the Principle, it's good to be with a man again!' he said. 'If you knew how sick I am of these chattering decadents—'

'Enough!' snapped Ganch. 'I am here on business. Operation Lift.'

Fraybiner's surgically slanted and darkened eyes widened. 'So it's finally coming off?' he murmured. 'I was beginning to wonder.'

'If I get away with it,' said Ganch grimly. 'If I don't, it doesn't matter. Exact knowledge of the enemy's strength will be valuable, but we have sufficient information already to launch the war.'

Fraybiner began operating concealed studs. A false wall slid aside to reveal a safe, on which he got to work. 'How will you take it home?' he asked. 'When they find their files looted, they won't let anyone leave the planet without a thorough search.'

Ganch didn't reply; Fraybiner had no business knowing. Actually, the files were going to be destroyed, once read, and their contents go home in Ganch's eidetic memory. But that versatile ethnographer did not plan to leave for some weeks yet: no use causing unnecessary suspicion. When he finally did . . . a surprise attack on the Hermesian bases would immobilize them at one swoop.

He smiled to himself. Even knowing they were to be attacked, their whole planet fully alerted, the Hermesians were finished. It was well established that their fleet had less than half the strength of Dromm's, and not a single supernova-class dreadnaught. Ganch's information would be helpful, but was by no means vital.

Except, of course, to Ganch Z-17837-JX-39. But death was a threat he treated with the contempt it deserved.

Fraybiner had got the safe open, and a metal gleam of instruments and weapons lay before their gaze. Ganch inspected each item carefully while the other jittered with impatience. Finally he donned the flying combat armour and hung the implements at its belt. By that time the sun was down and the stars out.

Chris had said the Naval HQ building was deserted at night except for its guards. Previous spies had learned where these were posted. 'Very well,' said Ganch. 'I'm on my way. I won't see you again, and advise you to move elsewhere soon. If the natives turn out to be stubborn, we'll have to destroy this city.'

Fraybiner nodded, and activated the ceiling door. Ganch went up on his gravity beams and out into the sky. The town was a jewelled spiderweb beneath him, and fireworks burst with great soft explosions of colour. His outfit was a nonreflecting black, and there was only a whisper of air to betray his flight.

The HQ building, broad and low, rested on a greensward several kilometres from Arkinshaw. Ganch approached its slumbering dark mass carefully, taking his time. A bare metre's advance, an instrument reading . . . yes, they had a radio-alarm field set up. He neutralized it with his heterodyning unit, flew another cautious metre, stopped to readjust the neutralization. The moon was down, but he wished the stars weren't so bright.

It was past midnight when he lay in the shrubbery surrounding a rear entrance. A pair of sentries, armed and helmeted, tramped almost by his nose, crossing paths in front of the door. He waited, learning the pattern of their march.

When his tactics were fully planned, he rose as one marine came by and let the fellow have a sonic stun beam. Too low-powered to trip an alarm, it was close range and to the base of the neck. Ganch caught the body as it fell, let it down, and picked up the same measured tread.

He felt no conscious tension as he neared the other man, though a sharp glance through darkness would end the ruse, but his muscles gathered themselves. He was almost abreast of the Hermesian when he saw the figure recoil in alarm. His stunner went off again. It was a bad shot; the sentry lurched but retained a wavering consciousness. Ganch sprang on him, one tigerish bound, a squeezed trigger, and he lowered the marine as gently as a woman might her lover.

For a moment he stood looking down on the slack face. A youngster, hardly out of his teens; there was something strangely innocent about him as he slept. About this whole world. They were too kind here, they didn't belong in a universe of wolves.

He had no doubt they would fight bravely and skilfully. Dromm would have to pay for her conquest. But the age of heroes was past. War was not an art, it was a science, and a set of giant computers joylessly chewing an involved symbolism told ships and men what to do. Given equal courage and equally intelligent leadership, it was merely arithmetic that the numerically superior fleet would win.

No time to lose! He spun on his heel and crouched over the door. His instruments traced out its circuits, a diamond drill bit into plastic, a wire shorted a current ... the door opened for him and he went into a hollow darkness of corridors.

Lightly, even in the clumsy armour, he made his way towards the main file room. Once he stopped. His instruments sensed a black-light barrier and it took him a quarter of an hour to neutralize it. But thereafter he was in among the cabinets.

They were not locked, and his flashbeam picked out th categories held in each drawer. Swiftly, then, he took th spools relating to ships, bases, armament, disposition ... b ignored the codes, which would be changed anyway whe the burglary was discovered. The entire set went into a sma pouch such as the men of Kwan-Yin carried, and he had micro-reader at the hotel.

The lights came on.

Before his eyes had adjusted to that sudden blaze, befo he was consciously aware of action, Ganch's drilled reflex had gone to work. His faceplate clashed down, gauntle snapped shut around his hands, and a Mark IV blaster was at his shoulder even as he whirled to meet the intruders.

They were a score, and their gay holiday attire was somehow nightmarish behind the weapons they carried. Wayland was in the lead, harshness on his face, and Christabel at his back. The rest Ganch did not recognize; they must be naval officers but— He crouched, covering them, a robot figure cased in a centimetre of imperviousness.

'So.' Wayland spoke quietly, a flat tone across the silence. 'I wondered – Ganch, I suppose.'

The Dromman did not answer. He heard a thin fine singing as his helmet absorbed the stun beam Chris was aiming at it.

'When my men reported you had been ten hours in the joyhouse, I thought it best to check up: first your quarters and next ...' Wayland paused. 'I didn't think you'd penetrate this far. But it could only be you, Ganch, so you may as well surrender.'

The spy shook his head, futile gesture inside that metal box he wore. 'No. It is you who are trapped,' he answered steadily. 'I can blast you all before your beams work through my armour ... Don't move!'

'You wouldn't escape,' said Wayland. 'The fight would rip alarms bringing the whole Fort Canfield garrison down on you.' Sweat beaded his forehead. Perhaps he thought of his niece and the gun which could make her a blackened husk; but his own small-bore flamer held firm.

'This means war,' said Chris. 'We've wondered about Dromm for a long time. Now we know.' Tears glimmered in her eyes. 'And it's so senseless!'

Ganch laughed without much humour. 'Impasse,' he said. 'I can kill you, but that would bring my own death. Be sure, though, that the failure of my mission will make little difference.'

Wayland stood brooding for a while. 'You're congenitally unafraid to die,' he said at last. 'The rest of us prefer to live, but will die if we must. So any decision must be made with a view to planetary advantage.'

Ganch's heart sprang within his ribs. He had lost, unless —
He still had an even chance.

'You're a race of gamblers,' he said. 'Will you gamble now?'

'Not with our planet,' said Chris.

'Let me finish! I propose we toss a coin, shake dice, whatever you like that distributes the probabilities evenly. If I
win, I go free with what I've taken here. You furnish me safe
conduct and transportation home. You'll have the knowledge that Dromm is going to attack, and some time to prepare. If you win, I surrender and co-operate with you. I have
valuable information, and you can drug me to make sure I
don't lie.'

'No!' shouted one of the officers.

'Wait. Let me think . . . I have to make an estimate.' Wayland lowered his gun and stood with half-shut eyes. He
looked as he had down in the traders' hall, and Ganch remembered uneasily that Wayland was a gambling analyst.

But there was little to lose. If he won, he went home with
his booty; if he lost . . . he knew how to will his heart to stop
beating.

Wayland looked up. 'Yes,' he said.

The others did not question him They must be used to
following a tipster's advice blindly. But one of them asked
how Ganch could be trusted. 'I'll lay down my blaster when
you produce the selection device,' said the Dromman. 'All
the worlds know you do not cheat.'

Chris reached into her pouched belt and drew out a deck
of cards. Wordlessly, she shuffled them and gave them to her
uncle. The spy put his gun on the floor. He half expected the
others to rush him, but they stood where they were.

Wayland's hands shook as he cut the deck. He smiled
crookedly.

'One-eyed jack,' he whispered. 'Hard to beat.'

He shuffled the cards again and held them out to Ganch
The armoured fingers were clumsy, but they opened the
deck.

It was the king of spades.

Stars blazed in blackness. The engines which had eaten light-years were pulsing now on primary drive, gravitics, accelerating towards the red sun that lay three astronomical units ahead.

Ganch thought that the space distortions of the drive beams were lighting the fleet up like a nova for the Hermesian detectors. But you couldn't fight a battle at translight speeds, and their present objective was to seek the enemy out and destroy him.

Overcommandant wan Halsker peered into the viewscreens of the dreadnaught. Avidness was on his long gaunt face, but he spoke levelly: 'I find it hard to believe. They actually gave you a speedster and let you go.'

'I expected treachery myself, sir,' answered Ganch deferentially. Despite promotion, he was only the chief intelligence officer attached to Task Force One. 'Surely, with their whole civilization at stake, any rational people would have— But their mores are unique. They always pay their gambling debts.'

It was very quiet down here in the bowels of the supernova ship. A ring of technicians sat before their instruments, watching the dials unblinkingly. Wan Halsker's eyes never left the simulacrum of space in his screens, though all he saw was stars. There was too much emptiness around to show the five hundred ships of his command, spread in careful formation through some billions of cubic kilometres.

A light glowed, and a technician said: 'Contact made. *Turolin* engaging estimated five meteor-class enemy vessels.'

Wan Halsker allowed himself a snort. 'Insects! Don't break formation; let the *Turolin* swat them as she proceeds.'

Ganch sat waiting, rehearsing in his mind the principles of modern warfare. The gravity drive had radically changed them in the last few centuries. A forward vector could be killed almost instantaneously, a new direction taken as fast, while internal pseudograv fields compensated for accelerations which would otherwise have crumpled a man. A fight in space was not unlike one in air, with this difference: the velocities used were too high, the distances too great, the units involved too many, for a human brain to grasp. It had to be done by machine.

Subspace quivered with coded messages, the ships' own electronic minds transmitting information back to the prime computers on Dromm – the computers laid out not only the over-all strategy, but the tactics of every major engagement. A man could not follow that esoteric mathematics, he could merely obey the thing he had built.

No change of orders came, a few torpedo ships were unimportant, and Task Force One continued.

Astran was a clinker, an airless, valueless planet of a waning red dwarf star, but it housed a key base of the Hermesian navy. With Astran reduced, wan Halsker's command could safely go on to rendezvous with six other fleets that had been taking care of their own assignments; the whole group would then continue to New Hermes herself, and let the enemy dare try to stop them!

Such, in broad outline, was the plan; but only a hundred computers, each filling a large building, could handle the details of strategy, tactics, and logistics.

Ganch had an uneasy feeling of being a very small cog in a very large machine. He didn't matter; the commandant didn't; the ship, the fleet, the grey mass of commoners didn't; nothing except the Cadre, and above them the almighty State had real existence.

The Hermesians would need a lot of taming before they learned to think that way.

Now fire was exploding out in space, great guns cutting loose as the outnumbered force sought the invaders. Ganch felt a shuddering when the supernova's own armament spoke. The ship's computer, her brain, flashed and chattered, the vessel leaped on her gravity beams, ducking, dodging, spouting flame and hot metal. Stars spun on the screen in a lunatic dance. Ten thousand men aboard the ship had become robots feeding her guns.

'Compartment Seven hit . . . sealed off.'

'Hit made on enemy star-class; damage looks light.'

'Number Forty-two gun out of action. Residual radio-activity . . . compartment sealed off.'

Men died, scorched and burned, air sucked from their lungs as the armoured walls peeled away, listening to the clack of radiation counters as leaden bulkheads locked them away like lepers. The supernova trembled with each hit. Ganch heard steel shriek not far away and braced his body for death.

Wan Halsker sat impassively, hands folded on his lap, watching the screens and the dials. There was nothing he could do; the ship fought herself, men were too slow. But he nodded after a while, in satisfaction.

'We're sustaining damage,' he said, 'but no more than expected.' He stared at a slim small crescent in the screen. 'Yonder's the planet. We're working in . . . we'll be in bombardment range soon.'

The ships' individual computers made their decisions on the basis of information received; but they were constantly sending a digest of the facts back to their electronic masters on Dromm. So far no tactical change had been ordered, but . . .

Ganch frowned at the visual tank which gave a crude approximation of the reality ramping around him. The little red specks were his own ships, the green ones such of the enemy as had been spotted. It seemed to him that too many red lights had stopped twinkling, and that the Hermesian fireflies were driving a wedge into the formation. But there was nothing he could do either.

A bell clanged. Change of orders! *Turolin* to withdraw three megakilometres towards Polaris, *Colfin* to swing round towards enemy Constellation Number Four, *Hardes*)— Watching the tank in a hypnotized way, Ganch decided vaguely it must be some attempt at a flanking movement. But a Hermesian squadron was out there!

Well . . .

The battle snarled across vacuum. It was many hours

before the Dromman computers gave up and flashed the command: Break contact, retreat in formation to Neering Base.

They had been outmanoeuvred. Incredibly, New Hermes' machines had out-thought Dromm's and the battle was lost.

Wayland entered the mapping room with a jaunty step that belied the haggardness in his face. Christabel Hesty looked up from her task of directing the integrators and cried aloud: 'Will! I didn't expect you back so soon!'

'I thumbed a ride home with a courier ship,' said Wayland. 'Three months' leave. By that time the war will be over, so . . .' He sat down on her desk, swinging his short legs, and got out an old and incredibly foul pipe. 'I'm just as glad, to tell the truth. Planetarism is all right in its place, but war's an ugly business.'

He grimaced. A Hermesian withstood the military life better than most; he was used not only to moments of nerve-ripping suspense but to long and patient waiting. Wayland, though, had during the past year seen too many ships blown up, too many men dead or screaming with their wounds. His hands shook a little as he tamped the pipe full.

'Luck be praised you're alive!'

'It hasn't been easy on you either, has it? Chained to a desk like this. Here, sit back and take a few minutes off. The war can wait.' Wayland kindled his tobacco and blew rich clouds. 'At least it never got close to our home, and our losses have been lighter than expected.'

'If you get occupation duty . . .'

'I'm afraid I will.'

'Well, I want to come too. I've never been off this planet it's disgraceful.'

'Dromm is a pretty dreary place, I warn you. But Thani is close by, of course. It used to be a gay world, it will b again, and every Hermesian will be luck incarnate to them Sure, I'll wangle an assignment for you.'

Chris frowned. 'Only three months to go, though? That' hard to believe.'

'Two and a half is the official estimate. Look here.' Wayland stumped over to the three-dimensional sector map, which was there only for the enlightenment of humans. The military computers dealt strictly in lists of numbers.

'See, we whipped them at the Cold Stars, and now a feint of ours is drawing what's left of them into Ransome's Nebula.'

'Ransome's ... oh, you mean the Queen of Clubs? Mmm-hm. And what's going to happen to them there?'

'Tch, tch. Official secrets, my dear inquisitive nieceling. But imagine what *could* happen to a fleet concentrated in a mess of nebular dust that blocks their detectors!'

Wayland did not see Ganch again until he was stationed on Dromm. There he grumbled long and loudly about the climate, the food, and the tedious necessity of making sure that a subjugated enemy stayed subjugated. He looked forward to his next furlough on Thanit, and still more to rotation home in six months. Chris, being younger, enjoyed herself. They had no mountains on New Hermes, and she was going to climb Hell's Peak with Commander Danson. About half a dozen other young officers would be jealously present, so her uncle felt she would be adequately chaperoned.

They were working together in the political office, interviewing Cadre men and disposing of their cases. Wayland was not sympathetic towards the prisoners. But when Ganch was led in, he felt a certain kinship and even smiled.

'Sit down,' he invited. 'Take it easy. I don't bite.'

Ganch slumped into a chair before the desk and looked at the floor. He seemed as shattered as the rest of his class. They weren't really tough, thought Wayland; they couldn't stand defeat; most of them suicided rather than undergo psychorevision.

'Didn't expect to see you again,' he said. 'I understood you were on combat duty, and ... um ...'

'I know,' said Ganch lifelessly. 'Our combat units averaged ninety per cent casualties, towards the end.' In a rush of bitterness: 'I wish I had been one of them.'

'Take it easy,' repeated Wayland. 'We Hermesians aren't vindictive. Your planet will never have armed forces again – it'll join Corrid and Oberkassel as a protectorate of ours – but once we've straightened you out you'll be free to live as you please.'

'Free!' mumbled Ganch.

He lifted tortured red eyes to the face before him, but shifted from its wintry smile to Chris. She had some warmth for him at least.

'How did you do it?' he whispered. 'I don't understand. I thought you must have some new kind of computer, but our intelligence swore you didn't ... and we outnumbered you, and had that information you let me take home, and—'

'We're gamblers,' said the girl soberly.

'Yes, but—'

'Look at it this way,' she went on. 'War is a science, based on a complex paramathematical theory. Manoeuvres and engagements are ordered with a view to gaining the maximum advantage for one's own side, in the light of known information. But of course, *all* the information is never available, so intelligent guesswork has to fill in the gaps.

'Well, a system exists for making such guesses and for deciding what move has the maximum probability of success. It applies to games, business, war – every competitive enterprise. It's called games theory.'

'I—' Ganch's jaw dropped. He snapped it shut again and said desperately: 'But that's elementary! It's been known for centuries.'

'Of course,' nodded Chris. 'But New Hermes has based her whole economy on gambling – on probabilities, on games of skill where no player has complete information. Don't you see, it would make our entire intellectual interest turn towards games theory. And in fact we had to have a higher development of such knowledge, and a large class of men skilled in using it, or we could not maintain as complex a civilization as we do.

'No other planet has a comparable body of knowledge. And, while we haven't kept it secret, no other planet has men able to use that knowledge on its highest levels.

'For instance, take that night we caught you in the file room. If we cut cards with you, there was a fifty-fifty chance you'd go free. Will here had to estimate whether the overall probabilities justified the gamble. Because he decided they did, we three are alive today.'

'But I did bring that material home!' cried Ganch.

'Yes,' said the girl. 'And the fact you had it was merely another item for our strategic computers to take into account. Indeed, it helped us: it was definite information about what *you* knew, and your actions became yet more predictable.'

Laughter, gentle and unmocking, lay in her throat, 'Never draw to an inside straight,' she said. 'And never play with a man who knows enough not to, when you don't.'

Ganch sagged farther down in his chair. He felt sick. He replied to Wayland's questioning in a mechanical fashion, and heard sentence pronounced, and left under guard.

As he stumbled out, he heard Wayland say thoughtfully: 'Three gets you four he suicides rather than take psycho-revision.'

'You're covered!' said Christabel.

Details

Imagine that we did learn how to end war and build an all-round decent world. It is conceivable. In fact, some people believe we already have that knowledge, as for example in the Sermon on the Mount. Given the program, though, can we put it into effect? The record of man's attempts to improve man is not especially encouraging.

The most austerely egalitarian societies – and the League is a mature culture which has put such games behind it – soon learn they must cater to the whims of their leaders. This is true for the simple reason that a mind on whose decisions all fate may turn has to function efficiently, which it can only do when the total personality is satisfied and unjarred. For Rasnagarth Kri the League had rebuilt a mile-high skyscraper. His office took up the whole roof, beneath a dome of clear plastic, so that from his post he could brood by day over the city towers and by night under the cold radiance of the Sagittarian star-clouds. It was a very long walk from the gravshaft door to the big bare desk.

Harban Randos made the walk quickly, almost jauntily. They had warned him that the High Commissioner was driven by a sense of undying haste and that it was worth a man's future to spill time on a single formality. Randos fairly radiated briskness. He was young, only a thousand years old, plumpish and sandy-haired, dressed in the latest mode of his people, the Shandakites of Garris. His tunic glittered with starry points of light and his cloak blew like a flame behind him.

He reached the desk and remained standing. Kri had not looked up. The harsh blue face was intent over a bit of paper. Around him the sky was sunny, aircraft flittered in dragonfly grace, the lesser spires glowed and burned, the city pulsed. For the blue man in the plain grey robe, none of it existed, not while he was looking at that one sheet.

After all, its few lines of text and paramathematical symbology concerned eight billion human lives. In another lifetime or so – say 10,000 years – the consequences might well concern the entire League, with a population estimated at ten to the fifteenth power souls.

After an interminable minute, Kri scribbled his decision and dropped the report down the outgoing chute. Another popped automatically from the incoming slot. He half reached for it, saw Randos waiting, and withdrew his hand. That was a gaunt hand, knobby and ropy and speckled with age.

'Harban Randos, sir, by appointment,' rattled off his visitor. 'Proposed agent-in-chief for new planet in Section two-three-nine-seven-six-two.'

'I remember now. Sit down.' Kri nodded curtly. 'Coordinator Zantell and Representative Chuing urged your qualifications. What are they?'

'Graduated in seventy-five from Nimë Psychotechnic Institute in the second rank. Apprenticeship under Vor Valdran on Galeen V, rated as satisfactory.' Damn the old spider! What did he think the Service was . . . the Patrol?

'Galeen was a simple operation,' said Kri. 'It was only a matter of guiding them along the last step to full status. The planet for which you have been recommended is a barbarous one, therefore a more difficult and complex problem.'

Randos opened his mouth to protest that backward planets were, mathematically, an elementary proposition . . . Great Designer, only a single world to worry about, while the Galeenians had reached a dozen stars at the time he went there! Wisely, he closed it again.

Kri sighed. 'How much do you know of the situation on this one?— No, never mind answering, it would take you all day. Frankly, you're only getting the job for two reasons. One, you are a Shandakite of Garris, which means you are physiologically identical with the race currently dominant on the planet in question. We have no other fully trained

Shandakite available, and indeed no qualified man who could be surgically disguised. Everyone I would like to appoint is tied up elsewhere with more important tasks. Two, you have the strong recommendation of Zantell and Chuing.

'Very well, the post is yours. The courier boat will take you there, and supply you en route with hypnotic instruction as to the details. You already know the Service rules and the penalties for violating them.

'I wanted to see you for just one reason ... to tell you personally what your job means. You're a young man, and think of it as a stepping stone to higher things. That's an attitude which you'll have to rub off. It's an insignificant planet of an undistinguished star, out on the far end of the galaxy, with a minimum thousand years of guidance ahead of it before it can even be considered for full status. I know that. But I also know it holds more than a billion human creatures, each one fully as valuable as you and I, each one the centre of his own particular universe. If you forget that, may the Great Designer have mercy on them and on you.

'Dismissed.'

Randos walked out, carefully energetic. He had been prepared for this, but it had still been pretty raw. Nobody had a right to treat a free citizen of a full-status planet like ... like a not very trustworthy child. Damn it, he was a man, on the mightiest enterprise men had ever undertaken, and—

And someday *he* might sit behind that desk.

Kri allowed himself a minute's reflection as Randos departed. It was so tinged with sadness that he wondered if he weren't getting too old, if he hadn't better resign for the good of the Service.

So many planets, spinning through night and cold, so many souls huddled on them ... a half-million full-status worlds, near galactic centre, members of interstellar civilization by virtue of knowing that such a civilization existed ... and how many millions more who did not know? It seemed that every day a scoutship brought back word of yet another inhabited planet.

Each of them had its human races – red, black, white, yellow, blue, green, brown, tall or short, thin or fat, hairy or bald, tailed or tailless, but fully human, biological human, and the scientists had never discovered why evolution should work thus on every terrestroid world. The churches said it was the will of the Designer, and perhaps they were right. Certainly they were right in a pragmatic sense, for the knowledge had brought the concept of brotherhood and duty. The duty of true civilization was to guide its brothers in darkness – secretly, gently, keeping from them the devastating knowledge that a million-year-old society already existed, until they had matured enough to take that bitter pill and join smoothly the League of the older planets. Without such guidance . . . In his younger days, Kri had seen the dead worlds, where men had once lived. War, exhaustion of resources, accumulation of lethal genes, mutant disease . . it was so hideously simple for Genus Homo to wipe a planet bare of himself.

The old blue man sighed, and a smile tugged at his mouth. You didn't work many centuries in the Service without becoming an idealist and a cynic. An idealist who lived for the mission, and a cynic who knew when to compromise for the sake of that mission. Theoretically, Kri was above political pressures. In fact, when there was no obvious disqualification, he often had to give somebody's favourite nephew a plum. After all, his funds and his lower echelons were politically controlled . . .

He started, realizing how much time had passed and how many decisions had yet to be made before he could quit for the day. His wife would give him Chaos if he stayed overtime tonight. Some damned card party. He bent over the report and dismissed from his mind the planet called Earth.

1

The doorman was shocked.

He was used to many people going in and out of the grey stone building, not only toffs and tradesmen but foreigners and Orientals and even plain tenant farmers, come down from Yorkshire with hayseeds in their hair. Benson & McMurtrie, Import Brokers, were a big firm and had to talk to every sort. He'd served in India as a young fellow and considered himself broad-minded. But there are limits.

' 'Ere, now! An' just where d'yer think you're going?'

The stocky, sunburned man with the tattered clothes and the small brass earrings paused. He had curly black hair and snapping blue eyes, and was fuming away on an old clay pipe. A common tinker, walking into Benson & McMurtrie cool as dammit! 'In there, ould one, in there,' he said with an Irish lilt. 'Ye wouldn' be denyin' me a sight of the most beautiful colleen in London, would ye?'

'That I would,' said the doorman. A passing car stirred up enough breeze to flutter the tinker's rags, flamboyant against the grimed respectability of Regent Street. 'On yer wye before I calls a constable.'

'Sure an' it's no way to be addressin' a craftsman, me bhoy,' said the tinker. 'But since ye seem to be sharin' of the Sassenach mania for the written word, then feast your eyes on this.' Out of his patched garments he produced a letter of admittance, dated two years ago and signed by McMurtrie himself.

The doorman scanned it carefully, the more so as McMurtrie was eight months dead, the nice white-haired old gentleman, struck down by one of these new-fangled autos as he crossed this very street. But it gave a clear description of Sean O'Meara, occupation tinker, and set no time limit.

He handed it back. 'In yer goes, then,' he conceded, 'though why they— Nev' mind! Behyve yerself is all I got ter sye.'

Sean O'Meara nodded gaily and disappeared into the building. The doorman scratched his head. You never knew, you didn't and those Irish were an uppity lot, a bad lot. Here Mr Asquith was trying to give them Home Rule and the Ulstermen were up in arms about it!

Sabor Tombak had no trouble getting past the private secretary who was a Galactic himself, but he sadly puzzled the lesser employees. Most of them concluded, after several days of speculation, that the tinker was a secret agent. It was well known that Benson & McMurtrie had sufficient financial power to be hand in glove with the Cabinet itself. They weren't so far off the mark at that.

The inner office was a ponderosity of furniture and sepia. Tombak shuddered and knocked out his pipe. Usrek Arken, alias Sir John Benson – grandson of the founder, who had actually been himself – started. 'Do you have to bring that thing in here?' he complained. 'The London air is foul already without you polluting it.'

'Anything would be welcome as a counterirritant to this stuff,' answered Tombak. His gesture included the entire office. 'Why the Evil don't you guidance boys get on orbit and guide the English into decent taste? An Irish peasant without a farthing in his pocket has better-looking quarters than this kennel.'

'Details, details.' The sarcastic note in Arken's voice did not escape Tombak. The word had somehow become a proverb in his absence.

'Better get hold of the boss and let me report,' he said. 'T've an earful to give him.'

'An eyeful, you mean,' replied Arken. 'Written up in proper form with quantitative data tabulated, if you please.'

'Oh, sure, sure. Gimme time. But this won't wait for—'

'Maybe you don't know we have a new boss,' said Arken slowly.

'Huh? What happened to Kalmagens?'

'Killed. Run over by a bloody Designer-damned petroleum burner eight months ago.'

Tombak sat down, heavily. He had had a great regard for Kalmagens, both professionally – the Franco–Prussian business had been handled with sheer artistry – and as a friend. He dropped into fluent Gaelic for a while, cursing the luck.

At last he shook himself and asked: 'What's the new man like?'

. 'Harban Randos of Garris. Arrived six weeks back. Young fellow, fresh out of his apprenticeship. A good psychotechnician, but seems to think the psychotechnic laws will cover every situation.' Arken scowled. 'And the situation right now is nasty.'

'It is that,' agreed Tombak. 'I haven't seen many news-papers where I've been, but it's past time Kaiser Wilhelm was put across somebody's knee.' He jumped back to his feet with the restless energy of two years tramping the Irish roads. 'Where's Randos now? Damn it, I want to see him.'

Arken lifted his brows. 'All right, old chap. If you really insist, I'll call him for you, and then I'll crawl under the desk and wait for the lightning to subside.'

He buzzed for the secretary and told him in English: 'Send Mr Harrison to me, please.' That was for the benefit of the non-Galactic employees. When the door had closed, he re-marked to Tombak:

'You know how complicated the secrecy requirement can make things. Bad enough to always have to look your Earth-age, and officially die every fifty years or so, and pro-vide a synthetic corpse, and assume a new face and a new personality. But when you're at the top, and the leading autochthons know you as an important man – Chaos! We have to fob Randos off as a senior clerk, freshly hired for nepotistic reasons.'

Tombak grinned and tamped his pipe. He himself was in the lowest echelon of the five thousand Galactics serving on Earth, and refused to study for promotion. He liked the planet and its folk, he liked being soldier and sailor and cowboy and mechanic and tramp, to gather knowledge of how the Plan was progressing on the level of common humanity. He did not hanker for the symbological sweat-shop work and the identity problem of the upper brackets.

A plump, undistinguished form, in sombre clothes that looked highly uncomfortable, entered. 'You sent for me, sir?' The door closed behind Harban Randos. 'What's the meaning of this? I was engaged in an evaluation of the political dynamics, and you interrupted me precisely as I was getting the matrix set up. How many times do I have to tell you the situation is crucial? What the Chaos do you want now?'

'Sir Randos . . . Sabor Tombak, one of our field agents, returned from a survey of Ireland,' murmured Arken. 'He has important new information for you.'

Randos did not bow, as urbanity demanded. He looked tired and harried. 'Then file it and mark it urgent, for Designer's sake!'

'Trouble is,' said Tombak imperturbably, 'this is not stuff that can be fitted into a mass-action equation. This concerns individual people . . . angry people.'

'Look here—' Randos drew a ragged breath. 'I'll take time to explain to you.' His tone grew elaborately satirical. 'Forgive me if I repeat what you already know.

'This planet wasn't discovered till seventeen ninety-eight, and three years went by before a mission could be sent. The situation was plainly critical, so much so that our men couldn't take a century to establish themselves. They had to cut corners and work fast. By introducing technological innovations themselves and serving with uncanny distinction in several countries' armed forces and governments, they barely managed to be influential at the Congress of Vienna. Not very influential, but just sufficiently to get a stopgap balance-of-power system adopted. They couldn't prevent the anti-democratic reaction and the subsequent revolutions . . . but they did stave off a major catastrophe, and settled down to building a decent set of governments. Now their whole work is in danger.

'We're too damned few, Tombak, and have to contend with too many centuries of nationalism and vested interest. My predecessor here did manage to get high-ranking agents into the German leadership. They failed to prevent war with Denmark, Austria and France, but a fairly humane peace treaty was managed after eighteen seventy. Not as humane as it should have been, it left the French smarting, but a good job under the circumstances.'

Tombak nodded. He had seen that for himself. He had been a simple krauthead officer then, moderating the savagery of his troops . . . less for immediate mercy than for the future, a smaller legacy of hatred. But rumours had filtered down, which he later gleefully confirmed: British pressure secretly put on Bismarck to control his appetite, and the pressure had originated with the Prime Minister's good friend 'Sir Colin McMurtrie'. And the Boer War had been unavoidable, but the quick gestures of friendship towards the conquered had not— The Plan called for a peaceful, democratic British Commonwealth to dominate and stabilize the world.

'Kalmagens' death threw everything into confusion,' went on Randos. 'I suppose you know that. You fellows carried on as best you could, but the mass is not identical with the sum of the individuals concerned. There are factors of tradition, inertia, the cumbersome social machinery . . . it takes a trained man to see the forest for the trees. Things have rapidly gone towards maximum entropy. An unstable system of checks and balances between rival imperialisms is breaking down. We have less than a year to avert a general war which will exacerbate nationalism to the point of insanity. I have to develop a programme of action and get it into effect. I have *no* time to waste on details!'

'The Turkish–Italian war was a detail, of course,' said Tombak blandly.

'Yes,' snapped Randos. 'Unfortunate, but unimportant. The Ottomans have had their day. Likewise this Balkan business.'

'Saw a paper on the way here. Sun Yat-sen's government is having its troubles. Are all those Chinese another detail?'

'No, of course not. But they can wait. The main line of development towards full status is here in Western Europe. It happened by chance, but the fact is there. It's European civilization which has got to be saved from itself. Do you realize that Earth is only a century or so from atomic energy?' Randos took an angry turn around the office. 'All right. I'm trying to work out a new balance, an international power alignment that will hold German ambition in check until such time as their Social Democrats can win an unmistakable majority and oust the Prussian clique. After that we can start nudging Europe towards limited federalism. That's the objective, sir, the absolute necessity, and your report had better have some relevance to it!'

Tombak nodded. 'It does, Chief, I assure you. I've talked with thousands of Irish, both in Ulster and the south. Those two sections hate each other's intestinal flora. The southerners want the present Home Rule bill and the Ulstermen don't. They're being whipped up by the Carson gang, ready to fight ... and if they do, the Irish–Irish are going to revolt on their own account.'

Randos' lunar face reddened. 'And you called me in to tell me this?'

'I did. Is civil war a detail?'

'In this case, Sir Tombak, yes.' Randos was holding back his temper with an effort that made him sweat. 'A single English division could put it down in a month, if it broke out. But it would take all Britain's and France's manhood to stop Germany, and we'd have to drag in a dozen other countries to boot. The United States might get involved. And the USA is the main line after Europe, Sir Tombak. They have to be kept out of this mad-dog nationalism, to lead the world towards reason when their day comes.' He actually managed to show his teeth. 'I'll forgive you this time on grounds of ignorance. But hereafter submit your reports in properly written form. The next time you disturb me with a piddling detail like Ireland, you'll go back to Sagittarius. Good day!'

He remembered to assume a meek look as he was opening the door.

There was a silence.

'Whoof!' said Tombak.

'Second the motion,' said Arken. 'But I warned you.'

'Where's the nearest pub? I need one.' Tombak prowled over to the window and looked gloomily down at the traffic. 'Kalmagens was an artist,' he said, 'and artists don't worry about what is detail and what isn't. They just naturally see the whole picture. This chap is a cookbook psychotechnician.'

'He's probably right, as far as he goes,' said Arken.

'Maybe. I dunno.' Tombak shrugged. 'Got a suit of clothes here I can borrow? I told the doorman I was coming in to make a date with a beautiful girl, and I noticed a most nice little wench with a sort of roundheeled look at a typewriter out there. Don't want to disappoint the old fellow.'

2

Peter Mortensen was born north of the Danevirke, but after 1864 his people were reckoned German, and he was called up in 1914 like anyone else. Men died so fast on the eastern front that promotion was rapid, and by 1917 he was a captain. This did not happen without some investigation of his background – many Schleswig Danes were not overly glad of their new nationality – but Graf von Schlangengrab had checked personally on him and assured his superiors of his unquestionable loyalty. Indeed, the count took quite a fancy to this young man, got him transferred to Intelligence, and often used him on missions of the utmost importance.

Thus the official record, and in the twentieth century Anno Domini the record was more than the man – it *was* the man. A few rebellious souls considered this an invention of that supreme parodist, the Devil, for now the Flesh had become Word. To Galactics such as Vyndhom Vargess and Sabor Tombak, it was convenient; records are more easily altered than memories, if you have the right gadgets. So Vargess became von Schlangengrab and Tombak called himself Peter Mortensen.

A thin, bitter rain blew across muddy fields, and the Prussian pines mumbled of spring. Out in the trenches to the west, it meant little more than fresh lice and fresh assaults, human meat going upright into the gape of machine guns. To the east, where Russia lay sundered, the spring of 1917 meant some kind of new birth. Tombak wondered what sort it would be.

He sat with a dozen men in a boxcar near the head of the sealed train. The thing was damp and chilly; they huddled around a stove. Their grey uniforms steamed. Beneath them, the wheels clicked on rain-slippery rails. Now and again the train whistled, shrill and lonesome noise across the graves of a thousand years of war.

Captain Mortensen was well liked by his men: none of this Junker stiffness for him. They held numbed hands towards the stove, rolled cigarettes, and talked among themselves. 'Cold, it's been a long time cold, and fuel so short. Sometimes I wonder what it ever felt like to be warm and dry.'

'Be colder than this in Russia, lad. I've been there, I know.'

'But no fighting this time, thank God. Only taking that funny little man towards St Petersburg ... Why the devil's he so important, anyway? Hauled him clear from Switzerland in his own special train, on orders of General Ludendorff, no less, one runty Russian crank.'

'What say, Captain?' asked someone. 'Are you allowed, now, to tell us why?'

Tombak shrugged, and the faces of peasants and labourers and students turned to him, lost between military caps and shoddy uniforms but briefly human again with simple curiosity. 'Why, sir? Is he a secret agent of ours?'

'No, I'd not say that.' Tombak rolled himself a cigarette, and a corporal struck a match for him. 'But the matter's quite simple. Kerensky has overthrown the Czar, you see, but wants to keep on fighting. This Ulyanov fellow has a good deal of influence, in spite of having been an exile for so long. Maybe he can come to power. If he does, he'll make peace on any terms ... which is to say, on German terms. Then we'll no longer have an eastern front to worry about.' Tombak's leathery face crinkled. 'It seems worth trying, anyhow.'

'I see, I see ... thank you, Captain ... very clever ...'

'My own chief, Graf von Schlangengrab, urged this policy on the General Staff,' confided Tombak. 'The idea was his, and he talked them into it.' He always had to remember that he was Peter Mortensen, doubly anxious to prove his Germanness because it had once been in doubt, and would therefore brag about the nobleman with whom he was so intimate.

What he did not add was that von Schlangengrab had been given the idea and told to execute it by a senior clerk in an English brokerage house, over an undetectable sub-radio hookup. This clerk, Mr Harrison, had checked Galactic records on Ulyanov – whom Kalmagens had once met and investigated in London – and run a psychotechnic evaluation which gave the little revolutionary a surprising probability of success.

'Maybe then we can finish the war,' muttered a sergeant. 'Dear God, it's like it's gone on forever, not so?'

'I can't even remember too well what began it,' confessed a private.

'Well, boys—' Tombak inhaled the harsh wartime tobacco and leaned back in a confidential mood. 'I'll tell you my theory. The Irish began it.'

'Ach, you joke, Captain,' said the sergeant.

'Not at all. I have studied these things. In nineteen fourteen there was a great deal of international tension, if you remember. That same year the Home Rule bill was so badly handled that it alienated the Ulstermen, who were egged on by a group anxious to seize power. This caused the Catholic Irish to prepare for revolt. Fighting broke out in Dublin in July, and it seemed as if the British Isles were on the verge of civil war. Accordingly, our General Staff decided they need not be reckoned with for a while, and—'

—And the Sarajevo affair touched off the powder. Germany moved in accordance with long-laid plans because she did not expect Britain to be able to fulfil her treaty obligations to Belgium. But Britain wangled a temporary Irish settlement and declared war. If the English had looked more formidable that year, the Germans would have been more conciliatory, and war could have been postponed and the Galactic plans for establishing a firm peace could have gone on towards their fruition.

'Captain!' The sergeant was shocked.

Tombak laughed. 'I didn't mean it subversively. Of course we had to fight against the Iron Ring. And we will conquer.'

Like Chaos we will. The war was dragging into a stalemate. Neither side could break the other, not when Russia had gone under.

If Russia did make peace, Randos had calculated, then the stalemate would be complete. Peace could be negotiated on a basis of exhaustion in another year, and America kept out of the mess.

Privately, Tombak doubted it. On paper the scheme looked fine: the quantities representing political tensions balanced out nicely. But he had lived in America some twenty years ago, and knew her for a country which would always follow an evangelist. Like Wilson – whose original nomination and election had hinged on an unusual chance. Randos assured him that the personality of the leader meant little ... was a detail ... but ...

At any rate, the main immediate objective was to get Russia out of the war, so that she might evolve a reasonably civilized government for herself. Exactly how the surrender was to be achieved, was another detail, not important. This queer, bearded Ulyanov with the bookish diction and the Tartar face was the handiest tool for the job, a tool which could later be discarded in favour of the democrats.

The train hooted, clicking eastwards with Ulyanov aboard.

His Party name was Lenin.

3

Tombak had not been in New York for three decades. The town had changed a lot; everywhere he saw the signs of a feverish prosperity.

On other planets, in other centuries, he had watched the flowering and decay of a mercantile system, big business replacing free enterprise. For certain civilizations it was a necessary step in development, but he always thought of it as a retrogression, enthroned vulgarity grinding out the remnants of genuine culture, the Folk became the People.

This was a brisk fall day, and he stepped merrily along through the crowds, a short, sunburned, broad-shouldered young man, outwardly distinguished only by a cheerful serenity. Nor was he essentially different inside. He was a fully human creature with human genes, who simply happened to have been born on another planet. His environment had affected him, balancing anabolism and catabolism so well that he had already lived two thousand years, training mind and body. But that didn't show.

He turned off on to Wall Street and found the skyscraper he was looking for and went up to the sacrosanct top floor. The receptionist was female this time, and pretty. Woman suffrage had eased the team's problems by allowing them to use their wives and girl friends more openly. For a moment he didn't recognize her; the face had been changed. Then he nodded. 'Hello, Yarra. Haven't seen you since . . . good Designer, since the Paris Exposition!'

'We had fun,' she smiled dreamily. 'Care to try it again?'

'Hmmm . . . yes, if you'll get rid of that godawful bobbed hair and cylindrical silhouette.'

'Aren't they terrible? Usrek ran a computation for me, and the Americans won't return to a girl who looks like a girl for years.'

'I'll get myself assigned back to Asia. Bali, for choice.' Tombak sighed reminiscently. 'Just worked my way back from there – deckhand on a tramp steamer to San Francisco, followed a harvesting crew across the plains, did a hitch in a garage. Lots and lots of data, but I hope the boss doesn't want it tabulated.'

'He will, Sabor, he will. Want to talk to him? He's in the office now.'

'Might as well get it over with.'

'He's not a bad sort, really. A basically decent fellow, and a whiz at psychomath. He tries hard.'

'Someday, though, he'll have to learn that— Oh, all right.'

Tombak went through the door into the office of the president. It was Usrek Arken again, alias the financier Wolfe ... a name chosen with malice aforethought, for wolf he was on Wall Street. But what chance did brokers and corporations, operating mostly by God and by guess, have against a million-year-old science of economics? Once Randos had decided England was declining as a world power, and become an American, Wolfe's dazzling rise was a matter of a few years' routine.

Arken was in conference with Randos, but both rose and bowed. The chief showed strain, his plumpness was being whittled away and the best total-organismic training could not suppress an occasional nervous jerk. But today he seemed genial. 'Ah, Sir Tombak! I'm glad to see you back. I was afraid you'd run afoul of some Chinese war lord.'

'Damn near did. I was a foreign devil. If it hadn't been for our Mongoloid agent in Sinkiang – well, that's past.' Tombak got out his pipe. 'Had a most enjoyable trip around the world, and got friendly with thousands of people, but of course out of touch with the big events. What's been happening?'

'Business boom here in the States. That's the main thing, so I'm concentrating on it. Tricky.'

Tombak frowned. 'Pardon me, but why should the exact condition of business in one country be crucial?'

'Too many factors to explain in words,' said Randos. 'I'd need psychodynamic tensors to convince you. But look at it this way ...

'Let's admit we bungled badly in 'fourteen and again in 'seventeen. We let the war break out, we let America get into it, and we underestimated Lenin. Instead of a republic, Russia has a dictatorship as ruthless as any in history, and paranoid to boot; nor can we change that fact, even if the rules allowed us to assassinate Stalin. We hoped to salvage a kind of world order out of the mess: once American intervention was plainly unavoidable, we started the "War to end war" slogan and the League of Nations idea. Somehow, though, the USA was kept out of the League, which means it's a farce unless we can get her into it.'

Thanks for the 'we', thought Tombak grimly. With the benefit of hindsight, he knew as well as Randos why the Russian revolution and the Versailles peace had gone awry. Lenin and Senator Lodge had been more capable than they had any right to be, and Wilson less so. That poor man had been no match for practical politicians, and had compounded the folly with his anachronistic dream of 'self-determination'. (Clemenceau had passed the rational judgment on that idea: *'Mon Dieu!* Must every little language have a country of its own?') But individual personalities had been brushed aside by Randos as 'fluctuations, details, meaningless eddies on the current of great historical trends.'

The man wasn't too stupid to see his own mistakes; but subconsciously, at least, he didn't seem able to profit by them.

'We still have an excellent chance, though,' went on Randos. 'I don't quite like the methods we must use, but they're the only available ones. Wall Street is rapidly becoming the financial capital of Earth, a trend which I have been strengthening. If finance can be maintained as the decisive power, within twenty years America will be the leader of the world. No one else will be able to move without her okay. Then the time will be psychologically ripe for Americans to get the idea of a new League, one with armed force to maintain the peace. The Soviets won't stand a chance.'

Tombak scowled more deeply. 'I can't argue with your math, Sir Randos,' he answered slowly, 'but I got a hunch . . .'

'Yes? Go on. You were sent around the world precisely so you could gather facts. If those facts contradict my theories, why, of course I'm wrong and we'll have to look for a new approach.' Randos spoke magnanimously.

'Okay, buster, you asked for it,' said Tombak in English. He returned to Galactic: 'The trouble is, these aren't facts you can fit into mass-action equations. They're a matter of, well, *feel*.

'Nationalism is rising in Asia. I talked with a Japanese officer in Shanghai . . . we'd got drunk together, and he was a fine fellow, and we loved each other like brothers, but he actually cried at the thought that someday he'd have to take potshots at me.'

'The Japanese have talked about war with the United States for fifty years,' snorted Randos. 'They can't win one.'

'But do they know that? To continue, though – people, Western people, don't like the present form of society either. They can't always say why, but you can tell they feel uprooted, uneasy . . . there's nothing about an interlocking directorate to inspire loyalty, you know. The trade unions are growing. If capitalism goes bust, they're going to grow almighty fast.'

'To be sure,' nodded Randos, unperturbed. 'A healthy development, in the right time and place. But I'm here to see that capitalism does not, ah, go bust. Mass unemployment— You know yourself how unstable the Weimar Republic is. If depression is added to its other troubles, dictatorship will come to Germany within five years.'

'If you ask me,' snapped Tombak, 'we've got too bloody damn much confidence around. Too many people are playing the stock market. It has a hectic feel, somehow. They'd do better to save their money for an emergency.'

Randos smiled. 'To be sure. I'll admit the market is at a dangerous peak. In this month, it's already shown some bad fluctuations. That's why Wolfe is selling right now, heavily, to bring it down.'

Usrek Arken stirred. 'And I continue to think, Sir Randos,' he muttered, 'that it'll cause a panic.'

'No, it won't. I have proved, with the help of games theory, that—'

'Games theory presupposes that the players are rational,' murmured Tombak. 'I have a nasty suspicion that nobody is.'

'Come, now,' chided Randos. 'Of course, nonrational elements enter in. But this civilization is in a highly cerebral stage.'

'What you ought to do,' snapped Tombak, 'is get away from that computer of yours and go out and meet some Earthfolk.'

Frost congealed on Randos' words: 'That is your task, Sir Tombak. Please report your findings and stand by for further assignment. Now, if you'll pardon me, I'm busy.'

Tombak swapped a glance with Arken and went out. He chatted for a while with Yarra and, silhouette or no, made a date for the next evening: Thursday, 24 October, 1929.

4

Now play the fife lowly and beat the drums slowly,
And play the dead march as you carry my pall.
Bring me white roses to lay on my coffin,
Roses to deaden the clods as they fall.

The flames jumped up, lighting their faces: grimy, unshaven, gaunted by wind and hunger, but American faces. Tombak thought he had fallen in love with America. A Galactic had no business playing favourites, and it was perfectly obvious that in another hundred years Earth's power centre would have shifted to Asia, but something in this country suited him. It still had elbow room, for both body and soul.

He finished the song and laid his guitar down as Bob Robinson gave the can of mulligan another stir. Far off, but coming along the rails near the hobo jungle, a train whistled. Tombak wondered how many times, how many places, he had heard that noise, and always it meant more lonesomeness.

'I looked at the schedule in the station.' A thin man with glasses jerked his thumb at the town, a mile away. 'Be a freight stopping at midnight, we can hop that one.'

'If the dick don't see us,' mumbled Robinson. 'They got a mean dick in this place.'

'I'll handle him, if it comes to that.' Tombak flexed

stumpy strong fingers. Maybe a Galactic shouldn't take sides, but there were some people whose faces he enjoyed altering. That storm trooper in Berlin two years ago, for instance, the lout who was kicking an inoffensive Jew around. Getting out of Germany had been like getting out of jail, and even riding the rods in the States was a welcome change.

'Be careful, Jim,' murmured Rose McGraw. She leaned against Tombak with a pathetic possessiveness.

In a better age, he thought, she would have been somebody's contented housewife, minding the kids in suburbia, not tramping over a continent in a ragged print dress, rain in her hair, looking for work . . . any kind of work. Too late now, of course, at least till the war with Japan made jobs. But Randos had predicted Japan would not attack till early 1942, give or take six months, and he was usually right about such things. Almost six years to go. True, initially he had thought the Japanese would never fight, but contrary evidence piled up . . .

'Don't worry about me,' said Tombak gruffly. He felt again the tugging sadness of the quasi-immortal. How many years on Earth, how many women, and with none of them could he stay more than a few months. They must not be taken off the road and fed, they must not be told the truth and comforted, Rose McGraw had to become a fading memory fast bound in misery and iron for the sake of her descendants a thousand years hence.

At least he had warned her. '*I'm not a marryin' man, I won't ever settle down.*' – Not till his tour of duty on Earth ended, another seventy-five years of it and then a hundred-year vacation and then another planet circling one of those stars blinking dimly overhead . . . Why had he ever gone into the Service?

'Think Roosevelt's gonna win?' asked Robinson. He mispronounced the name.

'Sure, Landon hasn't got a prayer.' The man with glasses spoke dogmatically; he had had some education once.

'I dunno, now. Old man Roosevelt, he's for us, but how many of us stay in one place long enough to vote?'

'Enough,' said Tombak. He had no doubt of the election's outcome. The New Deal under one name or another was foregone, once the Depression struck. Hoover himself had proposed essentially the same reforms. Randos had not even had to juggle the country – through propaganda, through carefully planted trains of events – to get FDR elected the first time. Tombak would be able to return from this trip and report that the changes were popular and that there was no immediate danger of American fascism or communism.

The main line of history, always the main line. Since the Rhineland debacle this year, war in Europe was not to be avoided, nor was war in the Pacific. Japanese pride and hunger had not been so small a factor after all. Tombak's mind slipped to the Washington office where Randos was manipulating senators and brain trusters.

'The important thing will be to keep the two wars separate. Russia will be neutral, because she has Japan to worry about, and Germany alone cannot conquer Britain. The United States, with British help, can defeat Japan in about five years while the European stalemate is established. Then and only then must Germany and Russia be goaded into war with each other ... two totalitarianisms in a death struggle, weakening as they fight, with America armed from the Japanese war and ready to step in and break both of them. After that we can finally start building an Earth fit to live on.'

An Earth which had so far gone from bad to worse, reflected Tombak. He didn't deny the bitter logic of Randos' equations; but he wondered if it was going to develop that way in practice. Roosevelt, who would surely run for a third term, had strong emotional ties – he *could* not see England fight alone, and he could make the country agree with him. And Hitler, now ... Tombak had seen Hitler speak, and met a lot of Nazis. A streak of nihilistic lunacy ran through that bunch. Against every sound military principle, they were entirely capable of attacking Russia; which would mean the emergence of the Soviet Union, necessarily aided by America, as a victorious world power.

Well ...

'Wonder if we're someday gonna find a steady job,' said someone in the night.

'Ought to have a guy like Hitler,' said another man. 'No nonsense about him. He'd arrange things.'

'Arrange 'em with a firing squad,' said Tombak sharply. 'Drive men like Einstein out of the country. At that,' he added thoughtfully, 'Hitler and his brown-shirted, brown-nosed bastards are doing us a favour. If this goes on, we'll have more talent in this country, refugees, than anybody ever had before.'

And if somebody had the idea of gathering it into one place, what would all that embittered genius do to Randos' plans?

Bob Robinson shrugged, indifference clothed in faded denim. 'To hell with it. I think the stew's about done.'

5

Harban Randos' eyes looked ready to leap out of their sockets. 'No!' he whispered.

'Yes.' Usrek Arken slapped the papers down on the desk with a cannon-crack noise. 'Winnis knows his physics, and Tombak and the others have gathered the essential facts for him to work on. They're making an atomic bomb!'

Randos turned blindly away. Outside, Washington shimmered in the heat of midsummer, 1943. It was hard to believe that a war was being fought ... the wrong war, with the issues irretrievably messed up, the Soviets fighting as allies of the democracies, Japan half shunted aside to make way for a Nazi defeat that would plant Russian troops in the middle of Europe ... and meanwhile gnawing away at Nationalist China, weakening the nation for Communists who had made a truce which they weren't respecting.

'They're able to,' said Randos huskily.

Tombak nodded. 'They're going to,' he said.

'But they don't *need*—'

'What has that got to do with anything? And after the uranium bomb comes the thermonuclear bomb and— Write your own ticket.' Tombak spoke flatly, for he had come to like the people of Earth.

Randos passed a shaking hand over his face. 'All right, all right. Any chance of sabotaging the project?'

'Not without tipping our hand. They've got his one watched, I tell you; we've not been able to get a single Galactic into the Manhattan District. We could blow up the works, of course ... fake a German operation ... but after the war, when they go through German records ...'

'Vargess can handle the records.'

'He can't handle the memories. Not the memories of thousands of people, intrinsically just as smart as you and I.' Tombak bit his pipestem and heard it crack. 'Okay, Randos, you're the boss. What do we do next?'

The chief sat down. For a moment he shuddered with the effort of self-control, then his body was again disciplined.

'It will be necessary to deal firmly with the Russians, force them to agree to a stronger United Nations Organization,' he said. 'Churchill already understands that, and Roosevelt can be persuaded. Between them, they can prepare their countries so that it'll be politically feasible. The West is going to have a monopoly of nuclear weapons at the war's end, which will be helpful ... yes ...'

'Roosevelt is not a well man,' declared Tombak, 'and I was in England only a month ago and can tell you the people aren't satisfied. They admire Churchill, love him, but they're going to want to experiment with another party ...'

'Calculated risk,' said Randos. His confidence was returning. 'Not too great.'

'Nevertheless,' said Tombak, 'you'd better start right away to handpick those men's successors and see they get exposed to the facts of life.'

'For Designer's sake, leave me alone!' yelled Randos. 'I can't handle every miserable little detail!'

Rasnagarth Kri did not want to spend time interviewing a failure. It seemed as if each day brought a higher pile of work to him, more decisions to be made, a million new planets struggling towards an unperceived goal, and he had had to promise his wife he would stop working nights.

Nevertheless, a favourite nephew is a favourite nephew.

He hooded his eyes until a glittering blankness looked across the desk at Harban Randos.

'We are fortunate,' he said, 'that an experienced man of your race was available to take charge. For a while I actually considered breaking the rules and letting Earth know the facts immediately. But at this stage of their society, that would only be a slower damnation for them; extinction is more merciful. Whether or not the new man can rescue the planet remains to be seen. If he fails, the whole world is lost. At best, progress has been retarded two centuries, and millions of people are needlessly dead.'

Randos stiffened his lips, which had been vibrating, and answered tonelessly:

'Sir, you were getting my annual reports. If I was unsatisfactory, you should have recalled me years ago.'

'Every agent is allowed some mistakes,' Kri told him. 'Psychodynamics is not an exact science. Furthermore, your reports, while quantitatively accurate, were qualitatively . . . lifeless. They conveyed nothing of the feel. Until the fact leaped out that nationalism and atomic energy had become contemporaneous, how could I judge?'

Feel! Randos thought of Sabor Tombak. The smug, pipe-sucking pig! He hoped Tombak would be killed; plenty of chance for that, in the next fifty or a hundred years of Earth's troubles.

No – he was doing the man an injustice. Tombak had simply been right. But Randos still couldn't like him.

'I used the standard methods, sir,' he protested. 'You have seen my computations. What else could I do?'

'Well—' Kri looked down at his desk. 'That's hard to answer. Let me just say that human nature is so complicated that we'll never have a complete science of it. All we'll ever be able to do mathematically is predict and guide the broad trends. But those trends are made up of millions of individual people and incidents. To pervert an old saying, in government we must be able to see the trees for the forest. It takes an artist to know how and when to use the equations, and how to supplement them with his own intuitive common sense. It takes not only a technician, but a poet to write a report that will really let me know what is really going on.'

He raised his eyes again and said mildly: 'You can't be blamed for being neither an artist nor a poet. I gather you wish to remain in the Service?'

'Yes, sir.' Randos was not a quitter.

'Very well. I'm assigning you to a chief technicianship in my own evaluation centre. Consider it a promotion, a reward for honest effort. At least, you'll have higher rank and salary. You may go.'

Kri thought he heard a gasp of relief, but returned to his papers.

One might as well face truth. You can't kick a favourite nephew anywhere but upstairs. The fellow might even make a good technical boss.

As for this planet called Earth, maybe the new man could salvage it. If not, well, it was only one planet.

Licence

Wars could not be fought were men psychologically unable to fight. An abolition of war, if such can be accomplished, will leave us with that potentiality of violence. How then shall we express it?

I landed at Wold-Chamberlain, on the edge of Twincity. It was mid-afternoon, but the air was mild; the summer here doesn't really get started till about July, and this was early June. The usual taxis were waiting for rocket passengers, just inside the crimeless area. I walked down the line till I found one whose polished armour and obviously well-oiled gun turret indicated a driver who knew his business. He jumped to open the door for me: I was wearing my union badge, and we're supposed to be good tippers.

'YMCA,' I said, entering. In the summers I usually lived at the Y; it's nothing fancy, but it's cheap and clean and there are some pretty decent guys around. Most important, though, once inside you're reasonably safe.

My cab nosed on to the fourth-level freeway and went on automatic. The driver leaned back and struck a cigarette. 'Working?' he asked.

'Not yet,' I said.

'You will be,' he predicted. 'It's been a lively year so far.' He jerked his thumb at the framed bootlegging and procurement licences. 'Business is good, you know. I wonder how come the crime rate jumps in boom times and drops in bad times. Sh'd think it'd be the other way around.'

'There are psychological reasons,' I told him. 'You can explain part of it by pointing to all the money floating about – hectic atmosphere and so forth, high living, eat, drink, and be merry. In a slump, people have to think more about simply eating.'

'You don't talk like a gangster,' he said.

'I'm only one in summer,' I admitted. 'The rest of the year I'm working for my Ph.D. at Harvard. Got to pay my expenses somehow.'

He grew less friendly, associating me with college kids, I suppose. I didn't bother explaining that my patty-raiding days were long past and that graduate students are still expected to earn their degrees. It had been fun once, but I think maturity consists largely in a shift of the pleasure principle. To me, at the ripe old age of twenty-four, there was delight in a psychodynamic equation and merely boredom in the thought of breaking down doors and toting a squealing coed into the bushes.

We passed a new school, steel and chrome and plastic leaping eighty storeys into the sky. I noticed a gym class having some machine-gun practice on the playground. The range was pathetically overcrowded. Where the hell are they going to put all the new children?

'Y' oughta be here in fall,' said the driver. 'We got a great team this year.'

'I don't care much for football, to tell the truth,' I replied. 'I see enough bloodshed without paying to watch somebody's face messed up with spiked knuckledusters.'

'Oh, the Big Ten are using goggles now. No more blindings. Though there's talk of legalizing switchblades . . . Here we are, doc.'

I got out on the ramp. The meter showed $250, which was not unreasonable, but I disliked adding the 25 per cent tip expected of me. People think a gangster sleeps on money mattresses. Well, he does get fat fees, but it's sporadic work and he has heavy expenses too.

After I had been frisked and had checked my weapons – I told you the Y is safe – I went over to the desk. Joe Green was on duty and said hello. 'How's things back east?' he added.

'As usual,' I said.

'How about that airport bombing?'

'You know I only hold a job summers. I hear the unions and the cops between them got the bastards in a few days, but it was no affair of mine.' I said that because I didn't care to make conversation; actually, I had been as outraged as anyone else. Unlicensed murder, and illegal weapons such as bombs – in this case, there were twenty innocent casualties – are an offence to every rule of human behaviour. Without law, we might as well go back to the caves.

'What kind of place you want?' asked Green. 'We've added a new wing: some nice three-room—'

'I'm trying to save money, for your information. Single with bath will do.'

'Okay. Two-seven-seven-three, then. Want a girl?'

'Not just yet, thanks. I want to take off my shoes and relax. When you get off, maybe we can go out for dinner and stuff.'

I picked up a fifth at the news-stand and looked for a book, but found nothing worth reading. I don't care about their covers, but these impurgated editions annoy me; nobody has a right to put clinical descriptions into *Romeo and Juliet* or provide Captain Ahab with a mistress. Oh, well.

I took the elevator up, entered my place, and checked the meters. Local water ration was thirty gallons a day; Minnesota still has plenty. After the grimy east, it was going to be good to bathe daily. While the tub was filling, I took my fifth over for a look out the window. The downtown area is new and spectacular, from the austere lines of the Retailers' Union skyscraper to the humorous fantasy of the Hamm's Building, shaped like a beer bottle. But I was high enough to see the grey miles of housing projects reaching beyond the horizon. They had expanded since last year, and I could understand why the cab driver had said this was a lively time. Unless we psychodynamicists come up with an answer, the curve of liveliness is going to keep on rising.

I didn't call union HQ till I was cleaned up. The face in the screen was unfamiliar. 'Hello, brother,' I said. 'Charles Andrew Rheinbogen checking in.'

'Hello, brother Rheinbogen,' he said. 'You're playing in the luck. All the boys out, and a large job just come.'

I sighed, having hoped for at least a day's relaxation. But you don't turn down an offer. 'Okay, I'll be right along. Only what happened to Sam?'

'Oh ... brother Jeffreys, you mean? He got his a week ago.'

'Hey, he was too old for anything but switchboard work.'

'This was a private murder. Somebody cooled him for personal reasons.'

'Damn! I liked him. Anything we can do about it?'

' 'Fraid not. Advance notification of intent was filed, the deed's been registered, and the weregild will be paid on schedule.'

Well, he'd had a full life, and the union would look after his family. But I was going to miss Sam. He had lived through the Smashup as a young man and, unlike most, always been willing to talk about it. Some of his stories would curdle your plasma, but he had kept his sense of humour too.

I slipped on clean pyjamas and shoes and went downstairs. In the lobby I bought a foodbar to keep going on; benzedrine I always carry. After getting my guns back, I took the slideway over to HQ on third-level Nicollet. The new operator had not lied about a big job. I was shown into the executive secretary's office at once.

Tom Swanson is a very high-class labour chief, managing not only the local and its benefit funds, but also its banks, stores, factories, and other business. He hasn't much formal education, but he looks like a middle-aged professor. That's due to plastic surgery, when he decided a mild, scholarly face was disarming and therefore useful. He shook hands with me and introduced me to the client: 'Mr James Hardy, this is Mr Rheinbogen ... one of our best.'

'Um,' grunted Hardy. 'Rather young, ain't he?'

I do have the misfortune – which will be an asset in about twenty years, if I live – to look like a slender blond sophomore. Maybe that was why I took a dislike to this customer. Or maybe it was his broad, carefully barbered and

assaged face, or the overly elaborate hairdo. He made me
ink of a shark at some Friendly Loan Company where
ey make you put up your wife's services for a year to
orrow a thousand. A bit of investigation next day was to
onfirm my hunch. However, a job is a job, so I merely sat
own and waited.

'Suppose you explain the situation yourself, Mr Hardy,'
iggested Swanson.

'Well . . . all right . . . if you guarantee this boy . . .'

'The union guarantees nothing except an honest effort to
ilfil the mission,' said Swanson gently. 'If we lose our men
n it, you'll need a fresh contract to try again.'

'Unless,' I said nastily, 'you want to try for yourself.'

'Don't give me that,' snorted Hardy. 'I'm a businessman –
ce chairman of the board, Teamsters' Union, Inc. I don't
o my own kidnappings any more than I do my own cook-
ıg in one of our restaurants.' It was a proper comeuppance
or me, but I didn't enjoy his tone. Arrogance ought to be
ıore courteous, a principle they understood back in the Re-
aissance.

'So it's to be a snatch,' I said. 'The season . . . no, wait,
idnapping season did open yesterday, didn't it? Okay,
ho's the goat?'

'A Miss Marie Dulac,' he answered. 'You've heard of the
ulac family? He's head of the Chemicals Union Trust.
hey have a summer home out at Lake Minnetonka, and
re there now.'

I suppressed an impulse to whistle – yanking a girl from
ıe house of her trillionaire father! But there must be a
hance of doing it, or Swanson wouldn't have me here.
Seems I've heard of the wench,' I said. 'But we can't lift her;
he's a minor.'

'Turned twenty-one last month,' said Swanson. 'I checked
ıe public records myself. She hasn't taken out first-class
itizenship, so she's immune to murder, beating, or criminal
ssault; but anything else goes.'

'How come you want her?' I asked.

'Business reasons,' said Hardy.

'I have to know why,' I explained. 'I'll need the whole picture. Professional confidence applies, of course.'

'All right,' grumbled Hardy. 'A simple matter of pressure on her old man. Both our unions are trying to merge with the Federated Nuclear Scientists. If I hold his daughter, he'll back out and let me have them.'

That was a very big picture indeed, and I felt more and more cold as I realized how well that house must be guarded. 'Any details on the girl herself?' I queried.

'Not too much,' said Swanson. 'I can't say how she'll react, Church, so you'd better handle with care and this side up. The Dulacs are French Canadian, mother died years ago, and she's been raised in a convent way to hellandgone in Quebec. Only sprung last month, and her debut is going to be pretty soon.'

Good. The confusion of preparing an orgy would help me. But old Frédéric Dulac hadn't got where he was without some hard and shrewd fighting. He was known to be a fair, even gentle boss, but when his goons had to shoot they only intended to shoot once.

Hardy produced the licence, and I scanned it carefully to make sure everything was in order. It certified that on payment of the usual (high) fees and filing of the usual notice of intent, he was hereby authorized to kidnap Marie Dulac within a period of not more than six weeks from date and to hold said person for a period of not more than one year from date, and was further authorized to use such force as necessary and legal on condition of paying the proper weregild for all damage done ... etc., etc., etc. They had changed the form since I last saw one; there was now a boldface notice that breach of the regulations governing any capital-crime licence meant full outlawry – anyone could kill you without penalty, and if the cops didn't get you first the gangsters would for the sake of their own good name.

Hardy had already made a contract with our local. Now he signed the licence over to me and I was committed. The fee, I knew, would be terrific, but I wondered what use money is to a dead man.

'You have my card,' said Hardy. 'You can deliver her to my New Chicago office.'

'Nothing doing,' said Swanson. 'We'll keep her.'

'What? But—'

'If you haven't read the union code, Mr Hardy, it's your own fault. In a case like this, we retain the victim to make sure no harm comes to her. Otherwise we'd occasionally find ourselves accessories to something illegal, like torture, or white slavery.'

I was pleased to see Hardy looking apoplectic. It was going to inconvenience him. Old Dulac might just be tough enough to wait a year till we had to release his girl. No – it would depend on how tough she was; if her father *knew* she could stand a year's comfortable arrest . . .

We got rid of our client after a while and settled down for a drink, smoke, and talk. Everybody knew that Dulac employed the American Freebooters' Laborunion. It's practically a mirror image of our own Criminal Industries Organization; I've bought drinks for many of their boys off duty, and some people wonder why the crooks don't merge. But then attack-defence-riposte would become impossible; you wouldn't fight your own brothers, would you? Dulac had to have his chance to guard or recover his daughter. Competition is the lifeblood of American free enterprise.

A job like this takes information, planning, and rehearsal, and the plan must be imaginative. Some locals rely on games theory computers, but there's still no good substitute for the skilled human brain. A machine can't *enjoy* thinking.

A week later we had our scheme fairly well rigged. Axel Nygard and I made reservations at a lakeside hotel and drove down. The rest of our boys had been trickling into the area, for days, under various names and faces. We ourselves didn't bother with surgery, because Intelligence had told us the Dulac goons rarely went scouting. The old man relied on his fortress-like estate, where you didn't get in without a retinal scan and a frisking. Just to add to his confidence, we'd sent a squad that made a deliberately bungled attempt on his home. No casualties except some flesh wounds on our side; if I had been in charge of Dulac's defences, that would have made me suspicious, but Swanson said his chief goon had an honest, straightforward mind. Both of them were prominent Rotarians, so he ought to know.

It was a pleasant drive once we got past the housing projects. Nygard is a big, burly chap, but he shuddered a trifle as we zoomed through. The tenements rose up on either side of the freeway; they seemed to have faces in every window, and the pedestrian levels below us were like a disturbed anthill.

'Christ!' he muttered. 'Can people really live this way?'

'Sure, they're doing it,' I told him. 'They've got to. Isn't much space left in the world. They're still eating, at least, and amusements are provided.'

'But the crowding— How many to a room?'

'Oh, not more than three or four. It's normal for them; they don't know anything else. I grew up in a housing project myself, and it really isn't so bad. Of course, my father had a good job, technician in a rocket factory. For twenty hours a week he was alone in a big roomy building with only a dozen other men. So he was a peaceful sort, didn't even take out a crime licence. Our neighbours were the usual working stiffs, and beguiled their leisure by robbing each other. Nice people. Ever since then, I've wanted to do something constructive for them and their kind.'

'It sounds like perpetual motion,' said Nygard suspiciously. He was new to gangster work. 'Bill robs Joe who robs Peter who robs Bill ... but dammit, money represents material goods and services. Transferring it that way is sheer lost energy.'

We went by a protein factory, processing the algae from Lake Superior. 'Not so,' I said. 'Work in places like that keeps the belly satisfied. But what makes you a man, instead of another machine, is what you do off duty. The Chinese failed to make the adjustment to the present phase of history, overpopulation *cum* technics, and are huddled up like hogs in a pen. The Russians spend their time bickering between a hundred religious cults. The South Africans march around with their rifles, knowing the Peace Authority won't let them go beyond their own borders and taking it out on any white person they happen to find.' At a distance I glimpsed a man talking to a woman – an obvious hetaera – on an upper-level ramp, while a boy picked his pocket. All three were smiling. 'I think we've got it better.'

We left the city and had only a short drive to Minnetonka. It's a fair-sized lake, and by piping their water from elsewhere they've kept it that way. That's expensive, and so are the several acres of trees and the fish they keep the lake stocked with; so it's a high-priced resort, the banks lined solid with hotels and summer cottages and fun houses. Coming in to Dirty Joe's Lodge, we passed the Dulac estate: a fabulous five acres between high walls, the house underground except for a sundeck. Little more than that was known about it, but Dulac had filed intent to shoot down any aircraft besides police or Peace Authority that went over his place, so he must have added guided missiles to his other defences.

Dirty Joe's was about a mile farther down the lake. We turned our car and a $500 tip over to the uniformed attendant and strolled into the lobby to register. The lodge lives up to its name with a backwoods, logging-camp atmosphere: plastic knottypine panelling, only one casino, the girls in the bar putting on their clothes to the accompaniment of folk ballads, and so forth. We were posing as young executives from the politicians' union. My studies make me talk like one, and Nygard was taciturn. The bellhop showed us to a twentieth floor room and asked if we wanted girls right away. 'Later,' I said, testing the taps. The Scotch faucet yielded a brand about as good as one can expect since the last of the great distilleries was wrecked in those clan feuds.

'Swanson won't like what the local fillies are gonna do to the expense account,' said Nygard when we were alone.

'Well, we have to maintain our character for a day or two while we case the joint,' I laughed.

Which we did, and had a fine time in the process. There was an undercurrent of tension, naturally, a watchfulness and an awareness that in a short while we might be just another three hundred or so pounds of material for the fertilizer plants. But once you get used to it, once your apprenticeship has scrubbed off nervousness and youth, you are seldom so much alive as when preparing a job. When I got my doctorate, I was going to hang up my guns – another phase of life outgrown – but I'd not be sorry I had worn them.

The rest of our band were elsewhere in the area; we saw them from time to time and exchanged a few quiet signals. It was on a Wednesday morning that I set the machine going with a single call.

As we'd been doing, Nygard and I hired a boat to go out on the lake fishing. We had seen that Marie Dulac went for a swim each day before noon. There were guards in her craft and another boatful next to it, and they never went far from their private beach. Nor did they allow anyone else within a hundred feet. The old man was careful, alright; but it seemed unfair to pit artists against him.

The lake was as crowded as usual with boats, their wakes creaming its carefully blued waters, and with swimmers. Overhead was always the maximum permissible number of rented copters. Today, I knew one of them was ours – that took substantial bribes to arrange – and not at all what it seemed to be.

Nygard and I steered to within fifty yards of the Dulac party and let our motor idle. Marie stood up in the bow of her vessel and peeled off her clothes. She was a tall slim girl with a vivid, tilted face, merry dark eyes, blue-black hair falling below her ears. From afar, I had seen her laughing and decided I liked her. She hit the water in a clean dive and came up whooping, happy simply to exist.

'Now?' asked Nygard.

I took a small swallow of whisky, a good relaxer, and nodded. 'Have fun,' he said.

'Same to you.' I was already stripped, and went over the side. We were trailing a net full of cold beer, but had laid an additional package in it. Working fast underwater, I got out the aqua equipment, adjusted it to my face, and breathed gratefully. Then I strapped the tank on my shoulders, slipped the paddles on my feet, and buckled a two-gun belt around my waist: a .30-calibre automatic and a sonic stunner. We had to assume nobody would notice I didn't come up again after my dive.

I swam easily, untensed, not allowing myself to think the job might go sour. The water was clear; I could see the boats wavering against sun-dazzle above me. Another aqua-man glided by, nodding to me. I felt a pulsing as Nygard steered away. His task was to divert attention by having a minor crackup with some other vessel. Then he was to head for the timber before Dulac's men started serious investi-gations; they would not be gentle if they caught him or any of us.

Now! I saw the two craft, like whales basking. The splin-tered sunlight made a roof immediately overhead. I slipped upwards, a few feet below the surface. Through the water I felt as much as heard the blunt shock of Nygard's collision. There would be angry voices raised for a minute, until urbanity returned with the recollection that a man can always take out a shooting licence, and people would be watching ...

She trod water, head and shoulders invisible to me, the rest graceful and faintly unreal. I drew my stunner and pulled her down with my free hand. She got a shock dose good for about half an hour and I let the gun sink, having too much else to do. My hands closed off her mouth and nose to keep water out – the metabolism is lowered by sonic so you can go several minutes without breathing – and my feet kicked us towards the middle of the lake.

With luck, I'd have done it quietly enough that her dis-appearance wouldn't be observed for several seconds. Without luck ... but it was pointless to think about that. I worked my legs hard, trying to keeep all muscles not con-cerned at ease, trying to keep my mind calm. The girl's body was cooling fast in my arms, I could feel the chill creep through it, her eyes were open and blank. She wasn't hurt, but I felt guilty, somehow. I told myself that this was the price you paid for being wealthy and having five landscaped acres to roam about in, but she looked pathetically young and murdered.

Here . . . I stuck my head out of water, keeping Marie below, and looked around. An uproar lifted a hundred yards back, the Dulac boats circling with engines ahowl, goons threshing the lake and cursing, people spilling out of the housegates. The boys in our copter had been watching through binoculars and saw me emerge. They swooped low, churning the water with the airwash, and snaked down a rope. I raised Marie's head into the air, transferred one hand to the cord, and hung on.

A winch pulled me up as the copter mounted skywards. I swung like a bellclapper, seeing brief crazy images below me, gaping faces, a guard shaking his fist but not daring to shoot, I heard a siren begin its clamour, then I was drawn up with my cargo and the hatch clanged shut behind me.

That was a special vehicle. It shed its rotors and a false rear end the moment I was aboard. I hoped they wouldn't do any damage as they fell; it would be a proud record for me if I could pull an important job without having to pay any claims. Our concealed jetpipe was now free and acceleration tugged at me as we got going.

Two other men were aboard, a pilot and a doctor. The medic bent over Marie and started artificial respiration in case she'd swallowed the lake after all. I shed my aqua stuff, jumped into the gun turret, and peered back. Two copters were lumbering up from the Dulac estate, but now that we were a jet we could show them our heels. What we had to do was shake any radar there might be, then streak for the hideout where Marie was to be kept.

'Nice job.' The doctor poked his head into my turret as Minnentonka vanished. 'Very neat. I've given her a reviver shot and put some clothes on her. She'll be fine.'

I shivered. 'I could use some clothes and a shot too,' I said, 'though maybe not the same kind of shot.'

He took the gun while I obtained the necessary. Marie was strapped into the bunk. She was wearing a coverall which gave her an even younger look, like somebody's kid sister. A touch of colour had returned to her cheeks and I could see her breathe.

'We're going to stop outside Duluth and transfer to another plane,' said the doctor after I resumed my post. 'Three gets you five old Dulac has a description and a reward offer broadcast inside half an hour.'

'Better not make such odds if you don't have a crooked-gambling licence,' I grinned.

We were flying illegally low to avoid radar, though of course we had a temporary permit to break traffic rules. Now and then a tree or a building whisked past us. I relaxed, feeling the alcohol glow within me, and fumbled out a smoke.

When I looked through the bubble again, I nearly swallowed the cigarette. A regular jet was after us, a Delta-wing job with the Dulac colours. 'Judas priest!' I yelped. 'What happened?'

Our pilot cursed and opened up his engine. That buggy could fly rings around us. But where did it come from? There wasn't a runway long enough for it in——

It neared, I could hear it whistle down the sky, and I made out a hook attachment. The old man had been more careful than we realized; he'd posted a mother ship in the stratosphere above his place, piggybacking this one.

Our communicator beeped and the pilot switched it on. I couldn't see the screen from where I was, but the voice came clearly: 'You there in that fakester! Land or I open fire!'

'Oh ... it's you, Bob,' said my pilot. 'How's every little thing?'

'Pretty good, Jack.' I gathered our opponent was an off-duty friend of his from the other union, in Dulac's pay. 'Damn nice try you made there, but not quite nice enough. Land and turn over the girl, and we'll call it quits. I'd hate to make Martha a widow.'

'Oh, I'm not married to her right now,' said my pilot. He

was being pleasant, stalling for time as we whined northward at five hundred per. I knew he must be operating the call button for all he was worth so that HQ would be aware of our plight. But it would take some time for our interceptors to scramble at Twincity and get here.

The jet walked around us and gave us a burst through the roof. I fired back without hitting anything. 'Just a warning, Jack,' said the radioed voice.

'Crack us up, and the girl goes too,' warned my pilot. 'It'd be a shame to hurt her, and I don't think her old man would appreciate your zeal.'

'I always liked to take chances,' said Bob. 'I think I got a way to force you down, but it's dangerous.'

'Go ahead and try, then,' said my pilot. 'I'm a poor man and I need my success bonus.'

The jet snarled around in a bone-cracking loop and came at us from the rear. I saw the tracer stream hosing from it, reaching for our control surfaces. It had to pull up in a few seconds, crossing over us, and I gave it a burst in the belly as it passed. My stomach muscles were knotted tight. I breathed deep and told them to relax. The jet came back for another try. That one chewed up our tailpipe a little. We lost speed and began to wobble in the air.

'The guy's good,' said the doctor. 'Maybe you better call it a day, Jack.'

'You're the boss, Chuck,' said the pilot to me.

I looked out, considering. We were on the fringe of the roadless area that reaches north of Lake Superior into Canada; we'd been flying longer than I realized. Most of it is second growth now, having burned off during the Smashup when people were too busy staying alive to fight forest fires. But it's still one of the biggest parks left on this continent.

The other man could disable us and force a landing, just as he claimed. Thereafter, unless our reinforcements arrived before Dulac's – which was improbable – we'd have to give up, since it would be illegal to use Marie for a shield. Prolonged resistance endangered everyone's life to no obvious purpose, and there was no disgrace to surrendering before these odds. On the other hand, the success bonus would put me through a good many months of school, and success itself under difficult conditions would raise the fees I could charge. I am no altruist – I want to be well-to-do, see my family grow up with room to breathe – but perhaps I also thought of funds for the psychodynamic research this poor crazy torn-up world so badly needs.

'If you two are willing,' I said, 'I have an idea.' Conversation was delayed while the jet made another pass at us. That time I was lucky and ripped up his rudder. He was still a tiger compared to us, but handled awkwardly now.

'I thought of doing our snatch in reverse,' I said. 'Skim each of these lakes that we go above. Pretty good tactics anyhow; at this speed, he'll have to pull up sharp if he doesn't want a dunk in the drink. On one of those skims, I'll bail out with the girl. You lead him on for a while, then land if you want to. You'll have nothing to conceal, and our planes'll be along before he or his buddies can get rough with you. Nobody's going to dogfight over an object of search which has disappeared.'

'And how about you, Chuck?' asked the doctor.

'Lots of hotels around here,' I said. 'If you play it right, the Dulac gang will think we already transferred the kid somehow and were decoying them; I shouldn't be molested. I can hoof it to one of the hotels and call HQ to send a plane after us.'

'It sounds kind of impossible.'

'A man might try,' I said. 'Take the gun.'

I went down into the hull and stuffed my pockets with foodbars. Boots for me and the girl I hung around my neck. She was warm again to the touch, breathing slowly and easily. I unstrapped her and dragged her over to the hatch and squatted there with her in my arms. Every time we swooped or swerved, she was flung against me, which was not a bit unpleasant. Even when a line of holes was stitched across the wall, I rather enjoyed myself.

Choosing the third downwards rush at random, I eased the hatch open. The water looked cold and brown; I thought it was filthy till I realized nobody had put bluing in it. A chill shriek of air buffeted up at us. Marie stirred and mumbled, her eyelids fluttering.

When we were a yard above the lake, I stepped out.

We went under like a dropped stone. I clawed my way back to the surface and raised Marie's head. She began to squirm as consciousness returned. I shook the water from my eyes and stared out over the lake. It seemed horribly empty, rimmed in with pine and spruce, no trace of man except the two planes vanishing over the treetops. We'd been dropped close to shore and not seen. The opposing pilot had enough to think about, manoeuvring his lame ship and crippling ours without killing our prisoner.

A few strokes brought the muddy bottom under our feet. I waded to shore and dropped Marie Dulac on a dense brown carpet of needles. She choked, sputtered and sat up.

'Here,' I said, extracting a pocket flask.

She took it, shakily, and got down a gulp. Her eyes widened, and she was white and shivering, but I liked the fact that she didn't scream.

'Better get those wet clothes off,' I suggested. 'They'll dry pretty fast with this breeze, but you might catch cold from it.'

'I've been immunized,' she said in a small hard voice. She sat for a while looking across the choppy dark bareness of the lake. 'Where are we?'

I shrugged. 'Somewhere in the Arrowhead.'

'I've been kidnapped, yes?' She had a faint, charming hint of Canuck accent.

I bowed. 'Charles Rheinbogen, at your service, miss. Now if you'll excuse me ...' I slipped off my garments. After a moment she did the same. Even at close range and without cosmetics, she was good-looking.

'Do you have a cigarette?' she asked.

'Mmmmm ... we're not supposed to smoke here, you know. It's summer and these trees haven't been fireproofed.'

'Please. I'll be careful.'

Swanson was always harping on the need for courtesy,

among other professional standards. 'Very well,' I smiled, and groped in my jacket where it lay. She moved closer. Her hand shot out and yanked my gun from its holster.

I caught the movement in time to snatch it away from her. Her features blazed at me. I laughed, put the weapon aside, and got out the cigarettes. 'Still want that smoke?' I queried.

'Y . . . y-yes.' I struck it for her and she inhaled raggedly and coughed. She had probably just been introduced to the vice. Holy Hermes, patron of thieves, she could still be a virgin!

'Look, Miss Dulac,' I said, 'you have nothing to fear. You're under the protection of the law and of my union. All we're going to do is keep you for a while in a certain place with an adequate staff and good facilities. I'm sorry to put you to this indignity, but there was no choice.' I told her how the job had been carried out. 'And I wouldn't advise your trying to escape,' I finished. 'It would be more trouble for you to do so than it would be for me to find you again. As far as that goes, if you haven't had a lot of practice, a pistol is an awkward weapon and you'd be lucky to hit a whale broadside on.'

She sat thinking for a while, her cheeks flushed and her dark head bent down. Somewhere a bird began chirping. Big puffy clouds drifted over us, the sun walking between them.

'Why have you done this?' she asked finally.

'Nothing personal about it. I was hired.'

'By who?'

'I can't tell you that. Professional ethics.'

'Ethics!' she spat. Her eyes lifted and challenged me.

'Certainly. And be glad we have them, too. Otherwise anything could happen to you. As it is—'

'I know!' She stood up and looked at me as if I'd crawled from beneath some abandoned garbage grinder. 'It's ethical to knock me out, and humiliate me, and endanger my life. It's ethical to let my father worry himself sick – *ugh*!'

I said in my best persuasive tone: 'Back in the old days, before the Smashup and the reconstruction, some people used to kidnap rich men's children – minors, even babies –

for ransom. But being amateurs, they often panicked and murdered the victim. Now ... well, if you and your father can both stand your being detained for less than a year, you'll go free, unharmed, and he won't have to yield a thing.'

She looked thoughtful. 'May I write him?' she asked.

I was surprised. She actually, automatically talked of writing a letter instead of making a call. That convent must be a pretty old-fashioned sort of school; I'll bet it even insisted the kids learn to spell the same way. 'Sorry, no,' I answered.

'But you don't understand. I've hardly seen him, except on holidays, till last month. He'll be ill with worry ... about how I take this ... if I could write and let him know I can stand it without mental damage—'

'Exactly,' I said. 'There'd be no point in snatching you if it didn't bring pressure to bear on him. After all—'

'Oh, be quiet!' she snarled, and turned her back.

I hunkered on the soft brown needles and squinted across the lake and tried to figure her. She wasn't reacting like others I'd heisted. Women, especially – either hysterical or 'Goodness gracious, how thrilling!' Marie was concerned about her father and plain boiling-over mad about herself.

After a while the neolon was dry, and we resumed our clothes and chewed a couple of foodbars. It was an effort for me to follow her casual example and drink from the lake ... sure, unpolluted, but *untreated*. I had a queasy feeling afterwards. The water tasted wild.

'Well,' she said scornfully, 'now what?'

'I guess we strike out till we find a hotel or ranger station,' I decided. 'We'll head due north by the sun. Bound to find something.' As a bold bad bandit, I seemed to be cutting a rather lame figure.

She nodded and we started walking. The trees were high and grave about us; the forest floor, springy and open, muffled our boots; sunlight spattered through the branches. Once I saw a live squirrel scoot up a tree. I nudged Marie and pointed it out. She nodded again, frigidly.

To hell with her.

The sun finally sank, molten gold behind the woods. A wind snickered in the pines. 'Don't tell me we'll have to sleep out,' I groaned.

'It seems that way.' Did I catch a bare overtone of gloat?

Our majestic trees began to look like black witches, much too tall and thin. 'Perhaps I made a mistake,' I said. 'We could have waited where we were. My own people would probably have backtracked, looking for us, after they'd got rid of yours.'

A smile curved her lips. 'I thought of that,' she said.

'Then for God's sake why didn't you tell me?'

'You're in charge, aren't you?' I have never heard so demure a voice.

Despite the law, I wanted to build a fire for the night. I'd have been glad to attract a ranger and pay the fine; at the very least, there would have been warmth. After some futile fumbling with green twigs, it was getting so dark that I quit. Marie had put her time to better use, cutting off slender spruce boughs with my pocketknife and making herself a bed. Now she stretched out on it, a blur in the dusk.

'Hadn't you better put that heap on top of you?' I asked. 'It's going to be cold.'

'If you have only one cover, sleeping out, it works best beneath you. I have often been camping. You will learn.'

'Hm,' I said. 'Frankly, I thought you'd spent your time in the chilly cloisters.'

She fairly threw at me: 'It was like old days up there – a little village, honourable men who lived off the land, a few people who really cared to know things and knew learning means work. The sisters and the villagers were more human than you are, Mr Rheinbogen!'

I think I surprised her by taking no offence. 'I realize that,' I said with a dim sadness. 'They were ... are ... the lucky ones.'

'So why do you live by killing and stealing and—'

'I'm afraid I wasn't born to be a child of nature. And I have my own work to do, you know.'

'Your *work*!' That was all the good night I got.

There was no danger that I would sleep so unwarily well that she could turn the tables. Not with the ground cold and damp and hard beneath me. I swore to myself and shifted position and counted up my separate aches. Ye gods – this was the natural life?

Sometime after midnight, the monotonous clatter of my teeth must have lulled me. I was wakened from a fitful doze by a bang that shuddered in the earth. Fire burst over the sky, and then God opened the taps up yonder.

We scrambled to what shelter we could find, under the heavy branches of a low spruce. The rain sheeted, blown on a skirl of wind, roaring in the needles, runnelling off the ground. Lightning lit the world, a moment's sharp white reality and then clamping darkness again, on and off, on and off; thunder went booming down endless hollow spaces.

Marie huddled against me, not scared but seeking warmth. In a moment's lividness I saw that she was smiling. And after a while I felt the same grin on my mouth. This was a wonder, it was the real cosmos breaking loose and roistering across the sky; I could not only realize intellectually, but *feel*, what ants we were, crawling over our mud-ball planet in a blaze of stars, and the knowledge was not terrifying but a sort of drunkenness.

Presently the thunderstorm rolled beyond us and we stood in a slackening rain. It felt strangely gentle and soothing after that heavenly hooraw. We were wet and cold and hungry, but the show had been so good that we didn't mind much.

'You know,' I said, 'now I understand what they mean when they talk about man being a forest animal. Ultimately all our art must go back to . . . this.'

Marie's voice came quizzical out of shadow, above the rainplash: 'You don't talk like a gangster.'

'How should I talk?' I chuckled. 'We're professional men, not walking clichés.'

'Well—' surprisingly, she laughed – 'you do seem to have more interests.'

I explained that I was only a hood as a means of putting myself through school. 'Someday I'm going to be a peaceful psychodynamics research man, looking for a scheme to reconcile the fact that seven and a half billion people on the Solar System's single habitable planet need technology to stay alive, with the fact that technology requires them to live under conditions for which they aren't biologically fitted. A better scheme than any we now have, I mean.' I looked out into the running gloom. 'It can't go on this way forever. The present system is frankly meant as a stopgap.'

'My father . . .' She hesitated.

'Yes?'

'My father said something like that a few days ago. He felt it was not right that we should have three separate houses while his workers were cooped into one room per family; and yet he would go crazy if he did not have space, and be unable to direct the chemicals union, and so there might be no artificial fertilizers and the workers would starve.'

'Your father is a wise man,' I said.

'But it's so unfair!'

'The universe never signed a contract with man requiring it to be fair. The old Jews knew that – read the Book of Job. Even you Christians don't imagine the wrong will be redressed in this life.'

She made no answer. We stood there while the rain ended and the clouds broke up and greyness became full sunrise. Then we had a bite to eat and started north again.

My unaccustomed body was tired, sore, and chilled. But that disappeared as we walked through the morning. I breathed unfouled air and saw no swirl of gaping faces around me; a jay was a vivid streak of blue against the dark spruce-green, a brook belled its way over mossy stones, something which Marie called a thrush whistled liquidly, unseen.

'This makes me wonder what possessed man to stop hunting and grub his food out of ploughed dirt,' I said.

Marie looked at me. We had not spoken for hours, but it had not been an altogether hostile silence. 'The food was more secure . . . more certain,' she ventured.

'Only in bad hunting territory,' I answered. 'Which was where agricultural civilization was invented, of necessity.' I like to hear myself talk, and in any event I wanted to make a good impression on this girl, justify myself if possible.

'Oh, there were reasons to become civilized, yes,' I continued. 'The power, the gadgets . . . Nevertheless, for almost a million years man was a hunter. He's evolved for it, biologically and psychologically. His eyes are most sensitive in the yellow-green, the colour of sunlight filtered through leaves. His feet are meant for a yielding surface, it's pavement that flattens them. His body wants to sleep when it's eaten a full meal, and otherwise run around freely. His soul wants the excitement of the chase and the kill; it wants a feast afterwards, rejoicing, the intimacy of a tribe . . . and the chance to be alone, too, sometimes. All this is instinctive.

'None of him wants to be crowded together, and chained to one tiny spot of the earth's surface, and be an anonymous unit, bossed and herded and jammed into an iron desert of a city, subordinating food and sleep and digestion and love and play to a single dreary job. He's not built for it, his whole organism revolts against it. And yet nowadays we haven't any choice, we can't go back.'

'Go back to the happy savage?' she jeered.

'I'm not a Rousseauist,' I said. 'The savage does have an impoverished, frightened, hard-working, short life. Civilization does have fantastically wonderful potentialities, if only we can realize them. But it has its drawbacks, too!'

We went on in silence for a bit. Finally she shook her head. The breeze ruffled her short black hair.

'What you call civilization isn't,' she said. 'You seem to think it means killing and stealing and tyranny.'

'But it does,' I answered. 'Civilization is an objective concept referring to a certain level of technology and a certain type of social organization. It has very good results – medical science, for example. It also has toxic by-products, the ones you mentioned.'

'It doesn't have to.'

'I'm afraid it does. Read your history. By and large, it's one long agony. Now, isn't it?

'It's a matter of scientific record that those primitive peoples who survived long enough to be studied were, on the whole, much more decent than any civilized race. If war existed at all, it was a game rather than a butchery contest. Theft, murder, rape, sadism, insanity were rare. Their morality may not have been that of the Decalogue, but they stuck closer to it than we've managed to stick to our own codes.'

'And so you think the Ten Commandments are wrong?' asked Marie.

'Not at all,' I said. 'An admirable ideal, but so far only workable for primitives. Being civilized, we're too full of tensions and hatreds to abide by it without a real effort, too great an effort for most people to make consistently. From petty chicanery and backyard malice, up to world war and the Almighty State, civilized man has to hurt his neighbour.'

We came out on the shores of another lake. Squinting against the sunlight sharded on the water, I saw a building on the farther side, a long low thing of tinted plastic. I felt a sagging within myself. The adventure had ended. The lodge stood blatant in the woods.

Well . . .

'We'll go and call my HQ for transport,' I said. 'Please don't make it necessary for me to confine you while I do.'

Marie's lips clamped together again. She went unspeaking by my side as we started around the lake.

'Take us a while to get there,' I said inanely. 'It's been a pleasant trip, hasn't it?'

No answer. 'Look,' I said, 'I'm only an agent. I'm terribly sorry to cause you this trouble. But it's not so different from being a cop and giving you a ticket for speeding, is it?'

Her voice was hard and remote: 'The policeman is protecting us. You're preying on us.'

'Believe it or not,' I said, 'I'm upholding the law. I exist for the public safety.'

'Oh, you're very smug about it,' she cried. 'You have your licence, you keep your greasy paws off me . . . thanks for that much!'

'If it weren't for the likes of me,' I said, 'you could well have been snatched by someone who would not feel bound to keep his paws off you. Or let's think about the Peace Authority.'

Her cheeks burned, but instead of swinging at me she couldn't help arguing. In some ways she was too intelligent for her own good, but a man would never be bored in her company. 'The Smashup was too much,' she said. 'People finally had it knocked into their heads what war means, and the Wastelands are still there to remind them. Don't you go taking credit for the Authority!'

'Oh, but I do. Consider, as merely one example, German history *after* the Thirty Years' War. People never learn. Ruins, Wastelands, historical records, memoirs, warnings, mean nothing. The Peace Authority is possible only because we've found a better outlet than war, at least a less harmful one, for the evil in man.'

'But man is not evil,' protested Marie. 'He's born to sin, yes, but he has the possibility of grace.'

'Maybe "evil" was the wrong word,' I agreed. 'Let's say, rather, the hatred in him which comes from being civilized.

'Just before the Smashup, psychodynamics had developed to the point where this could be shown to be a fact – that most men, if not all, hate their civilization, subconsciously but intensely; and that the hatred must be vented somehow. The old-time professional soldier, like the modern professional gangster, was usually a kind, friendly man because his tensions were discharged in wartime. But society can't afford war any longer.

'It was too late to prevent the Smashup, and civilization was lucky to survive. The destruction, chaos, and suffering

of it vented so much wrath that people were fairly peaceable
for a decade afterwards. That made it possible to institute
legalized, regulated crime, as the necessary safety valve. It
also, incidentally, abolished such cold-blooded wasteful
fiendishness as locking sound men into cages for one mistake – and, through the institution of outlawry, has begun
slowly to eliminate the incredible fat-headedness of turning
congenital psychopaths loose on parole. But that's minor.
Even the fun involved – and it *is* fun – is secondary.

'You seem to be more at peace with yourself than most,
Marie; you could live happily in a crimeless, warless world.
But not many people can. So we give them crime, and a
touch of freedom and colour and adventure in their lives,
instead of war.

'Therefore I insist, Marie, that in my own way I'm upholding the law and making the world a little safer, a little
cleaner. And someday I can have a hand in finding a better
answer than this.'

I stopped, quite hoarse from my oration. We walked for a
mile or so through summery quietness, rounded the lake and
found a path leading to the lodge.

'You may be right,' said Marie at last, quite softly.

My heart gave an irrational jump. It shouldn't matter
what a victim thought of me, but in this case it did.

Her eyes turned up towards mine. 'I have a right too,
though,' she said, 'and my father does.'

'I'm sorry for him,' I replied sincerely, 'and for you. But
aristocracy has always had its penalties as well as its privi-
leges.'

'You . . . you're not the sort I imagined you were . . . not
the sort to cause needless pain. You could let me go . . .'

I bit my lip. 'I could. But I won't.'

'Why not? If it's the money, you'll be paid ten times over;
I swear it.'

'No. It's a matter of—' I laughed, rather sadly. 'Honour.
May I use that word? I undertook to do a job, and my
brothers are depending on me to do it. I can't blacken their
name. It's socially important, too. I want to see more and

more people delegate their crimes to us pros. We can do it less messily, more considerately; and it helps get our customers out of the habit of violence.'

'But – you would work for that *cochon?*'

'The fellow who hired me? I don't like him one little bit. I wish to God your father had hired me against him. But yes, having given my word, I'll do his job to the best of my ability.'

Gravel scrunched underfoot.

'I'm sorry,' I said.

'If he could know how it is—'

'I'll gladly take a crack at him after this episode is over.'

'After he has got what he wants from my father, and is on his guard . . .' She turned her face. I saw her stiffen.

I walked on in anguish. It wasn't right, it wasn't fair. She was too much alive to be penned away for months. She would come out of it with her own tensions built up, already I could see it happening, another civilized creature with civilized hate to discharge on someone else. Wasn't I trying to build a society where no one loathed his fellow man, where folk worked together not because they were told to but because it was their free will? I had a member of that future right here, beside me, and I was going to ruin her for the sake of that same future. It didn't make sense.

We came up to the lodge. Its wealthy guests stared at our sunburnt griminess from their lounging chairs and their cocktail terrace. I wanted to stuff every fat belly in the place with lead.

Shifting my gun conspicuously near my hand, I took Marie into the lobby. 'I'm on a job,' I said to the clerk. 'Want to make a call from here.'

'Yes, sir, yessir, rightthiswaysir!' He jumped to it. I was disappointed, needing an excuse to bully someone. We were shown into the office and left in privacy.

I didn't dial HQ – our lines were undoubtedly tapped by Dulac's goons – but a laundry in Duluth. Our agent there relayed the call through a scrambler to Twincity. It took a minute or two to raise the operator at that end.

Waiting, I struck a cigarette and slumped. 'We'll have a plane here for you in half an hour,' I said. 'That'll finish my part of the job.'

She didn't reply, but stood behind me. I could hear how fast she breathed.

'You'll doubtless say no,' I went on, 'and I'll not blame you. But may I come see you in the hideout, now and then?' When she still made no answer, I smiled on one side of my mouth. 'At least let me buy you a proper breakfast here. It's on the expense account.'

The screen lit up before she could respond. I was put through to Swanson at once, and told him briefly what had happened.

'Good boy!' he said warmly. 'That was a beaut you pulled. It'll go down in the annals, believe me. We'll get a plane up there right away.'

'No hurry,' I said without tone.

'Ah . . . so. How well I understand.' Swanson bowed in the screen. 'Miss Dulac, my deepest apologies. I assure you—'

'Never mind that.' She drew a long breath and leaned over my shoulder, brushing me. Maybe it was just hunger, but suddenly I felt a trifle dizzy. Her voice was crisp, with a bare hint of laughter. 'Let me say something first.'

'By all means, Miss Dulac. We aim to please.'

'I have a job for you myself. I want a kidnapping done.'

I distinctly heard my jaw click against my Adam's apple.

'What?' Swanson recovered himself and sputtered: 'But this isn't— It's never been—'

'I insist on my civil rights,' snapped Marie. 'Merely being a prisoner hasn't removed them. I have the same right to take out a licence and sign a contract as anyone else.'

'Ah . . . to be sure . . . but—'

'We can settle it right here when your man comes. I want you to kidnap the one who had me kidnapped.'

'But we can't— We're *working* for him!'

'Are you, now? You contracted to do one task for him. You have done it. Aren't you now free to . . .'

'Well . . . let me think . . . yes, Chuck is under his contract and therefore can't operate against him till it expires. But anyone else in the union ... wait a minute!' The sparkle faded in Swanson's eyes. 'You can't sign a John Doe warrant, you know. You have to name the person you want heisted, and we can't tell you who he is.'

She made an impatient gesture. 'My father is no fool. When the notice of intent was served on me, I asked him who might be responsible and he explained how his affairs stood. Let's say, then, that I want the ... what you call it ... snatch put on one James Hardy of New Chicago. The ransom requirement will be that he, ah, arrange my release.' She paused, frowning. 'And yes, that he pay your fees for this job.'

Swanson leaned back in his chair and gasped with laughter.

We sat on the cocktail terrace, watching sunset smoulder into the lake. Around us went a muted buzz of conversation, clink of glasses, whisper of music. I didn't mind, in fact I felt quite kindly towards our fellow guests.

I raised my own glass. 'To success,' I said.

Marie nodded and clinked rims. Our shysters had pushed the licence, notice, and contract through in a hurry, and we were now awaiting news. Under the circumstances, I had declared that this lodge fulfilled the conditions of a hideout and that we could as well detain the girl here as elsewhere. It had been a good three days, I'd never had better ones.

'You're a strange man, Charles,' she murmured. 'The soul of honour about your profession, yes, but you helped me with a great deal of legal hairsplitting.'

'I had to see that everything was drawn up in proper form,' I said virtuously. 'Citizen's duty to respect the law.'

'The letter of the law, anyhow,' she grinned. 'But you were wearing such shining armour when we first met.'

'Armour is not awfully comfortable,' I said. 'I'd only wear it for someone like you.'

Her eyes darkened and she shivered. 'It is bad to think that you could be killed on your next mission.'

'I have to make a living. Several years to go yet before I can make it doing research.'

'My father . . .'

'Yes?'

'When I tell him how this was . . . he likes a clean fighter. He would be glad to offer you a summer position, one that paid well.'

'Sorry. He employs our friendly rivals. I couldn't fight my own brothers.'

The waiter oozed up with a phone extension and laid it on the table. 'Call for you, sir.' I lowered the privacy hood. In order to see the little screen under it, Marie and I had to have our heads together.

Swanson looked minutely out at us. 'All done, boy,' he said. 'Hardy was still in town. He'd figured Dulac himself put the bee on him, and wasn't looking for trouble from us. We lifted him right out of his hotel room, and you should have heard him squawk! He's met the terms, though. Had to, if his enterprises weren't to go to pot in his absence. You can take Miss Dulac home now.'

'Shucks,' I grinned, above a certain desolation, 'you needn't have been in that kind of a hurry.'

Swanson shook his head. 'An unprecedented business, this,' he muttered. 'It never happened before that a gang union acted against somebody who was employing one of its own members. There are going to be ICC hearings, and lawsuits, and— Lord knows what'll come of it.'

'That,' I said, 'is one reason why it's fun to be alive. I can rent a copter here. Never mind sending a plane for us. Cheerio.'

The hood lifted. Marie and I regarded each other for a long while. 'I hope you'll at least stay for dinner,' I said.

'Oh, yes. I should forego a genuine charcoal-broiled yeast mignon?' She laughed joyously and rose. 'I'll just call my father now. Be back at once, *mon ami*.'

I had time for some moody and lonesome thoughts while

she was gone, there in the twilight under the Japanese lanterns. She found me a poor companion on her return. 'But what is wrong?' she asked.

'Never mind,' I said. 'Or . . . oh, the deuce with it. I was thinking that I'll take you home in a couple of hours, and I can't accept that job you offered me, and there's an end of the matter.'

'But who said anything about a gunman's position?' she asked in surprise. 'Your psychodynamics has uses in industry, no? You know enough already to hold down a well-paid summer job, and . . .' Her voice trailed off. 'If you wish to cease being a gangster,' she concluded uncertainly.

I twirled the glass in my hands. It was no easy choice. I hadn't counted on hanging up my guns for years. I needed enough hunting to satisfy my instincts for the rest of an uneventful life . . .

But hell! Wasn't research a hunt? Had Newton or Darwin or Einstein ever felt the need to kill and steal? Hardly. They were after bigger game.

I lifted the glass and finished my drink.

Strange Bedfellows

*Progress does get made, however slowly and with
however many setbacks. It is the work of those who
are too brave to despair. Our descendants may yet
create a society more sane than any which has gone
before. But will this keep them from insanities of
their own?*

Suddenly the plain exploded. A pillar of steam shot sky-
ward, bone-white against darkness and the stars, tinged red
with incandescent drops of metal. Steel chunks from the
drill rig whizzed out of that boiling and roaring, struck the
ground and skittered murderously across kilometres. They
sounded like bees heard through thunder. Cracks opened
around the well, broadened to metres-wide ravines as they
ran outwards. The hole stretched itself into a crater and spat
ash and boulders. Then the rush of steam was hidden in
smoke, and in dust that whirled up from the shuddering
surface.

Don Sevigny had thrown himself prone when the con-
vulsion began. He clung in blindness to rock, felt it heave
against his belly and heard the shrapnel that had been
machinery go past. A taste of blood was in his mouth.
Poy, his mind stammered, *Erich, they were right on the
spot!*

What went wrong?

The explosions ended. Great hollow echoes rolled back
from the cliffs of the Caucasus, toned away and were lost in
the growl and seethe of the newborn volcano. The ground
still quivered, but the first dreadful seasick roll was over.
Sevigny jumped to his feet. Dust roiled around his helmet,
he was cut off from his men, from Earth and Moon, alone in
a night that clamoured.

'Report!' he yelled. 'By the numbers!'

Names trickled in, one, Aarons, two, Bergsma, three,

Branch, four ... nobody, Erich Decker was mute ... five, Gourmont, six ...

'... Twelve,' said R'ku's vocalizer.

Youkhannan finished with twenty. All accounted for but Decker and Leong.

The haze was leaving Sevigny's vision as the mineral flour settled. Bit by bit he made out the scene, the grey plain chopped off two kilometres away by the brutal upsurge of the Caucasus, the stars that glittered above those peaks, the scattered shapes of men and equipment. He turned to see the eruption and looked straight at Earth, not far above the near southern horizon. It was waning from full towards half phase, but the white-banded blue brilliance was nonetheless such that for a moment he was again blind.

The dazzle departed in ragged after-images. He saw a black geyser gushing from the riven soil. At five hundred meters it spread mushroom-like. By then it was pale azure in the Earthglow – ice crystals condensing at seventy-five degrees below Celsius zero. The cloud was not large; it melted at the edges, scattered by the thin swift wind that blew steadily east towards the sun.

There was no time to be afraid. Two men had been caught near the blast. They might be alive. Lava would soon come out of that hole. Sevigny plunged after the nearest moontrac. 'Three of you help me,' he called. 'Maybe we can hook Poy and Erich out of there.'

Even under Lunar gravity, it was an awkward scramble in his airsuit to reach the high-mounted cab. He leaned panting over the control board for several seconds before he realized that no one had joined him.

Huh?

The canopy was raised, the cab exposed to a wintry heaven. Camp had been established some time ago. Given inflated domes, covered with Lunar dust against the heat and radiation that would come at sunrise, people had no need to maintain vehicles at pressure or keep their screen generators in operation. Sevigny had only to lean over the edge and shout, 'What's ailing you? I want three helpers.'

Some heartbeats passed when only the volcano spoke. Then Branch replied, his sound amplifier tuned to maximum, as if in extra defiance: 'Are you out of your brain? Those jims are dead!'

'Maybe not,' Sevigny barked. 'We'll find out.'

'And kill four more? That thing's going to spit molten rock any minute.'

Briefly, Sevigny failed to understand. The situation just didn't make logic. It was like being caught in a dream.

His gauntlets closed on the cab rim, so hard that the thermo wires in them creaked. 'You—' All at once he understood. 'You *Earthlings*!'

'By God, Boss, you're right.' Aarons came over the plain in kangaroo bounds. Dust puffed where his boots struck. One by one, some others began to follow. Sevigny could only identify them, through the long shadows, by the phosphorescent numbers on their chests.

'Youkhannan and Nakajima,' he rapped. 'You're closest. The rest of you get our stuff to a safe distance.' Anger lifted fresh and he finished with a chosen insult: 'R'ku, you're in charge.'

'Very well.' The Martian had not stirred. Now his gaunt shape got into motion, a few jumps that no human could have matched, a sweeping overview, and a series of cool orders.

I don't blame him for not volunteering, Sevigny thought. *He'd be no use the minute that much water hit his skin; and Martians don't go in for romantic gestures. The rest, though – I didn't take them for crawlguts.*

But it struck him that Earthlings did not, after all, have clan bonds like Cythereans. For that matter, if he'd simply been one of the crew, he too might have hesitated to risk his neck for somebody with whom he had swapped no oaths. As boss, of course, he was in a different situation.

Aarons, Youkhannan, and Nakajima reached the flat bed of the trac and grabbed the cargo kingposts for support. Sevigny threw himself into the pilot's seat and gunned the right engines. Electric power surged from the accumulators massed below. The vehicle turned until its blunt nose pointed at the geyser. Sevigny cut in the left engines. Eight huge, soft-tyred wheels rolled forward.

A crevasse had opened in the ground between. Sevigny didn't pause to gauge distances. After a year on the Moon, his eyes were well trained. He threw a switch at a moment which he felt with his bones rather than his intellect was correct. Two metal arms lifted the portable bridge off the trac bed, carried it over the cab and laid it down precisely as the trac arrived at the verge. Wheels trundled across, with a boom and a rattle that resounded dimly through the cataract noise of the eruption. When weight was off the bridge, the arms swung it back into place.

Wind-whipped ash drove across the view. Sevigny heard it click against his faceplate. The trac lurched over tumbled stones, wallowed in new-formed mud. He leaned forward, straining to see, while his hands and feet wrestled with the machine. There— He steered for the dim bulk on the crater's edge, reached it and braked to a halt.

Half buried in wet cinders, the other trac lay broken on its side. A section of pipe had been coughed from the well and rammed through the hoist engine block. Close by was the drill rig's force unit, grotesquely canted, the casing scarred by energetic debris. He saw no human figures. The wind squealed faintly through the volcano roar.

He turned his amplifier to max and asked, 'Anybody see either of them?'

'No, sir.' Youkhannan's voice was only identifiable by the Iraqi accent. 'Likely they were pitched downslope and buried.'

'Grab shovels and go look,' Sevigny commanded. 'I'll scratch around here.'

He ignored the ladder, vaulted over the canopy edge and fell with maddening slowness. Heat gusted from the crater to bite through his suit's insulation. The thermostatic units switched over to cool-off; their pump-throb went in time with his pulse. He stumbled through black shards that grated underfoot and slipped beneath his soles.

Wait! Under the cab of the wreck ... a boot projected! Sevigny knelt and dug with his hands, dog fashion. Sweat was sharp in his nostrils, painful in his eyes, clammy in his undergarment. Somewhere far off a stranger cursed without cease and another stranger remembered how Mount Victory loomed over green Carlo's Lake, beautiful and irrelevant on Venus. The brawling around him deepened; there came a fresh moonquake and cinders shot forth to turn the murk nearly absolute.

Sevigny freed both legs, rose and heaved. The breath was harsh and dry in this throat. Almost at the end of his endurance, the body came loose with a suddenness that tumbled him on his rear. He crawled back, unclipped his flashlight, squatted and squinted through the ash rain. It was Leong. Air oozed in a vapour cloud from a rip in the man's suit, but some bubbles of blood on the lips behind the faceplate still seemed to move. Sevigny got him in his arms, pulled himself erect, and lurched towards his own vehicle.

With a deliberate and terrible drumfire, the first magma spilled from the hole. Sevigny dragged Leong on to the trac bed, laid him down and fumbled with a patch from the kit at his belt. The teakettle stream came to an end. On shaking legs, Sevigny rose to switch on the floodlamp above the cab. *Should'a done this before. How else can the boys find me? I'm beaten stupid.* Now he could again make out the force unit, through the mineral rain and swirling primordial dust. On a half animal impulse, he activated the crane that extended from the left kingpost. It swung out, hovered above the two-metre steel cube, dipped and grappled. He raised it. The trac swayed beneath such a weight. Metal sang in the cables.

The lava was very close now, a dully glowing glacier. Sevigny got into the cab. 'Nakajima!' he cried uselessly against the reverberations. 'Youkhannan! Aarons! Get back here, for everything's sake!' Momentarily he – rather, his clansman's reflexes – debated the ethics of abandoning them. They should be able to reach safety on foot . . . No. Someone had to give first aid on the way, or Leong might be dead before he reached the camp wagon.

A blackened shape came out of the whirl, and another and another. They hadn't found Erich, then. *Well, we did what we could*. Sevigny gunned the engines. He barely waited for his gang to climb aboard before he engaged the transmission.

'One of you get Poy here and treat him,' he said. 'The rest hang on!'

He dared not go full speed on this terrain, though the Mare Serenitatis might open beneath him at any time. And what a hell of a name that was, he thought in the back of his head. So lost was he in his driving that he didn't notice what went on around him. When he emerged from the smoke into clear vision, on to safe and stable rock, he was actually surprised to find the canopy dogged down and the air tanks opened to make full pressure.

He glanced behind. Leong's airsuit had been peeled off. The man sprawled on the rear seat, eyes closed, breath fast and shallow. Aarons knelt beside him, helmet and gloves removed. The lean hooked face dripped sweat down on to the blood that trickled from Leong's nostrils.

'Well?' Sevigny asked.

'Decompression, of course,' Aarons said in an exhausted monotone. 'Probably shock, concussion, maybe a fracture or two.' He opened the medikit, got a hypodermic needle, and filled it from an ampoule. 'I'll give him twenty cc. of ADR to play safe, but looks like you got him in time. Where was he?'

'By his own trac. I imagine he hit something when it was knocked over, and therefore simply slid down. Erich got thrown a distance.'

Aarons looked back at the pillar of smoke and the slow flood of fire. He shivered. 'No use hunting any more for him.' After a silence: 'I'm glad you made us come along, Boss, even if we didn't have much luck.'

Sevigny grunted.

The four remaining vehicles – camp and service wagons, 'dozer and scoop – were close now, box-like shapes on the plain with the men huddled around. R'ku stood a little apart. His long thin legs were crouched as if to leap, but folded arms and lowered abdomen bespoke repose. Earthlight shimmered off the metal-blue hide. His unhuman head seemed crowned with stars.

As Sevigny pulled alongside the camp wagon, which held bunks and some sickbay equipment, the Martian stirred. A single spring brought him to the trac. Seen thus in flight, the mantis-like form was no longer stiff or grotesque, but fluid elegance, an abstract statue cast in mercury. When he landed, his head was level was Sevigny's; and the cab seat was 150 centimetres off the ground.

His stare had long stopped bothering the Cytherean; it had merely been that those big turquoise eyes were made so unlike a man's, and never blinked. That narrow insectoidal face had always seemed more handsome than otherwise. At present it was largely hidden by the air helmet. Lunar atmosphere had by now got so thick that Martians didn't require suits, but the composition remained wrong. Not enough nitrogen to breathe, poisonous methane and ammonia; and while they needed small amounts of water as men need vitamins, there was too much of the vapour around these days for their metabolism to handle.

'What success did you have?' R'ku inquired. His words penetrated the glasolite canopy with the expected flatness. Sevigny sometimes wondered if the Martians' reputation for unemotionality was due to no more than the fact that they must use vocalizers to make humanly recognizable sounds. On the other hand, they seldom showed excitement in their behaviour. ...

'We saved Leong,' he answered. 'Have 'em snake a tube from the wagon for him.'

R'ku gestured. Four men got busy. They avoided looking in Sevigny's direction.

'You brought back the force unit,' R'ku observed.

'Yeah. Maybe that's what caused the trouble. We'll take it on to GHQ. Nothing more we can do here. And Poy has to get to a hospital.'

'He is salvageable, then.'

'I hope so.' With an idiotic desire for conversation: 'What'd you do if he wasn't?'

'I understand that your custom is burial.'

'On Mars, I mean.'

'That would depend upon what culture was involved. We of the Great Confederation would dry and powder the body and scatter it on the winds. But in Illach they would process it to fuel their Biological Engine; K'nea would use it for animal fodder; Hs'ach—'

'Never mind.' The man sagged in his seat. Weariness rose and hit him like a fist.

He had not felt so alone since he first arrived at Port Kepler. Then he was a bright young terraform engineer, with no more than three standard years' experience in the Drylands to justify a job offer from the Luna Corporation. Subsequently, he'd been too busy learning the tricks of this world's trade, working his way up until he headed a deeptap gang, losing himself in riotous furloughs at Paradise, to think widely. But how little the clans of Venus knew about the rest of the universe, under their clouded sky ... how isolated they were!

A man lay dead under molten stone because *his* well had erupted.

He shook himself. 'Move along, you sons,' he said harshly. 'Get that tube connected.'

The Buffalo laid his cigar in an old-fashioned ashtray and said, 'Hi, there. You're Sevigny? I thought at first you were the wrath of God.'

'I feel like its results,' Sevigny mumbled.

The Buffalo laughed. 'Well, come on in, ease your freight ... and your black friend, too. I'm kind of curious about him.'

Sevigny blinked, startled a little out of his lassitude. 'Oscar? But how—'

'I got a visual to the outer office.' The Buffalo pointed at a screen set in his intercom box. 'I like to see who my secretary is telling I'm in conference.' Small eyes darted slyly towards the visitor. 'I also got an auditory to her. Earplug set; that's how come all my girls wear their hair long. In case I decide I'm not in conference. Besides,' he added thoughtfully, 'I like long hair on women.'

Sevigny felt himself under closer observation than he would have believed possible. Automatically, he bristled, and one hand edged the least bit nearer to his sidearm. A man did not pay that kind of heed to another man on Venus unless a fight was brewing. He remembered he was on Luna. But he still had the pride of his clan to maintain.

'As you wish,' he snapped, and turned on his heel with calculated insolence. The frosted glass on the door said

BRUNO NORRIS
CHIEF OF OPERATIONS

It opened for him and he stuck his head out and whistled. Oscar jumped from the chair on which he had been grooming himself and darted inside, up to Sevigny's shoulders in one low-gravity spring.

The secretary gave him a surprised look, which lingered. He was not handsome: a big, rawboned young man with jutting nose and chin, blue eyes under shaggy fair brows, sandy hair not as well combed as it might be. But the sun had browned him, and he walked like a soldier. Long tunic with clan insignia, bare knees, and buskins marked him out too, among the Russian blouses and bell-bottomed trousers currently fashionable on Earth. Cytthereans weren't often seen off their planet.

He returned the girl's look with interest, in both senses of the word. The Buffalo's fame for choosing spectacular female help had turned out to be quite justified.

A little regretfully, but also a little more cheerful, he let the door close and faced around again. The grey-thatched, kettle-bellied giant behind the desk waved at a chair. 'Squat yourself. Cigar?'

'No, thanks. I don't smoke.' Sevigny took the edge of the seat.

'What's the matter, you want to live forever? Well, how about a drink? I estimate the sun just went over the yard-arm. But let's see.' The chief activated a full-wall view-screen.

It scanned the surface, rather than the underground warren which Port Kepler mostly was. In the direction of the harsh morning sun, the crater floor lay almost untouched, naked rock reaching towards the stark ringwall. Elsewhere, though, entry turrets, radars, control towers, solar cell banks, rail lines, the whole clutter of man had overrun the landscape. Earth was a wan half disc in a deep-blue sky where a few tentative clouds drifted.

Crow's feet meshed in a broad ruddy visage. 'Um-m-m,' the Buffalo said, 'reckon we'll have to lower the yardarm a trifle. *Selah.*' He reached into a drawer for a bottle of brandy and tumblers, into another, refrigerated one for ice and soda.

'I don't know, Mr Norris,' Sevigny hesitated. 'This is a serious matter—'

'Good Lord, man! Have you no redeeming vices?'

'Oh ... all right. Thanks.' A nearly involuntary smile tugged at the corner of the Cytherean's mouth.

Liquid gurgled forth. Oscar sat up, curious. Silky mid-night fur tickled Sevigny's neck.

'Here's to our noble selves.' The Buffalo tossed off half a glass in a gulp and resumed puffing on his cigar. 'I concede What is that beastie?'

'A dirrel. They're kind of one-man animals, so I had to bring him with me.' That still looked frivolous. 'Everyone almost, keeps a dirrel in the Shaws, my home country. It' be too easy to get lost in the wilderness without somethir for a guide that can climb the tallest trees; and they're goc at finding game.'

'I thought Venus was mainly desert still.'

'Some regions were ripe for ecology as soon as the water had precipitated. Native organic matter in the soil. When life was introduced it multiplied explosively.'

'M-m ... yeah, I remember now. That's probably the source of a lot of your clan feuds, hey? Squabbles over land that didn't need so much work before it could be settled. What species did the geneticists make your pet from?'

Sevigny shrugged. 'I don't know. Some rodent. They bred to a mass of seven or eight kilos, hands of a sort, and a pretty good brain. Oscar can communicate with me, a little, in a special language.' He rubbed the large, sharp-nosed head between the ears. Oscar arched his back and elevated his magnificent plume of tail.

'Oh. Sure. I see. His ancestors— But *no importe*. This is a pleasure, meeting you,' said the Buffalo. 'I wish I could get back out in the field myself. Those crews are apt to be weird and wonderful mixtures. I recall one Nigerian . . .'

The tension which had been departing returned to Sevigny. He sat straight again and said roughly, 'I'm sure your time is valuable, Mr Norris. What did you want to see me about?'

'That accident . . . now hold on, son. Not so defensive, if you please. By all accounts, you did just fine. I know it was pretty much a shock, your first job as crew chief going sour that way. But you handled matters better'n a lot of veterans would have. What I'd like is your own story of what happened. From the beginning.'

'You have my report.'

'Pretend I haven't read it. Pretend I don't even know deep-tap procedure. I'll tell you why, later on, but right now go ahead and talk.'

Sevigny scowled. He didn't know what to make of this first encounter with his ultimate boss. *Okay*, he thought, *blame yourself for the consequences.*

'We reached Mare Serenitatis Site Four at sunset, as per schedule,' he bit off. 'While the drill rig was being erected and started, the rest of the crew made camp. Everything seemed normal until circa eighteen hundred hours of the second day past midnight. We cleared ground and dug channels for the expected outflow of liquid, according to the maps drawn by Survey. At the time of the accident, a work shift was ending. Decker and Leong were at the well, about to change the cutter. The eruption caught them. We managed to rescue Leong – he's recovering nicely now – but couldn't find Decker before the lava forced us back. We struck camp and proceeded directly here. R'ku, the Martian on the team, stayed behind to observe. His last radio report to me was that the well had collapsed and outflow ceased. I told him to return. He ought to arrive at Little Mars shortly.'

As he spoke he had a vision of that tall strange figure, imperturbably watching the volcano die, then loading the meagre gear he needed on his thorax and soaring off across barrenness, into lunar day. That was hot enough and bright enough to kill a man who wasn't careful; the atmospheric blanket was still too thin to moderate the climate as much as Earth's is moderated. But the Martians had never suffered, though temperature rocketed beyond anything they had ever known at home. It was one reason the corporation paid them so well . . . Somehow, the picture was an eldritch and lonely one.

Sevigny's attention switched back to immediacies as the Buffalo asked, 'In your opinion, what caused the accident?'

'Probably failure of the force unit. Survey had warned us, on the basis of sonic probes, that there was a layer of allotropic ice at the depth we were reaching. Without counterpressure in the bore the stuff exploded into the lower density form, and the released energy vaporized it. That left a cavity through which molten rock farther down could rise.'

'Sounds reasonable. You did damn well to snatch that unit away.'

'Have your technies learned anything from it?'

'I've had a lab report,' the Buffalo nodded. 'There was crystallization in the Terence head. It broke apart under stress.'

'What?' Sevigny started so violently that Oscar almost

fell off. The dirrel chattered an indignant remark and clung tighter with his small half-human fingers.

'But ... how did any such thing get by inspection at the manufacturer's?' Sevigny choked.

The Buffalo's fist clenched on his desktop. 'That,' he said, 'is what I'd like to know.'

He leaned over and refilled both tumblers. 'Son,' he continued, 'we got troubles. That's why I wanted to see you and listen to you. To size you up. This isn't the first accident the project ought not to have had.'

'But—' Sevigny realized he was gaping and drew his lips shut.

'I've QT'd them fairly well,' said the chief. 'Can't go on doing that, though, if the farce proceeds. Oh, there's been a semiplausible explanation every time. But the upshot is that I'm not sure any longer who the devil I can trust.'

He sighed; then his gaze nailed the younger man and he asked, 'How much do you know about the political background of this undertaking?'

'Why ... uh ... the Corporation's an international venture chartered under the Commonwealth, with the different governments holding most of the stock.' Sevigny hunted through memories. 'That's about all I know,' he admitted lamely.

'Guess I needn't've expected more. Where you come from, the clan is the economic as well as the political unit; and with so little to trade thus far, Venus doesn't have a lot of contact with Earth. Never mind. I'll try to fill you in.'

The Buffalo stubbed out his cigar and lit a fresh one. He didn't speak until several noisy puffs had got it well burning.

'We're in a funny situation nowadays,' he said. 'People haven't quite realized it yet, but the era of stability has begun to end. (Hey, ain't that a lousy hunk of rhetoric?) Our hyperballyhooed world order was really a peace of exhaustion, following the global wars and their aftermath. Problems weren't so much solved as swept under the carpet, while the leading countries proceeded with their glorious conquest of space. Now the human race is getting restless again. The fact that nobody resisted hard when you Cythereans declared your independence is considered a textbook example of how Man Has Matured and such-like brain grease. Actually, though, if you'll excuse me saying it, the significant fact was not that you got away with breaking loose, but that you got the idea in the first place. Since then, more cracks have appeared in the system.

'Well—' He filled his mouth and blew rings. 'You needn't look so alarmed. I'm not about to read you my Lecture Number twenty-seven–B, Theory and Practice of Declinesmanship. What matters is that the project of terraforming Luna had enemies from the start. Setting up the Corporation was a necessary dodge. We'd never've swung it as a straightforward public enterprise.'

Sevigny took a long and badly wanted swallow from his tumbler. 'I don't understand,' he said. 'Why, the Venus project was far bigger and less directly rewarding—'

The Buffalo shook his massive head. 'Nuh-uh, son. The cost was relative peanuts in your case, even with spaceships as crude and expensive as they were at that time. Those algae only had to be seeded. Oh, sure, when they'd finished their job, a hellful of work remained. Still does, after all these decades. But ... it can be done piecemeal, by private outfits. There's the origin of your clans. And then, too, Venus is quite a way off. A morning and evening star, no more. It doesn't hang overhead, it doesn't rise big as a pumpkin over anyone's personal hills, to keep him reminded.

'You'd be surprised how much purely sentimental opposition there was to changing the looks of the dear old Moon. How many older people who remember have stayed resentful to this day. And also, when a world hasn't got an atmosphere to start with ... well, you should hear our cost accountants squeal every time the latest budget is presented. Mainly, though, various interests on Earth have their own sound, coldblooded reasons for not wanting this to go through.'

Unnoticed by himself, Sevigny's hand dropped to the butt of his gun. 'Are you implying sabotage, Mr Norris?'

'I don't know. I really don't. Still, a series of major setbacks for us would make very nice political ammunition, don't you think?'

Sevigny shook his head. 'Sorry, but *I* should think Earth is committed. I mean, uh, with the enormous investment already made – that can't simply be written off. Can it?'

'One of our own best talking points,' the Buffalo agreed. 'Please don't think I'm being paranoid. Just because everybody picks on me . . . I only thought I'd mention the general background, and ask you to read a few books and articles I'll list. They're kind of interesting in their own right, regardless.'

'Frankly, what little I know of politics bores me like an auger.'

'Which shows how little you know about politics, son. It's the only game in town. I do wish you'd study up a bit before you go to Earth.'

'What?'

'Would you pick his jaw off the floor, please, Oscar?' The Buffalo grinned. 'Sure. After what you did at Site Four, you rate a vacation. Need one, too. Human nerves don't unstretch overnight, and that was a rough cob for you.'

'But I hadn't planned—'

'Eh? You didn't mean to drop in when your contract expires, at least? See the green hills of Earth, the ocean Columbus sailed, Westminster Abbey, the Taj Mahal, the Brisbane Follies?'

'No. Why spend a lot of money on tourism, when what I want is heavy reclamation equipment to use at home?'

'If you'd let me show you some pictures from the Follies, you'd know why. But no matter.' The Buffalo jabbed his cigar in Sevigny's direction. 'You'll go at Corporation expense, and we aren't gonna look too squinch-eyed at your accounts.'

He grew serious. 'I can't leave right now, with everything there is to do,' he explained, 'and as I told you, I'm no

longer sure who I can trust. But you're outside these factions, you're a bright boy, presumably a tough fighting man,
and the Treaty of Toronto gives you the right to bear arms
anywhere. All I want you to do is convoy that force unit you
rescued to World Safety Corps headquarters, and ride their
tails to make certain they conduct a thorough investigation.
That crystallized metal looks mighty like sabotage to me. A
heavy dose of radiation 'ud cause it, and how could that
happen by chance? I could ask the Corps to send someone
here, but the evidence would have to go Earthside anyway,
and without one of my boys riding along. Not that I don't
think the Corps is honest; however, if the news is simply that
I've sent an engineer to discuss possible changes in machine
design, then no one will be tempted to try some fancy stunt.
You'll have an easy trip, a couple of weeks' layover, a
chance to wash some of that damned Swede-faced serious-
ness out of your system – and serve the project better than
you could here. How's about it?'

'Oh!' exclaimed the girl. 'I beg your pardon.'

Sevigny held stiff the arm against which she had stumbled
until she regained balance. Her floor-length gown and curl-
toed silver shoes were made to throw anybody.

So were their contents. She was bronze brunette, with
spectacular half-Oriental features, and the décolleté dress
fitted her like another skin. He had spent several seconds
after he stepped out of his room, admiring her as she undu-
lated down the hall. 'Quite okay,' he said. 'In fact, frankly, a
pleasure.'

She laughed. The synthodiamond necklace sparkled no
more brightly than her teeth. 'I didn't know a wild Cytherean
warrior could turn so pretty a compliment.'

In spite of what the Buffalo had said, Sevigny had a
normal capacity for fun. But to maintain his clan's good
name, he responded, 'Is that what they believe on Earth?
Not true, my lady. We work hard and don't fight except
when we have to.'

'Poof.' She wrinkled her nose. 'There goes another illusion. Did you arrive today? I'm sure I would have noticed otherwise.'

'Yes, on the Lunar packet.'

'The Moon?' She widened an incredible pair of eyes. 'Then you must be connected with the terraforming.' He nodded. 'But this is wonderful. How long will you be here?'

'Only till tomorrow, my lady. I've business elsewhere.'

He had intended to go directly from Pacific Spacedrome to Paris. But for some reason no transplanetary flight was available for days which could accommodate the ponderous engine he had in charge. Swearing, he had got a surface boat to Honolulu and arranged a private charter. Now the crate rested in a hotel storeroom and he had a loose evening.

It didn't worry him. A few dollars to the service captain had let him leave Oscar on guard. The dirrel was quite able to chatter an alarm into a short-range sender in the unlikely event that something suspicious happened; and the receiver lay in Sevigny's tunic pocket. He hadn't told the quarantine inspector about that piece of equipment. It might be illegal, and he didn't intend to do without it.

'Damn,' said the girl. She frowned, charmingly. Then: 'Please don't think I'm forward. The mores on Venus are probably different from here. But . . . have you got anything particular to do tonight?'

'No. I was about to have dinner.' Sevigny's pulse quickened. 'Is there a chance of your joining me, my lady?'

'More than a chance, thank you. I know this looks like rushing matters, but you see, the whole interplanetary situation fascinates me. One hears so many arguments and, oh, documentaries on TriV and so forth, but all second hand. This is my first encounter with someone who's actually lived it.'

Sevigny managed to harness his delight and say in an academic tone, 'That's surprising. I thought you upper level people knew everybody.'

Her lashes fluttered. 'I'm not upper level, if you mean the ten or twenty per cent who keep civilization running. My father has money, yes, but he got it in entertainment.' She laughed anew. 'So I've a date with a man whose name I don't even know. I'm Maura Sumantri – born in Djakarta, educated in Chicago, and here for the surfriding.'

'Donald Sevigny, Clan Woodman of the Shaws, at your service.' He made a formal bow.

Her hand rested lightly in his before she said, 'I was supposed to eat at the Kamehameha tonight with my club. Nobody will be mad if I don't show, but I'd better call to tell them. 'Scuse. I'll be right back.'

With conscious pleasure, Sevigny watched her walk off. He had grown used to Earth weight faster than expected, but had forgotten how much it added to the female gait. The analytical part of him considered ways and means. She could prove expensive. However, he had a goodly piece of cash on him, and had been told to indulge himself a bit. . . . Why not? He hadn't relished the idea of a solitary evening. Now, with luck, he might have company till his jet took off tomorrow. Judging by how gracefully she moved, she hadn't tripped against him by accident.

Maura returned in a few minutes. She took his arm and they strolled to an elevator. 'I suppose I ought to decide where we're bound,' he said, 'but as a complete stranger . . .'

'Don't worry about clothes,' she said. 'On Earth a uniform is correct any place, from the Imperial Saturn to a Subchicago pot mill, and that outfit of yours is really a uniform, right? I like the Moon Room here myself. The view is gorgeous.'

'Quite,' he said, looking downwards.

At the top of the elevator's range, they were met by an expertly obsequious headwaiter and conducted to a table next the glasolite dome. Sevigny had stopped being surprised at the amount of live service in an automated society. What else was the bulk of the population able to do? He was also getting used to being stared at. The stares were discreet here, and largely veiled by dimness, but he knew he was a conspicuous object.

Seated, he turned eyes away from the shadowed people and caught his breath. Left and right at the foot of the Gold water's soaring skyscraper, Honolulu stretched farther than he could see, a galactic sprawl of light, ruby, old gold, topaz, emerald, turquoise, sapphire, amethyst, flashing and glistening across night-purple hills. Southwards the ocean sheened beneath a sky crowded with softened stars, and a lowering second quarter Moon turned the Waikiki surf to what he guessed a snowstorm must be.

Maura regarded him gravely. 'Yes,' she said, 'old Earth is beautiful, isn't she?'

'Here, at least,' he answered.

'M-m-m ... all right, I daresay you've seen pictures and statistics. Most of the planet has become rather awful. Too many people, too little opportunity. Your ancestors were right in going to Venus. But will you ever make it over into this?'

'Someday.' He thought, with an unawaited pang, of forests that roared in the wind, leaves that gleamed with raindrops, and a wild bull shaking his horns against nacreous heaven. 'Here and there, in its own way, it already is – no, not the same. Can't be. But we've got *room*.'

He pointed at Luna. Atmosphere fuzzed its edge, made the dark part glimmer and the bright part shine as men had never seen before. 'You Earth people, though, will have the same thing, yonder, in not too many more decades,' he said.

'Do you really believe that?'

'Why, of course. The Lunar area equals a fourth of Earth's land surface ...'

Cocktails arrived. Maura smiled and clinked glasses. 'I'm afraid you're an idealist, Don. But welcome, nevertheless.'

The martini was cold and pungent on his tongue. He studied the menu with scant comprehension. 'I must admit our eating habits are barbaric on Venus,' he surrendered, 'and the Corporation is more interested in nourishing our bodies than our souls. What do you suggest?'

'By Sol, a man who doesn't have to pretend masculinity! Let me see. ... Whale teriyaki looks good. With that we'd probably want consommé Mexique, filet of mahimahi, tossed salad, and may I be greedy and have ice cream with that wonderful Martian herb sauce for dessert?'

'Uh, champagne's right, isn't it?' He selected one by the simple criterion of price and gave his order.

Appetizers were set down, Pâté de fois gras, smoked oysters, marinated artichokes, and thousand-year eggs were separate adventures for Sevigny. 'A whole dimension of living,' he exulted. 'How can I thank you for programming me?'

'Show me around your planet in exchange, if I can eventually promote a ticket there.'

'You must. Frontiers don't happen often in history. The Moon's more accessible, true. But it won't have breathable air for a long time.'

'If ever.'

He gave her a puzzled look. 'Why are you so doubtful?'

'Oh ... one hears so many things. Like, well, doesn't Earth's magnetic field shield us from a lot of radiation? And the Moon hadn't got any to speak of.'

'Nor Venus. Given enough atmosphere, that doesn't matter. Ours amounts to a good bit more than yours.'

'But the Moon's so small! How can it hold on to gases?'

'Loss to space isn't that fast. They won't have to worry about it for an estimated half million years. As for atmospheric shielding, the Moon actually has an advantage over Earth. So low a gravitational field makes a correspondingly lower gradient. A surface pressure equal to three-fourths of Earth sea level, which is what's planned, means that there will be a measurable concentration at altitudes which correspond to open space here. Charged particles won't penetrate deep, and actinic rays will be absorbed.'

'I've heard, though, that there isn't enough gas to be had.'

'The selenologists swear there is. Not as such, naturally. As buried ice; water of crystallization; carbon, nitrogen, and sulphur compounds released when minerals – and the organics left over from the original nebula – break down. What we're doing, actually, is using deep wells and atomic bombs to start vulcanism. The same process that gave all the smaller planets their atmospheres. Only we're going to tickle Luna so much that everything will happen several orders of magnitude faster than it did in nature.'

'But suppose your figures are wrong?'

'That's been thought of. It won't be hard to deflect some comets into collision orbits, if necessary, and they're mostly big balls of frozen gas.' Sevigny chuckled. 'One way or another, the final stages ought to be quite a show – from this safe, comfortable distance!'

'And what will you have when you're finished?' she argued. 'Poisons.'

She can't be that ignorant. Can she? Must simply be making conversation. Letting me show off my male knowledge.

'Venus didn't have anything else,' he reminded her. 'Nitrogen, carbon dioxide, and a certain amount of water in the clouds. But the photosynthesizing algae grew exponentially once they'd been seeded in the upper atmosphere. They released oxygen; also, they kept sinking to lower levels where it was so hot they decomposed into carbon and water. The greenhouse effect dropped off until temperatures went below a hundred; and for ten years it rained without pause. Given liquid water, the Urey process operated, raw rock consumed still more CO_2 and at last there was air that men could breathe.' He sipped from his glass. 'Solar protons and ultraviolet radiation helped, too, especially in breaking down hydrogen compounds. In other words, a weak magnetic field is an asset to the terraformer.'

'Do you plan the same thing for Luna, then?'

'What else? Different in many details, of course. Luna isn't identical with Venus or ancient Earth. Right now the air we've already given it is a lot like Mars'. Radiation's been releasing oxygen from water; the free hydrogen goes up and the free oxygen promptly attacks methane, ammonia, sulphites and hydrogen sulphide. This yields carbon dioxide, free nitrogen, and more water to split. But once the atmosphere is thick enough – anyhow, that part is quite well understood, what has to be done. Far more so than the present stage of operations.' He thought of Decker, buried under the ruins of his own, Don Sevigny's, well, and his fingers tightened on the stem of his glass.

'What's wrong?' she asked gently.

'Nothing.' He drank. 'I was reminded of an accident we had recently. Rather not talk about that.'

There was a slight bustle as a pair of men were shown to a table close by. Sevigny couldn't help gawking. They were in ordinary clothes, but if the pictures in his school anthropology text hadn't lied, one was an Arab and one from India ... He recollected his manners. Besides, Maura was prettier.

'I hear rumours about your having trouble,' she was saying. 'That could get many people angry, the ones who claim the project has already cost more than it's worth.'

'I can't understand that attitude,' he said, and congratulated himself on how neatly he could dodge the question of accident rates. 'Seems to me a whole new world is worth a billion times any conceivable price you'll have to pay.'

'How many people will get any use out of that world? That's becoming a political issue too. They say only the rich will be able to live there.'

'Pure demagoguery, my lady. The corporation charter' – Sevigny was glad now that his chief had made him read it before departure – 'says that one fourth of the Moon is reserved for recreational purposes, and that there's to be adequate housing at decent prices for all residents. Who'll make a sizeable number, you realize. The Moon has rich mineral resources. Once it's habitable, those will really be exploited.'

He began to plagiarize other literature that had been given him: 'Also, the project develops sciences and technologies which'll be useful elsewhere. As an example of international co-operation, it strengthens the Commonwealth. The fact that a great deal of the Moon will be left in woods and meadows is important; Earth has very little greenscape any more. And ... not altogether pleasant to think about ... but nuclear weapons do exist and times of trouble may come back again. The more worlds colonized, the better the race's chances of lasting.'

'You've convinced me,' she said merrily, 'and here comes the soup. So let's talk about other things. Like yourself.'

'You're a more interesting subject . . . Maura.'

• 'Very well, we'll take turns.'

Clan culture discouraged individual boasting but Sevigny found it remarkably easy to glamorize himself. He didn't need to embroider his reminiscences much. She had never hunted, camped in a forest or a desert, trucked fish to a new ocean, built a dam, fought a battle . . . And he found that he had never gone submarining or seen an opera or been to a happy-pill party or—

'*T'ki!*'

The wind glass dropped from his hand and shattered.

'Don,' Maura cried low, 'what's the matter?'

He snatched the vibrating little box from his pocket and laid it to his ear. '*R-r-rik-ik-ik, t'ki, t'ki, ch!*'

Oscar the dirrel had no words for a great concrete chamber five levels below ground, or a ramp leading out, or a truck with a hoist. But it had to be that. *Men come, four men come, machine, fright, chase Oscar, thing-Oscar-watch go, Don, come, t'ki, ki, ki!*

Sevigny was half out of the room before Maura screamed.

The headwaiter, a blurred shape, a hand to shake off, 'Can I help you, sir?'

'No! Emergency!' The engineer burst from among the tables and plunged to the elevator.

It wasn't there. He stabbed the button again and again, while Oscar chittered fear and rage from the overhead pipes where he crouched.

Maura reached him. He saw her across an immenseness, hardly felt her hands drag at him. The tears didn't register either. 'Don, Don, what's wrong? Are you banzai? Please come back—'

The elevator door opened. He shoved her aside. 'I may be back in a while,' he got out.

Another shape brushed past her. The man was slender, chocolate-skinned, full lips curved very slightly upwards. 'May I?' he said, and entered the cage.

Sevigny recognized the Indian from the table near his. He tried to thrust him out, and grasped air. The man had dodged like a bird. 'Emergency,' Sevigny snarled once more.

'Perhaps I can help,' said the Indian blandly.

No time to waste on him. Sevigny punched for sub-Five. The door closed on Maura. Her face had lost its strickenness.

Weight decreased. 'May I suggest notifying the hotel detective?' the Indian said.

Jarred from his haste, Sevigny made himself think about that. It hadn't occurred to him; the clans took care of their own. 'Will you do so?' he asked. 'And the, uh, city police. There's a theft being committed in sub-Five Oh One.' He took his gun from the holster. 'I'll get out and see what I can do. You go straight back to the lobby and holler for troops.'

'Is the matter worth such a risk to yourself?'

A man of Clan Woodman was entrusted with that crate. 'Yes.'

'As you will. If you wonder, sir, why I left my own dinner to accompany you, may I present myself as a physican.' The narrow dark head bent in a slight bow. 'Dr Krishnamurti Lal Gupta of Benares, at your service. I was afraid you might have been taken ill.'

Rik-ik-chik-ri-ch, Don, come, fast come, screamed the box that Sevigny held.

He stuck it back into his pocket. The elevator slowed. *Sub-five* flashed on to the indicator panel. 'Stand by to raise her,' Sevigny said. The door glided open. He sprang into a bare, grey, coldly lit corridor.

Something stung him between the shoulders. He whirled with a curse. Gupta stood in the cage, a tiny flat pistol in one hand. He was still smiling. Sevigny's world dissolved in surf and darkness. He tried to raise his gun and couldn't. Its clatter when it hit the floor reached him as a remote and tiny thud. His knees gave way and he fell on top of it. He ceased to be.

Awareness was first of the same countenance, hovering above him with the same friendly expression. He struggled to sit up and Gupta stepped back. This time he held a hypodermic needle.

Crazily through the fog, Sevigny remembered Aarons bent over Leong while the volcano drowned Decker. Because someone had bombarded the keystone of a machine with X rays ... Rage rose in him, so strong that it had a taste. Adrenalin joined the counterdrug in his bloodstream. Strength and senses rushed forth. He bounded to his feet.

'Stop right there,' said a man across the room. He was the Arab who had been with Gupta. His eyes were the most intent that Sevigny had ever seen. The gun in his hand reined the Cytherean to a halt.

'That's better,' said the third man. He was sumptuously clad, in gold and scarlet that contrasted with Gupta's white simplicity and the gunman's sombreness; at the end of middle age, he was bald, wattled, and pot-gutted. But his jaw was like a ram and he spoke in a young voice. '*Mama mia!* When did a person come out from under a sleepy jolt this fast, Kreesho?'

'Rarely, Mr Baccioco,' said Gupta. 'But he is both strong and excited. Please relax, Clansman. We have no intention of harming you.'

A door opened. Maura came through. Sevigny paid more immediate attention to Oscar, who zoomed past her, went up his tunic in one streak, hugged him around the neck and unburdened his own soul so noisily that nothing else could be heard.

Sevigny got the dirrel quieted down at length, with much stroking and reassuring. Most of him, meanwhile, studied the surroundings. He was in a rich man's room, which seemed to be part of a suite. He couldn't identify the pictures that glowed from the walls, but they were likeliest totirepros of medieval European masters. The windows were blanked out, and no sound penetrated from beyond. A clock said 2345.

Maura had settled into a relaxer. Her gown was changed for slacks and blouse. The effect remained explosive. She smoked a cigarette in short hard puffs and did not return his look.

Gupta sat at ease on a couch upholstered in what Sevigny thought must be genuine leather; cheap on Venus, but he'd been told that an Earthman might go through life without seeing any. The older man, Baccioco, prowled back and forth, hands tightly clasped behind his back. The Arab waited in a corner, weapon now pointed at the floor but eyes never leaving Sevigny.

'Well, are his fears allayed, the little fellow?' Gupta said. 'Fine, fine. You will, I hope, Clansman Sevigny, take his presence as earnest of our good intentions. When you were brought unconscious into the storeroom and laid in the truck — what else could we do? — your pet stormed down from his hiding place and fell upon you. I was forced to anaesthetize him too, his distress was so noisy, but had not the heart to leave him behind.'

'Thanks for that,' Sevigny said curtly.

'Please do not be too discomfited at your present situation—'

'Mainly I'm disgusted. With myself.' Sevigny stared so long at Maura that she had to turn her face to him. 'I walked right into the oldest trap in the universe, didn't I?' He spat at her feet.

'*Maròn!*' Baccioco gestured indignantly. 'Is that a decent way to behave? Watch yourself!'

'We must make allowances, sir,' Gupta soothed him.

Maura bit her lip. 'We never meant to hurt you, Don,' she said in a flat voice. 'I was only supposed to keep you busy till the thing had been removed. And as long afterwards as possible. I wish it had gone that way. I was honestly enjoying your company.'

'How did you learn?' the Arab demanded.

'Shut up, Rashid,' Baccioco said.

'Well, it is a question we meant to ask,' Gupta said. 'Do you mind telling us, Clansman?'

They don't know Oscar can— That might be a hole card. Barely might. Sevigny held his face rigid and shrugged. 'I put a scanner among the overhead pipes, connected to a microcaster. You doubtless found the receiver in my tunic.'

Baccioco studied him. Silence grew, under the white fluorescents, among the thick red drapes, until the slither when Rashid shuffled his feet was startlingly loud. A whiff of Maura's cigarette drifted to Sevigny, acrid when he remembered the perfume of earlier. Without his gun he felt naked, lopsided; and Oscar's warm weight on his shoulder was not much comradeship.

'Well,' Baccioco said, 'that sounds reasonable. I will have a man search for your scanner tomorrow, to make quite certain. As for now, though, here we are, no? You don't want to be here and we don't want to have you here. What to do?'

'I suggest we all begin by reducing our tensions,' Gupta said in his mild fashion. 'Maura, would you be so good as to fetch coffee? Or would anyone prefer something stronger?'

Nobody replied. The girl rose and left the room. Her head drooped a little.

'Do be seated, gentlemen,' Gupta went on. Baccioco snorted but threw himself into an armchair. After a moment, Sevigny took another. Rashid remained standing in his corner.

'We should show our guest the courtesy of further identifying ourselves,' Gupta said. 'Signor Baccioco is—'

'No!' the Italian broke in.

'Yes!' Gupta responded. 'Please consider. If Clansman Sevigny remembers your name at all, or even your appearance, he need only ask the first alert person he meets in order to be told that Ercole Baccioco is chairman of the board of Eureclam S.A. You must not be so modest about your reputation, sir ... Having inevitably revealed that much, I trust I can do no harm in describing our friend Rashid Gamal ibn Ayith as a representative, in our organization, of the Fatimite Brotherhood. As for myself, I am actually a physician, but may have gained a small prominence through my activity in the Conservationist Party of my native land.'

A corporation head, a politician, and some kind of religious fanatic. The girl, I suppose, a hireling, like those workers who removed the force unit. What are they doing together, tonight? As Sevigny's muscles tautened, Oscar bristled on his lap. He stroked the dirrel into calm. Oscar had to remain very, very inconspicuous.

'The matter must be important, to bring people like you here,' he said slowly.

'Critical indeed,' Gupta nodded. 'It was essential for us to obtain possession of that engine.' *Then they knew I was bringing it to Earth. So there's a spy in the Buffalo's top staff. He could have sent a coded radiogram without attracting notice; that's common enough. Still, if we get a chance to check the Comcenter records ...* 'Through various connections, we arranged that you would be delayed in Honolulu overnight.' *Thunder and fury, how many tentacles have they got?* 'But believe me, I beg you, there was no idea of involving you otherwise. That was pure misfortune.'

'Why did you want the unit?' Sevigny asked.

No one replied. Maura came in with cups on a tray. She went among the men, lingering briefly by Sevigny. He took his cup without regarding her. Rashid refused his. She sat down again.

'This is ridiculous,' Baccioco grumbled. 'Far past my bedtime, and here I sit talking with a ... an outplanet savage.'

'Not the least ridiculous, sir,' Gupta said, 'and in many respects the Cytherean culture is preferable to any on modern Earth.' He took an appreciative sip. 'Ah! Do notice the coffee, Clansman. Hawaiian kona is one of the glories of this planet ... Information for information. If you will tell us what you know and surmise, we shall reciprocate. Gladly. We want you to understand that our motives are altruistic. Who knows, you may even enlist in our cause.'

'Can you believe him?' Rashid growled.

'What do you have against me?' Sevigny flung at him.

The gun lifted a few centimetres. 'You defile God's work.'

'As you may readily learn by watching a few newscasts, the Fatimite Brotherhood takes a fundamentalistic view of terraforming,' Gupta said. 'A change in the appearance of the moon is especially distressing. Little can be done to reverse the process, but it should not be allowed to go any farther.'

'And you?' Sevigny inquired.

Gupta uttered a short laugh. 'Now, now. Pray do not look for vast, complicated motivations. Such things occur only on the TriV. The Conservationist Party of India, like its counterparts in numerous other countries, maintains quite openly that the Luna Corporation is wasting enormous, badly needed resources on a utopian scheme that, if it can be realized at all, will not make any difference to Earth for decades to come.'

'Isn't your own government a major stockholder?'

'True. The Vishnuists unfortunately command a parliamentary majority.' Lightness left the voice and the big dark eyes turned incandescent. 'City dwellers! They have not been out in the hinterlands, have not watched children starve because soil is exhausted and water tables are emptied and raw materials too costly for chemosynthesis. *There* is the place to begin reclamation!' He finished his cup in one draught. His hand shook.

'And ... hum.' Sevigny rested his gaze on Baccioco. 'Eureclam S.A. Chartered and equipped, no doubt, for work on Earth only. There'll be plenty of fat contracts to make the deserts fertile and so forth, if the Moon job is abandoned. Hey?'

Baccioco reddened. 'The question is not of money but of sound policy.'

'So you say. But look, you must realize that in the long run the Moon'll pay off ten times what Earth can.'

'Too long a run,' Gupta said. 'It will dehumanize us to plan in such terms.'

'I told you, Don, a political fight is going on.' Maura could barely be heard.

'Which your side is losing,' Sevigny pounced.

'What makes you think so?' Baccioco retorted angrily.

'Otherwise you wouldn't have to resort to sabotage.'

'That is a most serious accusation,' Gupta said.

'Why else did you steal that force unit?' Sevigny challenged. 'You couldn't afford to let me bring evidence of your work to the Safety Corps. An investigation would blow your gang open.'

Gupta spread his hands. 'I cannot tell you everything,' he said, 'and hence cannot at this moment refute your statement, however false it be. I will swear by anything you wish that you would not have missed your engine, had all gone well. But come, now, I offered information for information. Your turn, Clansman.'

'What the devil have I got to tell you? I was only an errand boy.'

'You had numerous confidential talks with Mr Bruno Norris. How much hard data does he possess? How much does he surmise?'

Sevigny leaned back and grinned at them. Inside, hatred made a cold lump in his stomach. Erich Decker, a man under command of a Woodman, had been murdered by agents of these.

Rashid took a step forward. 'You will talk,' he said. 'There are ways.'

'Please.' Gupta lifted a palm. 'Nothing violent. Means have a sorry habit of affecting ends.'

'There has been too much kitten play,' Baccioco declared. 'He will most certainly talk.'

Okay, we might as well bring it out in the open. 'I'm bound to talk when you let me go, am I not?' Sevigny said. The hatred left scant room for fear, but the blood thrummed in his veins. 'That fairly well proves you won't let me go, alive at any rate. So what have I to gain by helping you?'

In the return of the stillness, where Baccioco's breath rattled with rheum, he thought: *Maybe they always intended to kidnap me. The theft of my evidence would itself be evidence — No, wait. If I'd not burst in on them, they could have substituted another force unit, also damaged but in a way that'd look like ordinary failure, that'd give no clues to the Safety Corps labs. ... That must be it. So Gupta wasn't lying when he said I'd never have missed my engine.*

But now I can tell what's happened, under truth drug, and an investigation will start regardless.

If I can get away whole, that is.

Maura lit another cigarette. Her free hand clenched.

Gupta leaned forward, elbows on knees, fingers bridged, and peered amiably at Sevigny. 'Clansman,' he said, 'we serve a humane cause. But we are determined that it shall prevail. No one will wonder at your disappearance for days. The message to Corps headquarters in Paris, that you were coming, never left the Moon. Mr Norris will not expect to hear from you until you have something definite to report. Meanwhile, as you doubtless know, there are certain potent psychopharmaceuticals which will elicit information even from unwilling subjects. There is also a treatment to remove memories. And ... I am a mdical man.'

He paused. 'The experience of being interrogated under drugs is admittedly unpleasant,' he said. 'Memory removal involves a grave risk of removing too much. Moreover, at best you would be found in the gutter, apparently at the end of a monumental debauch, in the course of which you had lost the object entrusted to you. It would do credit to neither yourself nor your clan.

'You are a foreigner, owing no duty to any organization on Earth. If you consider the matter objectively, you will surely, as a reasonable man, see that justice lies with us. Not to mention the prospect of substantial material reward. Think well.'

He stood up. 'The hour is late,' he said. 'Everyone is tired. Please accept our hospitality for the night. I will discuss the subject with you again tomorrow. Through that door, if you will be so kind.'

Now!

Sevigny slid a hand under Oscar. He poked with a hard thumb. The dirrel hopped to his hind legs and chattered out a protest.

'What ails him this time?' asked Baccioco sourly.

'Excitement. Let me cool him off,' Sevigny said. He began murmuring.

'You remember, your pet is a hostage, too,' Baccioco said. 'Nasty things could happen to him.'

'*Tk-tk quee ch-rik, k-k-k-ti-oo—*' Oscar crouched like a cat. Sevigny picked him up in one arm and rose. Rashid glided near, gun aimed at the Cytherean's breast.

'You will rest sounder if you take a sleeping tablet,' Gupta smiled. 'I shall come along to your room and give you one.'

'Better than chains, huh?' Sevigny looked around at Maura. Damn, but she was a dish! 'Good night, my lady.'

'Good night,' she whispered.

Rashid passed Sevigny, two metres away, to get behind him.

'*Ki-ik!*'

Oscar leaped. Sevigny went to one knee. But the bullet did not fly where he had been. It cracked into the floor. Oscar had already landed on Rashid's wrist.

The Arab cursed and struck, Oscar sank teeth into his hand. Rashid yelled. Sevigny charged across the distance between. Gupta clawed at him. Sevigny's left fist met the Indian's face. Gupta lurched aside. Sevigny kicked Rashid in the larynx. The Arab fell in a heap. The gun clattered free. Sevigny scooped it up and jumped back out of reach.

'Okay,' he panted, 'stay where you are.'

Maura screamed. 'Be still!' Sevigny told her. He didn't know if there was anyone else in this apartment. Slowly, he moved to the wall until he covered every approach.

'*Tu porco—*' Baccioco was aiding Gupta to rise. Blood dripped heavily from the doctor's mouth. Oscar joined Sevigny and gibbered at the whole world. His fur stood on end.

Rashid got to hands and knees. He stayed there a second

or two, fighting for breath, before he climbed to unsteady feet.

Gupta shook his head. The daze cleared from his eyes. 'What do you plan to do?' he mumbled through puffed lips.

'Call the police,' Sevigny told him. 'Where's your phone?'

Rashid pulled a knife from inside his blouse and moved towards the Cytherean. He made mewing sounds and his eyes were crazy. Maura's mouth opened again where she huddled in her relaxer.

'Stop or I'll shoot,' Sevigny said to the Arab.

'He won't stop,' Gupta said. 'You will have to kill him.'

Rashid edged closer, he held the knife in an expert underhand grip. His tread wobbled, but . . .

'For that matter,' Gupta said, 'I intend to make a break for help. I recommend that Miss Sumantri and Signor Baccioco do the same. Since you do not know where the alarm buttons are that will summon others, you will have to shoot the three of us. The American police do not look kindly upon homicide. You may have some difficulty in proving self-defence.'

Sevigny moved crabwise along the wall until he was near a footstool. He snatched it with his free hand and threw it at Rashid. The Arab fell as the object hit him in the abdomen, staggered erect again, and resumed his weak, relentless advance.

'All right!' Sevigny yelped. He passed his hand above the plate of what seemed to be the main door. It opened for him and he saw a corridor beyond, an elevator waiting not far down.

'If that lunatic chases me I will shoot,' he said. 'I'll try only to disable him.' He backed through the door with Oscar and let it close. The other entrances he could see along the short length of the hall were on the same side, probably every one leading back into the suite. He retreated fast.

Fifty floors down, the elevator let him out into a lobby, small and empty despite its polished marble. 'Blastula,' he muttered, 'I'd hoped this was a hotel.' But no. You couldn't get away with as much in one as you could in a sound-proofed apartment. Baccioco probably maintained a number of those, around the planet. Sevigny debated whether to borrow someone's phone here. If he left this exit unwatched, his enemies could escape before the police arrived.

On the other hand, if he hung around they might well find some way to recapture him. And as for their escape, come to think of it, men as prominent as Baccioco and – he supposed – Gupta couldn't disappear. Rashid was little more than a tool. And he found himself hoping a bit that Maura would go free.

Oscar made comforting noises on his shoulder.

He walked out on to the street. It was wide and softly lit, lined with tall residential buildings. An occasional car went by, the whisper of its air cushion blending with the warm breeze that rustled in palm fronds. He was high above the ocean, which he glimpsed at the edge of the city glitter beneath. The Moon was no longer in sight, but he made out a few stars.

Where was the nearest public phone? He chose an eastward course arbitrarily and began striding. His buskins thudded; the slight jar and the sense of kinaesthesia helped shake a little tightness out of him. But his skin was still wet, his stink sharp against a background of jasmine.

At the end of the block a pedestrian belt lifted him over the street. From the top of its arc he spied some glowsigns to the north, and headed that way. Before long he reached a cluster of shops. They were closed for the night, but even in his hurry he lost a few seconds gaping at their display windows. Was such luxury possible on an Earth that everyone called impoverished? *Wait. Remember your history classes. Inordinate wealth for a few has always gone along with inordinate want for the many. Because the many no longer have the economic strength to resist . . . .*

That recalled him to his purpose. A booth stood at the corner. He went in, fumbled for a half dollar, and dropped the coin in the slot. The screen lit. He needed a minute to figure out how the system worked. On Venus and Luna they used radio for distance calls, intercoms when indoors. Finally he punched the button marked Directory and spelled out POLICE on the alphabet keys. A set of station numbers appeared. He dialled.

A face and a pair of uniformed shoulders came to view. 'Honolulu Central. Can I help you?'

'I want to report a theft and a kidnapping,' Sevigny said. It felt odd not to be telling his troubles to a clan elder.

The voice and eyes sharpened. 'Where are you?'

Sevigny peered out at the signs and read them off. 'I don't know where the nearest station would be. I'm a stranger here.'

'Name, please?' The man droned through a maddening series of questions. 'Very well,' he ended, 'stay where you are and we'll dispatch a patrol.'

Sevigny fretted for a time which seemed a deal longer than it was. When two dark teardrop shapes halted by the curb his heart slugged.

A large sergeant with an unexpectedly amiable brown face got out of one. 'You the party sent for us?' he asked. Sevigny nodded. The officer took a minitaper from the pouch at his belt and thumbed the switch. 'Tell me about it.'

Sevigny went through the account in as a few words as possible. When he spoke Baccioco's name, the policeman pursed his lips in a soundless whistle. At the conclusion he turned to the car he had come from and said, 'What you make of this, Bradford?'

'Damfino,' said the indistinct shape within, 'but sounds creaky to me.'

'You're serious, Mr Sevigny?' the sergeant wondered.

'I sure as hell am,' the Cytherean rasped. 'And I suggest, instead of a lot of silly questions, you arrest them before they take off.'

'Well, we can't do that on your bare word unless you make a formal complaint. Want to come down to the station with us? I ought to warn you, you being outplanet, if this isn't the truth you're in bad trouble.'

'I'll confirm what I said under drugs, damn you!'

'Hey, hey, take it easy. I'm not calling you a liar. The boys in the other car will go talk to these people and follow them if they leave. So let us be on our way.' The officer opened the rear door and gestured at Sevigny to enter first. The plain-clothesman in front fed instructions to the pilot and the car got moving.

Turning around, the detective gave Sevigny a hard look. 'Maybe your side is fighting back, huh?' he said.

'What do you mean?' With an effort, the engineer kept his hand away from the gun at his hip.

'Making up stories to discredit the people who're campaigning against the Luna Corporation. Everybody knows President Edwards has been trying to get the Commonwealth Council to revoke its charter; and this is an election year, here in the States. A nice ripe scandal could toss Edwards out and shoo Hernandez in – and *he* wants to sink more American money into Corporation stock.'

Oscar sensed hostility, fluffed out his tail and clicked his teeth together.

'Whoa, there, Bradford,' said the officer in back. 'You're letting your prejudices run away with you.' He turned to Sevigny. 'Me, I think this work on the Moon is the greatest thing that's happened since Maui's time. My grandchildren'll have elbow room like my grandfather used to talk about. Uh, my name's Kealoha, John Kealoha.'

Sevigny shook the big hand. 'Glad to meet you,' he said. 'I'd begun to wonder if anybody on Earth wanted us to succeed.'

'Sure. Anybody who can see past the end of his own snout. Why else would the opposition have to turn criminal?'

'That story's plain fantastic,' Bradford said. 'I'd like to interrogate you, Sevigny, the two of us alone.'

The Cytherean's jaw closed. He'd taken more than he would have imagined possible without drawing a weapon. 'Any time!'

'Slack off, you two,' Kealoha urged. 'Bradford, he said he'd take babble juice. Let the doc quiz him.'

A waiting silence fell. Eventually the car stopped before precinct headquarters. The building was dwarfed by the apartment houses around, but thickly formed in concrete, doubtless a relic of the Unrest years. Mass aberration could come back again, Sevigny thought; and it would, if Earth's population didn't find some outlet. Not that the Moon would relieve crowding here, to any noticeable degree. But a place for temporary escape . . .

As they debarked, Bradford grasped the engineer's arm. 'Come along, you,' he ordered: and let go with a yell. Sevigny had cracked the blade of a hand across his wrist.

'You—'

Kealoha shoved his bulk between them. 'None o' that,' he rumbled. 'You had no call to hustle him, Bradford. And you, Sevigny, don't ever resist an officer. Not ever.'

'Even when I'm in the right?' The Cytherean was so astonished that half the anger drained from him. It flowed back and his mouth twisted. 'Judas! I can't get off Earth too fast.'

Under Bradford's glower, he entered the building. A lieutenant of police, evidently in charge at night, waited by the sergeant at the desk. 'Sevigny?'

The curious, pale-cheeked tensions of him registered only faintly through the engineer's emotions. 'Yes. I want to file some charges.'

'Well, that takes time. We have to get hold of a judge, you know, before you can swear out a warrant.'

Bradford's expression froze. Kealoha's mouth fell open. The lieutenant frowned at him and made a slight negative gesture. Behind his desk, the other sergeant sat as if cast in metal.

'I'll make the call right away,' the lieutenant said. 'Meanwhile, turn your gun over to us.'

Sevigny shook his head. 'No. I have the right, by interplanetary agreement.'

'And we have regulations. Do you want our help or don't you?'

A sense of being caught in some purposeless machine

overwhelmed Sevigny. Without a word, he laid Rashid's pistol on the desk. It hadn't fitted his holster very well anyway. He sagged into a chair and stared across the bleak, harshly lit room, at nothing. Bradford grinned. Kealoha seemed puzzled and distressed.

The lieutenant went behind the desk and dialled. 'Mac-Ewen speaking, twelfth precinct station,' he said. 'Sevigny's here.' He cut the circuit before there was a reply, came back, and extended his hand with a smile. 'The judge is on his way,' he said. 'Glad to meet you, Clansman.'

Something strange ... But all Earth was an abyss of otherness. Sevigny shook hands unenthusiastically. 'Did you alert him in advance, then?' he asked.

'Yes.' MacEwen sat down, offered a pack of cigarettes, and took one for himself. 'The, um, the situation was peculiar. We didn't know whether it'd be best to take you here or to main headquarters. So we asked Judge Hughes to stand by.'

'Lieutenant ...' Kealoha began.

'Shut up,' MacEwen said. His voice was quiet but edged. Turning to Sevigny: 'This is as odd a case as I ever heard about. You mustn't blame us for being careful.'

'Too damn careful!' A little life returned to the Cytherean. He sat straight. 'I don't know anything about police methods, but what are you idling here for? That force unit is important evidence of ... sabotage, murder, conspiracy. Why haven't you got a crew, squad, whatever you call 'em, at the Hotel Goldwater this minute, finding out how the devil those men got in with their truck and loaded a piece of goods registered to me?'

'Don't worry, Clansman,' MacEwen said. 'There've been calls burning the lines throughout Honolulu.' He hesitated. 'And beyond. But don't you see, this is an international case. If your story is true, some mighty important foreigners are involved. It may be too big for us, may need the Safety Corps.'

'So call them. They must have a local office.'

'Please, Clansman. I promise you we've got things under

way. You'll have to be patient. While you wait for . . . for the judge, suppose you report what happened to you.'

'I already have. Twice.'

'That must've been pretty brief, though. You were in a hurry. We'll need to know everything you can recall. Best to put it on tape now, while it's fresh in your mind.' MacEwen went back to a shelf for a recorder. 'Sergeant Kealoha, how about getting us some coffee?'

'You're not even going to put him in an interrogation room?' the policeman asked incredulously.

'Get. That. Coffee. Sergeant.'

Kealoha went out. He looked defeated. MacEwen started the recorder. 'Go ahead, Clansman,' he invited. 'Start as far back as possible.'

Sevigny yielded. 'That would be on the Moon,' he sighed. 'I was in charge of a deeptap gang . . .'

'. . . so we went to dinner and talked. Not about anything significant.' It hurt even to tell this much. 'Suddenly . . .'

'. . . a needle gun. I passed out.' Kealoha, who had been standing close by, refilled Sevigny's cup.

'. . . he claimed . . .'

The door opened. Two men in unobtrusive clothes entered. They were both young and hard-featured. 'Excuse me,' MacEwen blurted, jumping to his feet. The fifth successive cigarette smouldered between his fingers. 'Are you the Federals?'

'Yes.' One of them flashed a badge. The other nodded at Sevigny, who crouched forward in his chair. 'That him?'

'Right.' MacEwen stepped aside. There was awe in his expression.

The two men walked quickly over to the engineer. 'Donald Sevigny,' one said, not a question but a statement which didn't wait for reply. 'We're from the Federal Police Agency of the United States.'

'So?' Sevigny rose, balanced on the ends of his feet. He sensed a wrongness; his skin prickled. Oscar poised humpbacked on his shoulder, tail flicking from side to side. Kealoha, MacEwen, and the desk sergeant grew altogether motionless. Bradford grinned afresh where he sat. For a space the silence was broken only by the remote drone of a freight-craft lumbering overhead.

'You are under arrest. Come along.'

'What?' In spite of every premonition, the words struck like lightning. Sevigny took a backwards step. His right hand grabbed for the gun that was no longer there, his left lifted as if to plead. 'Are you crazy on Earth?'

'Come along, I said.' A needler seemed to appear from nowhere in the first man's fingers.

'Wait a minute!' Kealoha bellowed.

'Be quiet, sergeant,' MacEwen ordered.

Huge and blue in his uniform, the policeman stood his ground. 'You've already took too much advantage of him being ignorant. He's got a right to know the charge. I can't let you make an improper arrest.'

'Conspiracy to violate the sovereignty retained by the United States government under the Commonwealth,' clipped the second man.

'Nothing doing.' Kealoha shook his head. 'Too vague. I know the law. What's he supposed to have done?'

'Go to quarters, sergeant, or I'll break you,' MacEwen said. 'Damn it, these are *Federal* officers! Take him away, gentlemen.'

Conspiracy indeed, it tolled through the thudding in Sevigny's skull. *Baccioco and Company got on the phone the minute I left. They must have partners in Washington. The President himself is anti-Lunar. Word went back, the city police were to keep me for these . . .*

The second agent took a pair of handcuffs from his pocket. 'You Cythereans have a reputation for violence,' he said. 'Hold out your wrists.'

'God damn you, no!' Three generations of pride sent Sevigny recoiling. 'Not on a clansman!'

The first man aimed his needler.

Oscar the dirrel knew only that his boss was threatened. He shrieked and launched himself. The anaesthetic dart flew wide. Oscar swarmed up the agent's blouse and went after the eyes. The other man whipped his handcuffs across the animal's nose, got hold of the tail and hurled him to the floor. Bradford left his chair, pistol out. It coughed twice. Blood spurted.

'K-ti,' said the ragged thing which had been Oscar, and died.

There was no time for thought, caution, anything but revenge. Sevigny leaped. His right fist buried itself in the solar plexus of the first Federal. He could feel the shock, distantly and impersonally, in his shoulderblade. The agent sank to his knees, retching. Sevigny twirled. The other one's needler was out. Sevigny's foot lashed. The weapon arced across the room. Sevigny moved in, grabbed collar and belt, and threw the man against Bradford. Both went down.

'Stop!' Kealoha shouted. His own gun barked. A star rayed out in the wall where the bullet smote.

'Shoot to hit, you idiot!' Bradford rolled free and scrabbled for his pistol.

Sevigny went out the door. He was a dead man if he stayed. Kealoha was not far behind. The officer's shots whanged right and left. He stopped in the entrance, blocking it.

'Get out of the way!' Bradford screamed.

Kealoha stood where he was and fired at the night. Sevigny ran across the street. Lamps glared everywhere— No, that dark building across from him, surrounded by garden, tall stands of bamboo, and he was a hunter from the Shaws— He fled towards darkness.

Flat on the ground beneath a rose hedge that raked at him, he watched two policemen go a metre past his nose. Their footfalls vibrated through the damp grass and their flashlights made bobbing spears in the murk. When they were beyond him, he started to crawl.

The grounds opened on another street. He peered from the shadow shelter of a hedge. Cars whirred by against shimmering store fronts, but he saw no pedestrians. He had to get out of this district fast, before a cordon was established. In spite of having spent a year under Lunar gravity, he could doubtless outrun any urbanite: not a needle or a bullet.

A vacant taxi came cruising by. He sprang out and waved. For a ghastly moment he thought its scanner had missed him. It stopped and he tumbled inside. The robot voice of a central monitor asked, 'Where do you wish to go?'

'Head for the harbour,' he panted. That area should be safely distant from here, though the safety wouldn't last. The machine purred into motion. A police car wailed and Sevigny huddled low. But they didn't think to stop his vehicle for a search. That would soon occur to them. His one lonely asset was a habit of swift action.

The avenues, seen on the edge of vision, took on a flickering quality as the taxi gained speed. He had already used this kind of transportation, from the dock to his hotel – God of time, scarcely twelve hours ago! – and knew how it worked. He fed money to the phone and punched for information on automats. Comparison of addresses with the posted city map gave him the location of one near the waterfront. He told the monitor to send him there, sat back, and tried to rest.

The first rage and grief were past. Poor loyal Oscar had come a long way to die; but it was up to him to use the dirrel's last gift. He wondered, briefly, if he could have escaped without that stimulus of *berserkergang*. Consciousness might never have got so reckless. But now the fighting man's reflexes had taken him as far as they could. Only brain would keep him free.

There was no use arguing with himself whether he should have done what he did. His act probably was right. The more he considered the behaviour of the Federals, the less aboveboard it looked. Once in custody, he would most likely not have been taken to a nice public jail and allowed to call for legal help. He didn't relish guessing what would have happened instead. But no difference that. The fact was he had resisted arrest, assaulted law officers, and made himself a fugitive who could be shot on sight by the most honest of constables.

He stared out at the city. It was so gigantic, so inhuman, that he must choke down panic. What to do now, where to hide, whom to trust anywhere on the turning planet.

One step at a time, he scolded. That reminded him, in his friendlessness, of his old drillmaster in war school; of parade grounds dusty in the hot grey light of day, enchanted through Venus' long, aurora-lit night; horseplay in barracks, the clean oil smell of weapons, manoeuvres and marches and companionship in bivouac; and he calmed himself with the chant that had gone over so many kilometres, *Left, right! Left, right! It's seventeen marches to water, it's twenty-eight farther to beer. But when we come toddling to Helltown, the hell girls will see us and cheer. Left, right! Left, right . . .*

The taxi stopped. He gave it thirty dollars, took his change, and went quickly out when the door unlocked for him. He'd need transportation again soon, but best not use this one. Though his image was wiped by the monitor as soon as it ascertained everything was in order, the record would remain that a fare had been picked up close in space-time to the escape episode. The cab droned off to seek other trade, leaving him alone in a satisfactorily asleep neighbourhood.

A depressing one, though. The darkened tenements that lifted around him, blocking off world and all but a string of sky, were not tumbledown like many he had seen pictures of. This was no slum, must in fact be a lower middle class district. But they were uglier and less personal than Lunar domes, the spacing of windows bespoke the crampedness of apartments, and a faint stench hung in the air of too many bodies too close together.

Yes . . . Earth needed a living Moon.

As Sevigny had hoped, there was no watchman in the automat – everything must be equipped with alarms that went directly to the nearest police station – and no other customer at this hour. Compared to the one in Port Kepler, the place was stupefying. He zigzagged around for minutes before locating the tailor booth. Once inside, he took off his clothes and activated the measure. From the fabric samples

he chose something cheap and dark blue, from the styles the
one that seemed most conservative. The price appeared on a
screen, he stuffed in money, machines hummed, a door
opened in the wall and a parcel slid forth. He donned the
outfit, wrapped his clan garments, and – not without a sense
of guilt – pitched them down the first waste chute he came
upon.

Now I won't be quite so easy to find.

He wasn't hungry, but he felt the beginnings of weakness
and his hands trembled. A drug vendor displayed more
brands of pills than he had known existed. Its battered appearance suggested that it saw a lot of use. He chose a stimulant combined with a mild euphoriac, and tapped himself a
cup of coffee at the lunch dispenser to play with while the
pill took effect.

And while he groped for a plan.

*Once beyond American territory, I should be safe. If the
Federals then want me on their damned charge, they'll
have to apply to the World Safety Corps. And they aren't
likely to do that; it'd provoke too many questions. So I
shouldn't have anything to fear except assassins.* Scornfully:
*If what I've met is a fair sample, that's nothing to fret a
clansman.*

Worry returned. *How am I going to get away, though? I
haven't got the price of a flier, even if I dared try to buy one.
Every outgoing common carrier will be under surveillance.
Give a robot at headquarters my description, hook a motion
analyser into the circuit to watch for characteristics like
walk and gesture, which've been well documented by the
socioanthropologists, then feed in continuous data from
scanners at every ticket office and embarkation point . . . I
can't possibly disguise myself well enough.*

He could try to reach the local Corps office . . . No. If it
had not itself been corrupted, it would be staked out in an
ticipation of just such an attempt. At least, he had better no
assume otherwise. Suppose he phoned and asked for a
escort there . . . That was out, too. The Commonwealth'
peace officers had, he remembered from reading, no author

ity to keep a man wanted on a strictly local warrant. And it would take too long to convince them that this was an international problem. The most he could hope to do was get them interested, and an eventual investigation started. Meanwhile he would have been taken off by the Federals, who served a desperate set of masters.

The same argument applied even more strongly to the Luna Corporation's Honolulu agents.

The whole planet wasn't hunting him. He must hang on to that fact, must remember powerful men like Norris and humble ones like Kealoha. If he could get in touch with those who were influential, there would be lawyers, publicity, political and financial pressure on his behalf. Only, who? It had to be someone in town to begin with, and he didn't know anyone. Besides, you didn't simply buzz a vip, you hacked your way through an abatis of underlings, and during that time the police closed in.

The Buffalo was easily accessible to him, and could perhaps tell him where to take cover, but he hadn't the cash to commission a message to the Moon over a pay phone.

Sanctuary, breathing space, a man of some importance who could act for him—

Wait!

Sevigny's breath quickened. He dashed to a call booth, punched for the directory, and spelled out CONSULATES.

So few of their people visited Earth that the Cytherean clans kept nothing more than a joint embassy in Paris. But Mars did a considerable amount of trade, especially since the Lunar project began, and the Great Confederation of Y had long agreed, for a fee, that its local representatives would look after any Cytherean problems that arose. Also, the Martians had extraterritoriality . . .

There was only one outplanet listing. 'Mars.' Sevigny scratched his head in wonder. Every major society maintained its own diplomats, he knew, not only an ambassador to the Commonwealth but a minister to each important nation . . . Well, evidently a mere city consulate was different. Y and Illach and Hs'ach and the rest could save money there by employing a single person together.

Sevigny consulted Public Data and learned that in this case the person wasn't even Martian by race. Again, though, it made sense. Why build an expensive dome and supply expensive sealed cars and antiweight drugs for an agent who doubtless worked part time and on largely routine business?

The Who's Who file informed him that Oleg N. Volhontseff had been born fifty-eight years ago in the Ga'ea'm region of K'nea, child of a biologist in the scientific colony; had received his elementary education there, taken degrees at Moscow and Brasilia, returned to Mars as a xenologist, and only in the last few years retired to work on his books. An impressive catalogue of scholarly publications marched over the phone screen ... why, wait, Volhontseff was the man who had translated the *T'hu-Rayi*, he must think as much like a Martian as was possible for a human brain; no wonder he'd never married!

'Better and better,' Sevigny exulted, sent for a cab and left. He didn't think the pill alone had put bounce back into his stride.

Volhontseff's office was at home, in the hills above the university. The neighbourhood was lawns, bowers, individual houses of some architectural distinction. To a Cytherean it felt crowded; nevertheless, on today's Earth this must be a wealthy district. Half-time consular pay couldn't be lavish, nor the royalties from monographs on things like Illachi fosterbirth practices. Had the man inherited a private fortune?

Sevigny glided from the cab into the darkness under a tree and stood for a while straining his senses. Nothing moved but leaves in the breeze, under a velvety dark sky embroidered with constellations. A window spilled yellow light on to Volhontseff's yard. *Good, I was afraid I'd have to wake him.* Sevigny walked up a gravelled path, that scrunched louder than he liked to the front door. As he mounted the porch, he heard the bell peal. For the benefit of the viewer screen he tried to look harmless.

The door opened. A small man in a brown robe glared at him from disconcertingly bright green eyes, set in a nut-cracker face beneath a high hairless skull. 'Well, sir?' Volhontseff crackled.

'I'm sorry to bother you so late—' Sevigny began.

'I should hope so. I always do my writing at night. Had half a mind not to answer. Who are you and what do you want?'

'May I come in?'

'Not without stating your business.'

'I'm Donald Sevigny of Clan Woodman on Venus—'

'Yes, yes, your accent is obvious. No one but a Shawdweller treats English diphthongs thus. Why are you not in national costume?'

'Well, I – oh, hell. I claim sanctuary. Frisk me for weapons if you like.'

Volhontseff didn't so much as blink. 'Sanctuary from whom?'

'Enemies of the Luna Corporation,' Sevigny snapped, exasperated, 'and you know how important that's become to the Martian economy. This is your affair as well as mine.'

'Indeed? The project has enabled Martians to earn out-planet exchange for their societies, and of course, once Lunar mining starts in earnest, they will be able to buy minerals cheaper there than from the asteroids. But otherwise . . . well.' Volhontseff's irritation seemed to vanish. Suddenly he had no expression, and his voice was robotic. 'Come in and let us discuss the matter.'

He led the way down a corridor wainscoted in genuine oak, where eerily carved staffs hung as ornament, to a study walled with books. 'Sit down.' He waved at a deep antique armchair. For himself he took a seat behind a desk cluttered with papers and library apparatus, lit a cigarette without offering one, leaned back and watched Sevigny through a blue cloud.

'Proceed with your story,' he directed.

As the Cytherean stumbled through it, Volhontseff began to show animation again. Now and then he nodded, a few times he interrupted with highly perceptive questions. At the end he sat for some while before stating, with a scowl:

'This puts me in an awkward position. I am not an American national, you realize, and do not wish to have my residence permit revoked. The climate here is too good for ageing bones that grew under Martian gravity. And my references, my collections, no, moving them would be quite unfeasible. So I must not exceed my legal prerogatives; and those are limited.'

Sevigny slammed a fist on the desktop. 'What the devil do you mean?' he exploded. 'You're the Martian consul. You have extraterritorial jurisdiction.'

'Only over Martians, and that only because it is manifestly impossible to apply human legal concepts to them. Cythereans – hm, they are supposed to lack special privilege except for what was granted by the Treaty of Toronto. On the other hand, perhaps one could argue that my authority extends to everyone whom I represent, regardless of affiliation. I do not know, and in fact I do not know if the question has ever arisen in court.'

Hope hatched in Sevigny and chirped. 'Well,' he said, 'that's a talking point. You can refuse to hand me over till you get a top-level decision. What we need is delay and publicity. The enemy can't survive that.'

Volhontseff gave him a narrow look. 'Young man,' he murmured, 'for a colonial you are developing a remarkable shrewdness. Very well. I must have the support, or at least the involvement, of an important organization. But I can get in direct touch with the Martian ambassador . . .'

'Which one?'

'What?'

'All of them? Might be best.'

Volhontseff stubbed out his cigarette and made a production of igniting the next. 'I must think about that,' he said. 'Intersocietal relations on Mars are complicated. The don't have wars, but rivalries aren't the less real for being subtle.'

'Oh, well, something else is equally important,' Sevigny said. 'To get a message to my boss on Luna, Bruno Norris at Port Kepler. He'll have reliable contacts in the Commonwealth hierarchy.' He showed teeth in a dog's grin. 'Those poor, bought Feds won't know what blasted them.'

Volhontseff drummed nervously on his desk. 'They do raise a problem, however,' he said. 'Whether or not they acted lawfully, they were officers and you are guilty of resisting them. If I do not notify them at once of your presence, I will have been harbouring a fugitive from justice. Yet if I do notify them, they may forcibly remove you before the influences on our side can be brought to bear, and tell me to appeal to the courts.'

And what can a dead man, 'shot in a second attempt to escape', prove? Sevigny thought grimly. *Volhontseff here has nothing but my unsupported word to go on. The Buffalo can try to raise a stink, and maybe in time he'll get the Safety Corps interested. But meanwhile the anti-Lunar faction will have been alerted, will have had a chance to cover its tracks, to cry that it's being smeared by the dirty opposition . . . Yes. I'm afraid that if the police arrest me now I won't see another Moonrise.*

'So they're not going to,' he said aloud.

'Eh?' Volhontseff said. His air of calculation had gone, as mercurially as his previous moods; he looked very much an old professor, helpless against the savageries that lived outside his books.

'You'll postpone telling the locals I'm here until you've raised every possible ally and they've had time to act,' Sevigny informed him.

'But—'

Sevigny rose, loomed over the dwarfish shape before him, lifted one fist and said: 'I'm threatening you, understand? I'm bigger, I smoothtalked my way into this house, and now you have no choice but to do as I want. That clears you legally, correct?'

'Well . . . well . . .'

The Cytherean tapped the phone on the desk. 'Start call-ing, friend.'

Volhontseff looked away and gradually, as he sat rubbing his chin, Sevigny saw decision crystallize. *How much like R'ku he is*, the engineer thought; and that returned him for a minute to Luna and his work; and Oscar's wistful ghost was there. He blinked away tears and barked, 'You heard me.'

'Yes. I was thinking.' The mask came down on Vol-hontseff's countenance. 'About certain difficulties. Calls can be monitored. And we don't know how many spies the enemy has planted in key positions. If a call from the Moon was never sent, how can you be sure that one will ever be received?'

Sevigny teetered back on his heels. 'That's right. But damn the universe, we can't do nothing.'

'No. I have an idea. Let me simply get in touch with the K'nean Embassy. The hour must be about noon in Paris, the office is open, and that circuit includes a scrambler. I will give them the facts and request them to transmit messages elsewhere. You are quite correct about Mars' vital interest in the terraforming work. And on so high a level, they can make direct contact with the others.'

'Hm.' Sevigny pondered. It sounded good. 'Okay. But what about me?'

Volhontseff made a parched chuckle. 'You stay here and do not allow me outside. I am in your power, remember.'

His fingers danced across the lock on a drawer. It opened and he took out a notebook and ruffled through the pages. 'Here we are. The unlisted number of the ambassador's private office.' At once he closed the book and started dial-ling. Sevigny moved around the desk to stand at his back.

The screen brightened with the image of a room strangely furnished. A long, squatting figure swung luminous eyes towards the phone. Volhontseff unhooked a vocalizer at-tachment and began talking.

Sevigny jerked it from his hand. 'None of that. I don' understand any Martian language.'

'You must trust me,' Volhontseff said.

'As far as necessary. No further. Sorry.'

Impassive, the ambassador waited.

Volhontseff's narrow shoulders lifted and fell. 'No difference, I suppose. Ah ... Nyo, we shall use English, if you please. The matter is urgent and critical. Kindly record. I have here an employee of the Luna Corporation with a rather unusual story to relate.'

'Proceed,' said the transformed voice.

Once again Sevigny went through his narration. At the end, Volhontseff said, 'This must be transmitted to the following persons in strictest confidence: the head of the World Safety Corps, the president of the Corporation, the Cytherean ambassador, and Mr Bruno Norris, operations manager in Port Kepler.'

The chitinous Martian visage had not stirred. It could not. 'Yes,' Nyo said, 'I grasp your meaning.'

Volhontseff hunched forward and said in the most intense tone Sevigny had yet heard from him: 'You realize that no time can be lost. My guest and I will remain here, but the situation is obviously unstable. Can you dispatch a diplomatic flier for him? You must have a pair of reliable humans available to man it and fetch him to safety.'

Nyo reflected for a while, during which Sevigny's pulse grew loud. 'Yes,' the Martian said, 'I believe that can be done. We will assign someone near you if possible, *exempli gratia* from the San Francisco consulate, so that they can land at your house before dawn. Stand by.'

The screen blanked.

Volhontseff put another cigarette between his yellowed fingers. *I just hope he gets his cancer shots regularly*, Sevigny thought. 'Excellent,' the small man said. 'I expect you need not wait long. Two or three hours, perhaps. Ah ... do you suppose that my part in this affair can be ... hushed down, is that the idiom? It would simplify matters. But let me prepare a bed for you.'

Sevigny shook his head. 'No, thanks. I'm strung too tight. Besides, I don't dare sleep.'

'As you wish.'

'If you want to rack out, though—'

'Not in the least. Come, we shall have breakfast.' Volhontseff got to his feet and tugged at Sevigny's arm.

'I'm not hungry.'

'I am. You shall watch me eat and possibly gain appetite. Afterwards you will no doubt be interested to see some of my Martian relics.'

'Take my mind off my troubles, anyway.' Sevigny's gaze travelled around the room and lighted on a piece of sculptured crystal on a bookshelf. 'What's that?'

'From Illach. Nothing of great value.'

'But lovely.' The engineer went over to have a closer look.

'Come, I say!' Volhontseff jittered near the door.

Sevigny turned around. A tingle went along his spine. 'You're mighty anxious to get me out of here,' he said low.

'I am hungry, I told you.'

'Well, go eat ... Why'd you call the K'neans in particular?'

'I did most of my field work in their area as you can find out from my publications. I know them best. They are to be trusted.'

'I think,' Sevigny said experimentally, through a tightened gullet, 'we ought to buzz the Cytherean Embassy ourselves, just to make sure.'

Volhontseff became waspish. 'Ridiculous. That is not only unnecessary now, it is unsafe. I have no scrambler connection to them.'

'Why should any of your calls be tapped?' Sevigny retorted. 'If the cops suspect I'm here, they'll come in person.' He took a pair of giant steps back to the desk. 'What are you trying to do, anyhow?'

'Get away from my private papers!' Volhontseff yelled. He darted at the engineer, who shoved him staggering back.

'Retro yourself, jim,' Sevigny said. 'If I'm wrong, I'll apologize. But a hunted man can't take chances.'

He picked up the notebook. Volhontseff snatched at it. Sevigny warded him off without effort. The consul turned and ran. Sevigny beat him to the door, closed it, and growled, 'Were you after a gun?'

Volhontseff recoiled. His chest rose and fell with breathing. Sevigny flipped through the pages. Names, addresses, phone numbers, in Cyrillic script but he knew Russian . . .

Ercole Baccioco leaped at him, and an Earthwide list of residences. One was the apartment building where he had been a prisoner.

'So.' He stared at the little man's rigid figure. Sweat rolled from beneath his arms. Swiftly, then, he searched, and found Gupta entered. A local hotel had been pencilled under the Benares address.

He stuck the book in his pocket. 'All right, Volhontseff,' he said. The words fell like iron weights through the night silence. 'You belong to the enemy, too. And so must that Martian. Tell me about it.'

Volhontseff retreated. Sevigny sprang, grabbed a skinny wrist and twisted until the other fell to his knees. 'You bully!' Volhontseff squalled.

'Not so loud,', Sevigny said between his teeth. 'Your saboteurs have killed men on Luna. One of them was under my command. I've also lost another friend tonight, and my own life is on the block. Do you expect me to play pattycake with you?'

Volhontseff squirmed and tried to bite. Sevigny cuffed him so that the bald head rocked. 'Hold still and talk . , . quietly!'

A curse answered. Sevigny hesitated. Even now he didn't want to— His mind cometed through darkness, towards understanding.

'The outlines are obvious,' he said, word by word, reasoning as he went on. 'These different anti-Lunar factions have got together. Certain members of them, that is. Probably not many, or men as big as Baccioco and Gupta needn't have dirtied their personal hands with me. The ordinary anti-Lunar person doesn't know about the gang, of course, and'd be shocked if he learned. But religious nuts; those who want, fanatically, to reclaim the last open parts of Earth so as to fill them too with miserable trapped people; those who want contracts for that reclamation; and now K'nea.

'You're an agent of K'nea. They're slipping you money under the counter, so you can sit close to Pacific Space-drome and watch events and exert your influence and help direct any foul play that seems indicated. K'nea is wealthy, one of the first-rank Martian societies. I wouldn't be sur-prised but what they're financing most of the gang's oper-ations.

'And then there must be someone in the American government, so powerful he can order Federal police to arrest me on a trumped-up charge the moment his good friend Baccioco told him I'd got away. Who can probably arrange for me to be killed, or at least have my memory wiped. Who ... yes, who must have got a warrant issue in the first place, to have my force unit removed. It had to look official, that removing, or there'd've been too much ruckus. But "reasons of state" has always been the only excuse an overlord needed to order anything, as long as most people believe in the Holy State. Who is he?'

'Let me loose!' Volhontseff cried.

'With what I've now got to go on, my side can find out the answer. You might as well tell me. The President himself?'

'*Nyet*—'

'Who, then? Or we'll assume it is Edwards, and what'll that do in the election?'

Volhontseff crumpled. Sevigny had to hold him up. 'Gilman,' he whispered. 'Secretary of Resources. Appointed by Edwards, yes, but ... I swear he acts for himself.'

'Why? What motive? Same as Gupta? The United States has its problems, but I don't believe they're near as bad as India's. ... Ah! If the Lunar project is discontinued, there'll be more funds to spend at home. Gilman's bureaucracy will grow. He'll become even bigger than he is. Right?'

'I do not understand these Earthside motives.' Vol-hontseff began to sob. 'You are wild beasts, you humans. I only took the pay so I could finish my work. And K'nean policy is not evil, not evil.'

'What does K'nea want?' Sevigny snapped the fingers of his free hand. 'Never mind. I see for myself. The greatest hurdle the anti-Lunars have to face is the investment already made in the Moon. No matter how much trouble and discredit they heap on us, Earth can scarcely afford to stop. But if K'nea suddenly offered to pay off the shareholders of a failing enterprise, lease the whole satellite, and do what little more is necessary to make it over into a new Mars ... Sure! And that would make K'nea the most powerful society on the home planet by a light-year. They'd dominate their entire species.'

'They must protect their philosophy,' Volhontseff wept. 'The Confederation and the Illachi are more alien to them than you can c-c-comprehend.'

'Well, Mars will have to solve its own problems,' Sevigny said coldly. He let Volhontseff slide to the floor and lie huddled while he paced, back and forth in the cage of the office.

His temples throbbed. Now, more than he had imagined, the information he had was beyond price. And it would be scrubbed out of his brain, by drugs and electric potentials or by death, before sunrise. Nyo's men were plainly supposed to land soon and invite him, unsuspicious, to board their flier. He wouldn't fall for that stunt. But then they need only tell the Federals where he was.

Volhontseff, trembling at his feet, must have a car. That offered escape. He could bind the consul and lay him on the floor with a rug thrown on top.

But a ground vehicle wouldn't get him off Oahu, and as soon as the pursuit grasped what had happened they would check the registry and throw out their nets.

Shame hit him in midstride. He halted with an oath. What was he doing, a Woodman, worried about his own precious neck when he had contracted out his loyalty to the Corporation?

I'm no hero – Judas, I'm scared – but there'd be no returning home if I went coward. I can at least try to keep them from murdering my story.

*Besides, I've got anyway a couple of hours before the flier
arrives . . .*

He flung himself into the chair at the desk and searched
Volhontseff's private directory. En route, he was aware of
surprise when his glance fell on Maura Sumatri's name. He'd
assumed she was imported to beguile him and had used a
pseudonym; but no, there she was with a town address. Well,
the organization probably kept girls like her on the payroll
in most major cities, to use on local politicians and such. . . .
The Cytherean Embassy wasn't noted. Why should it be, at
that? The clans were apart from this power grapple. By the
same token, though, their diplomatic office must be free of
double agents.

He dialled Paris, got the number, and put the call through.
An Earthified young man regarded him with shock. *I must
look like a derailed hamburger*, Sevigny realized. *Dirty,
bristly, unkempt, red-eyed, and not even the memory of a
binge to show for it.* Curtly, he identified himself.

'Samuel Craik, Clan Duneland of Duneland,' the young
man said with elaborate formality. 'At your service.'

'Who's the highest ranking person I can talk to at once?'

Craik looked pained. 'Really, Clansman, when you aren't
even in proper garb—'

'All right,' Sevigny sighed. 'You record my message. I
warn you right off that you won't believe a word. But play it
for your superiors. Have them check with the Luna Corporation office on the Moon. That's the main thing I ask
you: pass the tape on to Bruno Norris in Port Kepler, and
make bloody damn sure that he himself gets it.' He drew a
long breath and intoned: 'This I lay on you for the right and
honour of the clans of Venus.'

Craik looked still more unhappy. *Oh, Lord, I'll bet that
fop thinks the Word is a quaint barbarian custom*, Sevigny
groaned to himself. He launched into the account.

'Clansman!' Craik protested after a few minutes. 'Do you
feel well?'

'I told you you wouldn't believe me,' Sevigny gritted.
'Now hold still and let me finish.'

The violence that churned in him suddenly spouted forth an idea. He gasped. Somehow he managed to keep talking while he thought with more and more excitement about it.

Why not? Secure Volhontseff out of sight and tell 'em he had to go on an errand. If there isn't a gun in the house, there must be some of those beautiful Martian dart knives. Nyo's agents won't know that I know their purpose. I can board the flier with them. Its diplomatic registry will pass it through national checkpoints without inspection. Once we're aloft, them not yet ready to take me and not expecting any trouble ...

Laughter coughed silent in him. *A good honest fight, a clear track to Paris, and won't brother Craik be surprised when I walk in on him!*

'... changed clothes,' his tongue formed, 'and got to the consulate here ...'

The door clicked shut again.

Sevigny was half-way there before he realized what had happened. Volhontseff! The withered little devil had crawled out when he wasn't looking!

The door was locked. He palmed the plate and it swung open with Inquisition slowness. The moment he could, he squeezed through; and tumbled flat on his belly. Volhontseff had laid half a dozen Martian staffs there for him to trip on.

The tiny shape was at the front entrance. 'Stop!' Sevigny bawled. The door began to gape. Sevigny grabbed a staff and threw it like a spear. It shattered where Volhontseff had been a half second before. He scampered from sight, yammering louder than seemed possible.

No use chasing him. He must already have awakened his neighbours. The police would arrive in minutes.

Sevigny hurried back to the phone. 'What's gone wrong now?' Craik asked superciliously.

'Record this!' Sevigny overran him. 'I know these are conspiring – Nyo, the K'nean ambassador; Ercole Baccioco of Eureclam; Kirshnamurti Lal Gupta of Benares and the Indian Conservationist Party; Gilman, the United States Secretary of Resources; the Fatimite Brotherhood. They want . . .' He outlined the scheme. 'In the name of God and honour, *get them investigated*.'

He snapped off the set and ran back through the house. Maybe his message would spread. And maybe it wouldn't. He had to stay free and make sure. Besides, he himself was the most important piece of evidence there was. Once repeated under truth drug, in the presence of so many Safety Corps officers that nearly all were bound to be honest, his accusations were certain to start their machine.

First, though, I've got to start a different machine. If time allows.

A rear door led directly into the garage. Volhontseff's car was impressive to see. But Sevigny was interested only in getting at the prime circuit. No chance of finding the key before the cops showed. However, any Cytherean must have mechanical skills, and there were tools on a wall rack. He flung back the hood and fairly ripped the cover off the pilot. Hotwire here? No. Here? The engine awoke. He sat down behind the wheel and eased in power. The garage door opened.

He was steering manually now, and that was illegal in town. Any prowl car that passed near would fail to register an active pilot and take off after him. So he couldn't go many kilometres.

But away!

He backed out into the street precisely as a police vehicle rounded the corner. 'Okay,' he spat, 'want to race?' The motor roared with energies.

Downhill he went in a shriek of wind and of pursuing siren, squealed around a corner, zigzagged up another twisting way as fast as he had once taken a gun car up a mountainside at the Battle of Jerry's Landing, swooped among the trees of a small park on his airblast . . . It was unfair to pit a lifetime driver on pavements against a Cytherean. In minutes Sevigny moved alone, slowly and quietly, through the nighted tangletown.

But the ether was acrackle with calls, he knew, and every road would soon be blocked.

What about those mountains, humping high in the north against a sky that had begun ever so faintly to pale? Honolulu had sprawled far into them, but there should be brush-grown empty areas yet, where a man might skulk. ... No. He'd never make it. His auto had to be abandoned fast. In any event, whatever wild section remained couldn't be so large that a determined search with modern manhunting equipment wouldn't soon flush him out. Nor would he have any way of knowing what went on in the world.

Left, right! Left, right! drummed senselessly through his head. *Good soldiers can always find cover when enemies menace their life. Our lovable sergeant has said it. Take cover, my lads, with his wife. Left, right! Left, right! I know you're a man of Clan Woodman, I know you are gallant and true. So don't turn your back in our army; they'll give you the royallest ...*

Sevigny snapped the Halt switch. He had half unconsciously been looking from side to side. When he saw what he wanted, dim in starlight, he recognized what it was. A garage stood open and empty. Some night owl was going to be surprised when he got home. With luck, that wouldn't be for hours; and meanwhile the hounds would cast about in vain for this car.

He slid it inside. For a space he slumped, and a tide of exhaustion rose in him. *Venus,* he thought, *morning star, even the fennecs of your desert have a place to lair. But you are forty million kilometres away. Goodbye, Venus.*

And then the remembrance came to him, and he sat up with a strangled yell.

Pre-dawn light seeped through a window at the end of the tenth-floor corridor. Sevigny stepped from the elevator and walked down its lushly carpeted length. On the way he noticed a mail slot. *Good. I won't have to wait till night to mail my letter. Any time that no one's around, I ... we ... can slip out.* Door No. 14 came into view. The directory in the lobby had given him that information.

Now for the tricky part. His walk had been long but uneventful. The police search was concentrated in the Manoa Road area, where there were roofs for a forester to hide on while men went beneath, gardens and byways for him to slip through. Afterwards a city map taken from the auto had guided him on a route avoiding important streets. Doubtless an alarm would be broadcast with the morning news, his description and perhaps a drawing based on what those who knew him could tell. Or a photograph, if Gupta had thought to take one while he lay unconscious. But to passersby in the last couple of hours he had only been a lone walker, belated or early as the case might be, nothing to take heed of. If afterwards some remembered him, little harm in a metropolis like this.

The next few minutes were what counted.

The automatic doorbell had been turned off for the night. He shoved the manual button. The chime sounded remote, not quite real. He hunched his shoulders and dropped his chin. With the help of the car mirror he had rubbed grime into his hair, brows, and sprouting beard. That, a change of clothes and posture, a lowered face, a disguised voice, might get him past the viewer.

If not, he was done.

'Wha' you wan'?' The voice from the speaker was blurred with sleepiness. Fine.

Aloud, with the best Russian accent he could muster: 'I am from Oleg Volhontseff. Please to let me in. I have a very fast message from him.'

'Ah-yaw . . . um . . . why di'n'e call?'

'He could not. I shall explain. It has to do with the Martian you know of, him from K'nea.'

'Oh! One minute, please.'

He gathered his muscles. So his guess was right. Volhontseff must have got in touch with Baccioco and Gupta by now, but lesser agents like Rashid . . .

The door opened. He hurtled through. Maura's lips parted to scream. He got a hand over them, held her locked in a wrestler's grip, and hissed, 'Keep still or I'll snap your spine. I haven't much to lose, you know.'

The door closed. He guided her to a chair in the luxurious room, released her, but kept one hand on her neck, letting her feel its weight and hardness.

'Don,' she shuddered, 'please, please—'

'I don't want to hurt you,' he said with entire honesty. 'Co-operate and you'll be okay. I need a hiding place. Where better than with a member of the opposition?'

'You can't, it's not possible, you've got to go away!'

'Quiet down, I said. You must be able to see I can't leave. Your friends sicked the Federal police on to me the moment I'd gone. But as I hoped, they didn't wake you later to tell you I'd had a run-in with Volhontseff. No reason for them to do so. I used his name to establish my bona fides here.' Sevigny let go of her, crossed to the door, and shoved a heavy couch across. 'There. You won't run loose as he did.'

He turned around, wondering how wild his appearance was. 'I repeat, I've no intention of hurting you,' he said. 'The most I'll do is tie and gag you while I sleep or am otherwise busy. I'm efficient at knots, by the way. I suppose you've got food in the kitchen to last the several days I'll need until this mess is straightened out. We'll stay inside, and I hope the TriV programmes aren't too dull.'

'No . . .' She saw her robe had come open, and gathered it with a calculatedly provocative movement. He was not unaffected, but had no urge to be fooled twice. 'Don,' she pleaded, 'I can't stay here that long, I've got appointments.'

'Call and cancel them. Say you're sick, or have to go out of town, or something. I'll stand by out of view, but in easy reach.'

'You wouldn't harm me if I got them to come here, would you? Not really.'

He grinned. 'Okay, my lady. A deterrent has to be credible, and clansmen don't attack women. But I plan to cobble together some weapons from whatever I can find around this place. If the enemy locates me, they'll have to force their way in, and I'll put up one Satan of a fight. You'll have an excellent chance of getting caught in the fire. Is that believable?'

She swallowed and nodded.

'I don't need too long,' he said. 'We are going to venture out once, very briefly, in half an hour or so, to post a letter I'll write, addressed to my boss at his private apartment in Port Kepler. It should get on the returning packet tomorrow sunrise. If I know him, he won't need much time to swing into action.' He paused. 'And then, Maura, you may be damn glad I was here, to put in a word for you ... or look the other way while you catch a jet to Djakarta.'

She considered him. A certain coolness descended on her. 'Djakarta might be a good idea at that,' she said, 'because I was born Mary Stafford in Chicago.' He choked. Cat-adaptable, she laughed. 'Or maybe Venus, hm?'

'God help Venus,' he muttered in awe.

She rose and said practically, 'You must be starved. I'll fix breakfast. Afterwards ...' Her gaze dwelt on him. 'Frankly,' she said, 'the TriV programmes *are* dull.'

'So I lay doggo till you appeared personally on the newscast to vouch that the charges against me had been dropped,' Sevigny concluded.

'What was this person's name you were with?' the Buffalo asked.

'Never mind,' Sevigny said.

The Buffalo gave him a look, shrugged, and remarked nothing but: 'You seem to've had a tough time. I haven't often seen a man so pooped.'

'It could've been worse,' Sevigny answered dreamily.

The Buffalo blew out his cheeks in an enormous snort and wallowed deep into the lounger. 'Whoof, but I'll be glad to get back!' he said. 'I'm far too old and fat for Earth weight. Fuel me, will you?'

'You must've been working pretty hard, too,' Sevigny sympathized. He opened the liquor cabinet and poured two drinks of Glenlivet. The Goldwater had seemed swank when he first got here, but that was before he was introduced to the Andromeda Suite.

'I've seen damned little on the news, though, about this

whole business,' he complained. 'Isn't the investigation getting anywhere?'

'All kinds of places,' the Buffalo replied. 'But don't expect ultra-sensational revelations. Enough little fish will get netted to put a crimp in the gang. The big ones will mostly go free, as usual.'

'Huh? But—'

'Calm down and give me my booze. What did you think would happen? High-explosive international and interplanetary implications. A first-class scandal would raise too much partisanship, too many hard feelings. They'd fight back almighty mean if they got desperate: same as you did, if you recall. So . . . ah, thanks.' The Buffalo drank, belched, and wiped his mouth with the back of one hairy paw. 'The Chinese had a proverb in their war lord era, that you should always leave your enemy a line of retreat. We'll do best not to pry too deep. Let some of those jims retire gracefully from public life. Let the rest know we're watching 'em close and they'd better reel in their horns. Make one or two stiff examples of secondary figures, to show we mean business. Who're your candidates for that? Eenie, meenie, minie, moe.'

'But the others'll try again!' Sevigny protested.

'Some of 'em might. I sort of doubt it – they're likelier to jump on our bandwagon – but they might. We're forewarned now, though, thanks largely to you. We didn't know, before, how strong and piratish the anti-Lunar coalition was. Hah! Wait till they see ours!'

'What?' Sevigny nearly dropped his tumbler.

'Of course. Remember, we still have to keep down the honest anti-Lunars, who had nothing to do with the gang. But there's a bucketful of organizations with a vested interest in moon development. Like the various national political parties who voted to establish the Corporation while they were in office. Like different bureaucrats – space commissioners, for instance. Like the companies which stand to make a profit when Lunar exploitation really gets going. Like the Great Confederation of Y. Like, maybe, a few million plain, ordinary people that daydream about some uncluttered place to go. We had an active lobby in the beginning, to start the project. But then we let it fall apart. Now we'll build a new one, stronger than ever, since the work is in fact well under way. We'll propagandize, and get our personal boys elected, and pressure their colleagues, and logroll, and drop a tiny bribe here and there where that'll do some good, and—' the Buffalo laughed, earthquake style – 'all in all, the other coalition ain't gonna have a marshallow's chance on Mercury.'

Sevigny went to the window and stared downwards. The street below crawled with dwarfed traffic. 'I suppose you know best,' he said in weariness. 'Me, I only want to get back to work.'

'That's what I was talking about, son,' the Buffalo boomed. 'Fitting you and me into our proper slots. Hey, don't look so bitter. If your chin dropped a centimetre more we could use it for a 'dozer blade. As soon as the Corps gets through with you and you've had a rest – I know a place in Canada, sho'nuff forest preserve, set aside for billion-aires and you – back you go to the air mines. Now drink up and let's go eat.'

Sevigny found himself grinning. The tumblers clinked together.

THE WORLD'S GREATEST SCIENCE FICTION AUTHORS NOW AVAILABLE IN PANTHER BOOKS

Poul Anderson

The Corridors of Time	50p	☐
Trader to the Stars	95p	☐

Philip José Farmer

The Stone God Awakens	80p	☐
Time's Last Gift	85p	☐
Traitor to the Living	85p	☐
To Your Scattered Bodies Go	£1.25	☐
The Fabulous Riverboat	£1.25	☐
The Dark Design	£1.50	☐

A E van Vogt

The Undercover Aliens	95p	☐
Rogue Ship	95p	☐
The Mind Cage	75p	☐
Moonbeast	85p	☐
The Voyage of the Space Beagle	75p	☐
The Book of Ptath	75p	☐
The War Against the Rull	70p	☐
Away and Beyond	75p	☐
Destination Universe!	95p	☐
Planets for Sale	85p	☐

P15481

ISAAC ASIMOV, GRAND MASTER OF SCIENCE FICTION – NOW AVAILABLE IN PANTHER BOOKS

P17481

THE WORLD'S GREATEST SCIENCE FICTION
AUTHORS NOW AVAILABLE IN PANTHER BOOKS

Ray Bradbury

Philip K Dick

THE WORLD'S GREATEST SCIENCE FICTION
AUTHORS NOW AVAILABLE IN PANTHER BOOKS

Robert Silverberg

Earth's Other Shadow	75p	☐
The World Inside	75p	☐
Tower of Glass	60p	☐
Recalled to Life	95p	☐
Invaders from Earth	80p	☐
Master of Life and Death	75p	☐

J G Ballard

The Crystal World	75p	☐
The Drought	80p	☐
The Disaster Area	95p	☐
Crash	95p	☐
Low-Flying Aircraft	75p	☐
Concrete Island	60p	☐
The Atrocity Exhibition	85p	☐

All these books are available to your local bookshop or newsagent, or can be ordered direct from the publisher. Just tick the titles you want and fill in the form below.

Name ....

Address ....

....

Write to Granada Cash Sales, PO Box 11, Falmouth, Cornwall TR10 9EN

Please enclose remittance to the value of the cover price plus:

UK : 40p for the first book, 18p for the second book plus 13p per copy for each additional book ordered to a maximum charge of £1.49.

BFPO and EIRE : 40p for the first book, 18p for the second book plus 13p per copy for the next 7 books, thereafter 7p per book.

OVERSEAS : 60p for the first book and 18p for each additional book.

Granada Publishing reserve the right to show new retail prices on covers, which may differ from those previously advertised in the text or elsewhere.

P12481

By the same author

One of the most popular and prolific of American Science Fiction authors, Poul Anderson was born in Pennsylvania in 1926. He graduated with an honours degree in physics from the University of Minnesota, but chose to write for a career. His varied and successful work includes both historical and conventional fiction.